The Pleasure
of His Bed

The Pleasure of His Bed

MELISSA MacNEAL
DONNA GRANT
ANNALISE RUSSELL

APHRODISIA
KENSINGTON BOOKS
http://www.kensingtonbooks.com

Contents

The Captain's Courtesan

Melissa MacNeal

1

London, 1717

"Babies are *not* made that way! Don't *tell* me I must subject myself to—" Daphne Havisham shuddered from the tip of her upswept ebony hair to the hem of her voluminous blue gown. "Mama, this is wrong! Don't make me go to America to become some man's . . . Oh, I'm going to be ill!"

From across the sumptuous bedroom, Sofia Martine bit back a snicker. She'd been packing the girls' trousseaux—Daphne and Beatrix were taking an *enormous* number of trunks—while Lady Constance educated her two oldest daughters in the ways of men and women.

As the indelicate sound of vomiting came from the corner, Beatrix eyed her mother with a raised brow. "So you're saying you've allowed Papa to do this to you. . . . Well, if there are four of us girls, at least four times he's dipped his stick into your—"

"Trixie! That's enough of your impertinence!" Constance Havisham's tight-lipped pucker became the martyred expression she assumed at the first sign of unpleasantness. "A woman

must endure inelegance—must rise above her own discomfort—to bring children into this world. It's our mission. It's
why we were created."

"I'm not going!" Daphne declared. "I cannot fathom opening my legs to allow—to be *violated* by—"

As the spoiled brunette gagged over the chamber pot again,
Sofia turned her head to keep from joining her—and to roll her
eyes. It was no secret among the household staff that Lady
Constance did *not* open her legs anymore, and that her husband found his pleasure elsewhere these days . . . below stairs,
when it was inconvenient to visit his mistress across town.

"I've finished here for now, milady," Sofia rasped. "If you'll
excuse me, I'll pack my own trunk. The girls will need me to
dress them *very* early in the morning."

Lady Constance covered her nose and mouth, nodding weakly.

Sofia threw open the window and then placed the rose-
patterned wash bowl beneath Lady Constance's pale, pinched
face. "There, there," she crooned, "you've done your motherly
best. It's up to the girls and their husbands to put it all together,
just as you did when you were a bride."

Sofia exited the bedroom then, aware of a rising hysteria in
that room—and the foxlike smile on Trixie's face. At fourteen,
Miss Beatrix was wiser in the ways of the world than her older
sister . . . contemplating a voyage away from her mother's
watchful eye, aboard a ship where brawny sailors might teach
her what Daphne didn't want to know.

For propriety's sake, there could be no babies—no spreading of virginal legs—before Sofia delivered the sisters to their
prospective bridegrooms! Which would be worse? Nursing
Daphne, who would puke and pout during the entire voyage?
Or keeping track of the devious Miss Trix? As she hurried
down the back stairs, Sofia wanted much more than fresh air:
she wanted *out*. Even in their finer moments, the Havisham sis-

ters tried her patience enough to dampen her excitement over this trip to America . . . this daring adventure!

Those sailors would appreciate a woman who could match them in for out, soft for hard. A willing woman like herself! Except she'd be playing nanny and nursemaid the whole time, unless—

At the sound of male voices, Sofia paused before passing the study doorway. Lord Havisham and the captain he'd hired spoke in low undertones, making the final arrangements before tomorrow's departure.

"—hope you'll understand, Captain Delacroix, that while the safe delivery of my daughters is my highest priority," the nobleman insisted, "I have loaded the *Lady Constance* with jewels, fine textiles, spices—not to mention the double dowries promised to my associates in New York who are betrothed to Daphne and Beatrix."

"And I thank you for equipping *my* two ships so generously, sir," came the suave reply. "You've entrusted me not only with your precious daughters but with a great deal of wealth, as well. I assure you my partner and I are committed to a safe and timely delivery."

There was a pause. A clinking of snifters.

"I see this voyage as . . . an investment in America and in my shipping interests there." Lord Havisham's voice and sense of importance were riding a wave of happy intoxication, yet he splashed more brandy into their glasses. "I trust you will take every opportunity to make this a *lucrative* venture . . . for both of us. Pirates notwithstanding."

Pirates? Sofia's eyes widened, and she shifted slightly . . . caught the men's reflection in the gilt-framed mirror beside the fireplace. Zachary Havisham, even in his high, white wig, came only to the shoulder of his companion, the captain. And what a fine, square shoulder it was, too.

"Dellakwahhhhhh," she murmured, tasting his name, just as he was savoring the costly brandy her employer had poured. Saints above, he was a sight! All dark, masculine curls and a cleft chin and blue, blue eyes.

He caught sight of her in the mirror with those stunning eyes and held her gaze as he replied to Lord Havisham.

"Yes, sir, of late the entire coastline of America has become Blackbeard's playground," he said calmly. "But my partner, Morgan O'Roark, and I are experienced in the ways of such brigands, and we know alternate routes to elude them. Should we encounter pirates, my lord, I guarantee you we shall have our way with them!"

"Yes, yes! Hear! Hear!" Havisham crowed, and then he clinked his snifter to Delacroix's again. "By Jove, were I a younger man, I'd be sailing with you! Nothing quite like the salt air—"

"The freedom of the seas."

"—and the rolling of the waves—"

"The validation of one's . . . manhood," the captain crooned. And damned if he didn't wink at Sofia!

"—to set the blood a-boil," her employer expounded. With a single gulp he emptied his snifter and then flung it against the hearth. "Here's to you, Damon Delacroix! And to your successes in America! Long may you sail!"

Delacroix raised his brandy in silent salute to the mirror—to *her*!—and then he, too, drained his snifter and shattered it against the bricks. "Here's to your daughters—to their fine *breeding* and the continuing of your lineage, sir."

Oh, but he was asking for it, wasn't he? Smiling coyly, Sofia ducked down the hall before she did something foolish to call attention to herself. Lord, but she was quivering and flighty and . . . wet. She could show Daphne and Beatrix a thing or two about how things *really* happened when a man and a woman felt the heat rising between them!

But it was time to help her mother dish up dinner in the kitchen. Sofia dearly wanted to dish up something hotter and spicier after the meal, too, before the dashing Captain Delacroix left the estate tonight. She'd be shirking her duties indeed if she let this fine man go away hungry!

2

"Psst! Captain Delacroix! Aren't you forgetting something?"

Damon turned at the hedgerow that grew along the estate's front lawn. Was it his imagination, or had someone whispered to get his attention? The tall bushes cast a large shadow by the light of the flickering street lamp, and he peered into the darkness. "Begging your pardon?" he asked in the same secretive tone.

"You didn't finish your dessert, sir. I've come to deliver it."

He wasn't surprised when Lord Havisham's serving girl stepped out of the shadows. When she removed her white cap, long, black hair fell in glistening waves below her shoulders. Even in her modest gray uniform, she was a saucy piece . . . ripe and lush and every bit as wicked as he'd guessed from her reflection in the mirror. Her skin glowed like a gypsy's, while her smile promised delights far beyond any confection the cook could've served up.

"On the contrary," he teased, "I've just enjoyed the most delicious meal I've eaten in weeks. Better than any I'll likely have until I reach New York with the Havisham girls. I'm quite . . . *full.*"

"I can see that, sir!" She cocked her head and planted a fist on her ample hip. "Daphne and Trix would drive your sailors stark raving mad before you've left the harbor!" she insisted. "And because our subject was dessert . . . something sweet and tart and satisfying . . . we ought not mention the Havisham girls in the same breath."

Caught up in her flirtatious game, Damon stepped toward her and then playfully looked all around. Her expressive eyebrows arched above bright, intelligent eyes that sparkled in the lamplight . . . signs of a woman who knew her power and went after what she wanted. And this minx was being anything but subtle about it! "Where's your dish, then? If you brought my dessert, why don't I see a bowl or a spoon or—"

"What I'm dishing up comes in its own bowl, Captain Delacroix." She straightened her spine, thrusting her breasts at him. Her gaze flickered to his bulging buttons, and then she focused coyly on his face. "You look ravenous, sir. Take what you're wanting—but please kiss me first! Best to sample and sip before . . . plunging in."

"Whatever are you talking about?" he murmured, inching closer. "I'm a man of honor, pledged to deliver the goods your employer has entrusted to—"

"Would you like me to deliver *my* goods, captain? Or shall we circle each other like dogs in heat until someone comes from the house looking for me? They will, you know."

Saucy little wench! He wove his fingers into her warm, black hair. "What's your name, then? I couldn't possibly kiss a woman to whom I've not been introduced."

She was on him in the blink of an eye. Her lips parted as she raised on her toes. "Sofia," she sighed.

And for the first time in many a moon, Damon Delacroix

fell passionately in lust with someone he was fated to take and then leave behind. A woman well worth playing with, if only he had the time to savor her feminine assets.

Her lips sought his, and he moaned into the kiss—wrapped his arms around her and squeezed her soft, ample body against his own. Lord, but she was luscious! Not one bit afraid of what he'd do to her, nor one bit shy about dishing herself up, as she'd put it.

Sofia, her name was, and she tasted as exotic as it sounded. Dusky skin and raven hair and secretive perfume lured him until his lips opened hers and his tongue ventured into her mouth.

When she sucked him deeper, Damon gasped—but Sofia took advantage of that, too! He opened his eyes to find her gazing directly at him as though willing him to behave as she would direct. Willing him to drop his drawers and release himself fast and hard without sentimentality.

She knew the value of a good fucking without expecting love in return! He admired that in a woman! His hands slid lower to cup her hips and hold her firmly against his hardness as the kiss continued. His member felt ready to pop every button that stood between it and a slit that would be warm and wet and welcoming. He swore he caught a whiff of it . . . rubbed himself against her as she began to undulate, too.

"Too many clothes," she rasped. "And if we sprawl on the lawn—"

Ah, but that brought wanton images to mind! Her body bared in the lamplight, and her clothing strewn in disarray as she spread her legs . . .

"—I'll have grass stains announcing what we've been doing—"

"Can't allow that." He silenced her with another kiss that made them rock against each other, crazed with need. "So perhaps, gentleman that I am, I should stop now, before either of us regrets—"

"You'll do no such thing, captain!" She fired a brazen, black-eyed gaze at him. "Any *gentleman* would see to his lady's preference first before—"

"And what would that preference be?"

She cupped his cock between her hot hands. "I think I deserve a licking because I delivered your dessert without being asked."

Desire surged through him. "Won't the sound of my hand smacking your ass bring someone running from the house to—"

"On your knees, knave! For that remark, you'll pay dearly!"

Damon bit back a laugh as Sofia led him deeper into the shadow of the hedgerow. Again he played along, kneeling obediently as she shoved his shoulders down.

When she raised her skirts and lifted one shapely leg to his shoulder, he was mere inches from a thicket of dark curls . . . the secretive scent of lips that demanded attention he was happy to give. Few women knew what a delectable treat this could be— for both of them!—because they were too repressed or too shy to let a man sample them. This wanton puss wasn't wearing a thing in the way of drawers, either.

He smiled devilishly at her. "You want me to lick you?" he teased. "I thought you felt penitent—the need to be punished— for your naughty behavior in the hallway. Such eavesdropping could get you fired from—"

Sofia chortled. "I'm escorting the girls to America because the missus suspects naughty behavior below stairs. Lord Havisham's going to miss me much more than she will!"

The thought of that barrel-bellied coot in the powdered wig nibbling this morsel made Damon harder still. And if she would be aboard the *Lady Constance* . . . he'd spend most of the voyage to America with more than his spyglass extended at full length. Daphne and Beatrix didn't tempt him at all, but this vixen—

"For a man who knows his way around the likes of Black-beard," Sofia challenged, "you're awfully hesitant about approaching *my* black beard. I'd never guessed you for a man who doesn't like the taste of—"

As Damon pressed his mouth hungrily to her warm nether lips, the maid's outcry gratified him. So responsive she was! So damned silky and wet and ready for bigger things—and his was growing despite the way his pants cramped it. He ran his tongue around the rim of her, nuzzling her soft curls with his nose.

Sofia panted his name. Her hips quivered, and his fingers closed more firmly around them as he lingered over her sweet, secret places . . . the opening that closed around his curious tongue and then the stiff little nubbin she rubbed insistently against him.

"Yes, please . . . right there!" she moaned. "Oh, captain, I can't stop throbbing for want of—oh! Oh, I'm clenching and ready to—"

Damon rose quickly and turned her to face away from him. "Bend over," he rasped as he unfastened his fly. "I'm coming in!"

When she flipped her skirts over her back and thrust her buttocks at him, Delacroix nearly shot all over her. What a pale, rounded moon shone before him, lit by the lamp and her playful passion! His finger found her wetness, and her desperation drove him wild. No gentleman in his right mind would leave a lass in such a state of uproar—not that he felt like a gentleman. Sofia had lit a wayward fire, and he wanted to ram himself inside her, ignoring her needs.

As if that could happen! The little tart thrust backward against him when his tip touched her moist flesh. She braced her hands on her knees, positioning herself to best advantage . . . pleasing herself with unbridled abandon.

He had no choice but to go along for the ride.

Damon gripped her rounded backside and gave her precisely what she wanted. He planted his thighs against hers and rocked in a steady rhythm . . . the in and out that would deliver the dessert they both craved. Saucy and sweet and warm she was, and if he'd ever had a woman so quickly possess him, well, he was too far gone to recall.

The urge closed in on him, and he surrendered, thrashed into her wetness until Sofia squeezed and held his cock captive. They surged and bucked and damn near toppled over with the force of their climax.

"Sweet Jesus," he rasped. As his after-throbs subsided, the night slowly came into focus again; Sofia was breathing as heavily as he, gripping his hands. They stood in the shadow of the hedgerow, but good God—anyone walking by could've spotted them! Had anyone in the Havisham house gazed outside, they'd have seen the pale froth of Sofia's petticoats raging like a storm at sea!

"We'd best be righting ourselves, in case—"

"I will never be right again, sir." Carefully she disengaged so her skirts fell back over her exposed parts. She then tormented him with a dewy-eyed gaze that could've implied utter joy or utmost desolation—or anything between. "How can I ever look at another man, now that I've had you, Damon Delacroix?"

He held her gaze as he buttoned himself in—no small feat, considering he was still half stiff. The tone of her voice made his neck prickle. Where was the wayward wench who'd only wanted a fast fucking? Had she played him for a fool? Expected something more?

Damon reached into his pocket and pulled out twelve pieces of eight—all the money he had on him. "No doubt you'll catch a better man's fancy, Sofia, just as he'll catch yours. I've no time before tomorrow to buy you— et yourself a remembrance of me! I've enjoyed our little 'dessert' immensely!"

When he closed her fist around the coins, he immediately regretted it: Sofia's face clouded over, and it didn't take a ship's captain to recognize stormy seas. Her lips, still pink from their kisses, tightened into a line.

"How dare you pay me like a—a whore?" she growled. And before he could reply, Sofia stalked across the lawn—right out in the open moonlight, where anyone at a window could see her.

Damon sighed tiredly. He hadn't intended to offend her, but perhaps it was best. No sense in having a hot-blooded wench cavorting in his wicked imagination during these weeks at sea. No sense in giving her any inkling that he'd leave his post—or relieve Sofia of hers—as they escorted the Havisham brides across the Atlantic.

Because he was the captain, and he *said* so, dammit!

3

"Mama! Mama, wake up!" Sofia whispered, although her mother was no more asleep than she was. "We've had a change of plans!"

Mama gripped her hand. She glanced around to be sure no one else in the darkened maids' quarters followed their conversation. "You're not going to America?" she whispered gleefully.

"*You're* going! In my place! I've left room for your things in my trunk—but not a word to anyone!" she insisted against her mother's ear. "Just play along! When the Havishams ask, you have no idea where I've gone!"

Sofia padded out of the low-ceilinged room before Mama's questions awoke the rest of the help. She grabbed the clothing she'd bundled into her sheet, and when she reached the bottom of the back stairs, she put her shoes on. A square of light on the lawn told her Daphne was still awake, bemoaning her maidenly fate, so Sofia kept to the shadows. As she stepped between the hedgerows to the street, her thoughts of Damon Delacroix reminded her to be bold—downright brazen! If he thought he could buy her off—

"Sir! Could you take me to the piers, please?" she called to the driver of a passing wagon. His crates of clucking chickens meant he had business to attend to—but so did she. She tossed a coin onto the seat and scrambled up over the wheel before he could refuse her.

"I'm to prepare quarters aboard the *Lady Constance* before the Havisham girls arrive, and I've overslept!" she declared. "They're going to America, you see, to wed Lord Havisham's partners in New York!"

The old codger's hand snaked toward the coin. "And how's the likes of you throwin' this silver around, eh?" he grunted.

"Never you mind." Sofia leaned toward him with a scowl. "We'd best be getting ourselves along, or you'll lose your stall at the market. The missus won't be happy about that, now, will she?"

A lopsided back wheel jostled them all the way to the waterfront, yet Sophia didn't care. While she'd been excited about escorting the girls to America, her plans were far grander now. As they approached the piers, where dozens of tall masts bobbed like skeletons against the gray sky, her heart thundered.

What if she couldn't find Captain Delacroix's ship? She'd helped Lord Havisham prepare new ships for his more prestigious customers, but in this darkness before dawn, one large, bobbing vessel looked much like the ones moored on either side of it.

"This'll do, thanks." Sofia hopped from the wagon with her bundle beneath her arm, praying her instincts—and her nerve—didn't fail her. There was no turning back. No alternate plan if her audacious idea backfired—or if she got left behind because she'd come to the wrong part of the harbor.

Sofia slipped into the shadows to get her bearings . . . accustomed her nose to the stench of dead fish and salt air as she tuned her ears to the male voices around her. At this hour, stevedores and sailors grunted beneath the cargo they carted up the gangplanks, their faces slick with sweat in the light from the flickering lanterns. If she weren't careful, they'd mistake her for a loose woman come hunting.

But she'd survived that slight already, hadn't she? Sofia squeezed the cool, hard coins in her skirt pocket and walked slowly along the boarded piers, craning to read the names painted on the ships' bows. These huge, hulking vessels, stretched as far as she could see along the docks, made her feel small and inconsequential. And the farther she walked, the lower her heart sank. Was that the first hint of dawn lighting the horizon?

By now, the Havisham household would be in an uproar as Daphne and Beatrix wailed their final good-byes—and maybe whined because their abigail was nowhere to be found. These fleeting images gave Sofia no pleasure, however. If she didn't find the *Lady Constance* soon, the opportunity of a lifetime would sail away without her—not to mention Damon Delacroix. And by the saints, she wasn't nearly finished with him!

Raucous laughter made her duck behind a lamppost: the last thing she needed was to be knocked into the water by a drunken sailor. As Sofia squinted into the shadows of the nearest ship, however, she spied familiar dark hair and heard an all-too-alluring voice.

"We'll make our fortunes, partner! Havisham's loaded his ship to the gills, with the idea that he—and we—are to profit hugely from this voyage!" Captain Delacroix wore a wicked grin in the flickering lantern light, and the man to whom he spoke laughed loudly again.

"It's time for a rendezvous with Teach, then. Shall we set our course for America, by way of New Providence?"

This fellow wasn't as tall as Delacroix, but his smile and catlike grace showed the same lust for life she'd felt in Damon. This must be the Morgan O'Roark he'd mentioned to Lord Havisham . . . a man she'd do well to watch—and not just because he was every bit as dashing and handsome as Delacroix.

"That's what we'll do, yes!" Damon replied. "I hope you got your fill of good food and female company tonight, as we'll be a long time without such luxuries."

"Two of 'em at once—and *they* provided the meal and the bottle!" O'Roark crowed. "I can't imagine you fared as well at Havisham's unless his wife availed herself?"

"Ha! Lady Constance is almost as enticing as her ship's wooden figurehead. But I did take my pleasure with a vixen serving girl who gave the name *Blackbeard* a whole new meaning!"

"Did she, now? You must fill me in over our next drink!"

Delacroix glanced around the piers, grinning. "I recall a bottle of fine brandy in your cabin, Morgan. Shall we toast our success before those simpering Havisham girls arrive? You'll be damn glad they're sailing with Ned Cavendish instead of on board the *Odalisque*."

"Let's drink to Blackbeard, then! Wherever he—or she!—may be found!"

You do that, gentlemen. Sofia watched the two laughing captains saunter along the boardwalk and then followed them in the shadows of the ships. When they started up a gangplank, she craned her neck to read the vessel's name. If this was O'Roark's ship, the *Odalisque*, then Captain Delacroix's vessel, the *Courtesan*, had to be nearby!

Sure enough, the *Lady Constance* swayed gently in the next slip, and when Sofia saw the bold red and black lettering on the *Courtesan*, she tucked her bundle higher beneath her arm. Her first impulse was to duck her head and dodge any questions from the bustling crew—but, then, they needed to know who she was! Who they were dealing with!

"Ahoy there, miss! Can't came aboard this ship, on account of—"

Sofia arched an eyebrow at the grizzled old sailor and then sidestepped the tobacco juice he spat. "I'm inspecting, on behalf of Lord Havisham himself!" she announced. "I'm to see that all is clean and proper aboard the two ships escorting his daughters to America—to report any irregularities before you set sail! And what might your name be, sir?"

"Never you mind," he muttered. He let fly with another stream of muck, deciding if he believed her. "How 'bout you carry on with your job, and I'll do mine, eh?"

"A wise choice. As you were, sir." Sofia watched him walk away with the uneven limp and the *thunk . . . ka-thunk* of his peg leg. Then she strolled purposefully toward the stern. Unless Delacroix's ship was different from the Havisham vessel, the captain's quarters were beneath the quarterdeck.

And as she approached, Sofia could hardly believe her luck! Not a soul was in sight! Sailors' voices echoed in the hold below, but all hands on the deck were busy loading near the bow.

Chuckling, Sofia padded down the steps and opened the nearest door. The furnishings shone with promise in the first light of dawn that peeked through the small, high windows. The captain's bed looked to be carved of mahogany and was far larger than any she'd ever slept in.

"Oh, this will do nicely!" Sofia closed the door—locked it, for good measure. Then she imagined how best to greet Damon Delacroix when he finally found her.

4

Damon bounded down the stairs toward his quarters and a much needed drink. *Hours* behind schedule they were, all because that feisty abigail's absence had thrown the household into turmoil. Another suitable chaperone had been found—and *then* Daphne and Beatrix had clung to their mother as if certain death awaited them aboard the *Lady Constance*. Such weeping, wailing, and carrying on like he'd never seen!

But when he'd suggested to Lady Havisham that they must be sailing while the tide was in their favor, her glare would've felled a lesser man—as if he had arranged her daughters' marriages in faraway America. As if he were separating her from her two oldest girls and had the audacity to keep a schedule they'd set weeks ago.

Women! He was happy to leave Lady Havisham and her last-minute instructions behind, bound for the open sea. With the nobleman's ship sailing between his *Courtesan* and O'Roark's *Odalisque* at last, some semblance of order had returned.

He twisted his doorknob and then banged into the door. "What the—? Why in God's name is—?"

He turned the knob again—shoved the door with his shoulder—but nothing moved! He never locked his quarters! Hired only trustworthy sailors, so he had no need to carry a key.

Damon stood at his door dumbfounded, growing angrier by the second. The only thing aboard the *Courtesan* he ever locked was the strong box in which they kept the valuables after plundering a prize—and this only to prevent accusations of petty thievery from running amok, come time to divvy up the spoils.

Scowling, he peered through the keyhole. Nothing amiss in his main room, far as he could see . . . so he'd have to tell Jonas Comstock his door needed unlocking. Jonas had cooked aboard the *Courtesan* since she'd been built: if any man knew the whereabouts of important keys, it was the gimpy old salt who ran the galley and kept the rum kegs locked up.

Muttering, Delacroix took the stairs two at a time. His mood didn't improve when Comstock quizzed him about where the deuce he'd put his own key and why the hell his door would be locked anyway. They then resurrected the damn key from a drawer of odd cooking utensils, wasting yet another half hour in the process.

When he returned to his quarters, his door stood ajar.

Damon kicked the damn thing and entered. Stood in the center of his main room, looking for reasons this whole damn day had gone wrong.

"What the hell's happening here?" he demanded aloud.

He couldn't find a thing out of place. His navigational instruments lay on his square table where he'd left them. His two baroque chairs sat on the Ottoman rug facing the matching settee—ornately carved pieces his sailors teased him about, but it gave the place a homier feel. This *was* his home, after all, and because he'd selected every book and tankard and tapestry himself, he thrummed with the sense that all was not right.

"I'm drawing my sword, dammit!" he warned, looking toward the half wall that separated his bed from the main room. "You've no place to hide, so you might as well—"

"I've seen your sword, captain, and you don't scare me one bit! Bring it on!"

Damon's jaw dropped. What was a *woman* doing in his bedroom? *Aboard his ship*? Where had he heard her voice?

And why was his cock already high and hard?

"You!" He gripped the edge of the low wall to keep from rushing at her in his frustration. "Haven't you caused enough trouble for one day by disappearing from your post?"

The raven-haired maid from last night lay naked against his headboard, swaddled amongst his pillows and sheets like a cat settled in for a nap—as if she belonged there! "Come, come, now, captain," she crooned, slyly raising her arms to rest her head on them. "Is there such a thing as 'enough trouble'? You didn't seem to think so last night."

"*You* brought it on! Claiming to deliver my dessert—"

"Which you gobbled shamelessly!"

"—when you intended all along to get into my pants—"

"So you got into mine! And you loved every moment!"

Damon blinked. "You weren't wearing any."

"At last! A rational thought from a man who finds me *distractingly* attractive." She flashed him an adorable grin while thrusting her bare breasts at him. "You can't tell me you're not happy to see me, Captain Delacroix. A man will say all manner of misleading things, but his cock never lies!"

"You can't stay here," he challenged in an ominous voice. "We don't allow women on our ship. It's bad luck."

Damned if she didn't sneer at him—and then she threw something! Hit him in the chest with it!

"What do I care about your silly superstitions?" she demanded. "You treated me like a slut last night—pressing money on me, no less! I've come to demand restitution."

He bit back his retort. Studied the lush woman with the raven hair cascading over her shoulders . . . spilling over his pillows in invitation. "And just what does that mean, restitution?"

"Aha! So you weren't paying attention in class, either!" Sofia crowed. "I know plenty of things that got past Daphne and Trix during their time with the tutors."

Damon shifted, aware of the light in her dark violet eyes and the flush on her pretty cheeks—and his body's reaction to them. This alluring domestic had no inkling of her *place*, which meant this conversation could continue down the primrose path for a long, long time. What man really wanted intelligent conversation from a fine, feisty female displaying herself so brazenly in his bed? Especially one who'd locked his own damn door on him?

He had half a mind to spank her. The thought of his hand landing a satisfying *smack* on her curvaceous backside made him shift his weight again. She *was* distractingly attractive, dammit, and she knew her power well.

"I apologize for my clumsy show of appreciation," he murmured. "Even as I gave you those coins, I realized such payment might offend you."

She pursed her lips in a pouty little moue, which made her extremely kissable. "Apology accepted—if you don't commit any further faux pas."

"You still can't stay, Sofia. I must follow the code of conduct my men have agreed to uphold," he insisted. Although, as she stretched, teasing him with her womanly attributes, a list of male rules was the furthest thing from his mind. "The Code states that any sailor who seduces a woman and brings her aboard shall suffer death."

Sofia's gaze didn't waver. She sprawled proudly, with her lovely shoulders back, contemplating his edict. "But that doesn't apply here, does it, captain? You own the *Courtesan!* And we've agreed that it was I who seduced *you.*"

How could he could he not like this woman? God love her, she was even more alluring by day than she'd looked in the twilight shadow of the hedgerow. "I doubt my men will make that distinction," he said, swallowing a snicker. "Even if I'm their captain—of a ship we plundered awhile back—it's unfair for me to have a lady at my disposal if they don't get the same—"

"Thank you, sir. Not many address me as a lady."

Damon stopped midsentence. Why should he care if she'd been treated poorly? She was a domestic—a servant who'd shirked her duties by running off and who'd cost him precious time this morning! "Stop leading this conversation astray! I'm telling you any man who has a woman aboard is to *die.* 'Restitution' of his life and rights is not an option!"

"So if the man dies . . . what happens to the woman?"

He gaped. Her distinctive eyebrow arched as she awaited his reply . . . studied him with unwavering attention . . . expected an answer at least as astute as her question. Damn! He didn't have an answer, but he had no doubts about the propositions this wench would receive before she was removed from the *Courtesan.* Just thinking about his men lusting after her made him seethe!

It was time to take charge by approaching her from another angle. "Why did you run off, obviously plotting to stow away on my ship?" he demanded. "Few serving girls are fortunate enough to sail to America with their—"

"Would *you* stay with Daphne Havisham?" she cried. "My God, the puking and bawling when Lady Constance tiptoed around the subject of 'wifely duties' and fucking! No, thank you!" Sofia declared, her cheeks flaring. "I'll take my chances at whatever punishment you serve up, sir!"

Damon clenched his jaw to keep from laughing, as it would give her more advantage than she already had. Any moment now one of his men might come looking for him, and the sound of a female voice . . . or of his bed creaking in that unmistakable rhythm of . . .

Damn! He had to keep his mind on discipline! He was the captain here! "What punishment would you suggest, Sofia?" he asked slyly. "If you were one of my crew caught at wrongdoing, I'd clap you in irons on the deck, at the mercy of the wind and rain. Or I'd sic the cat on your back. What a pity, the scars our cat-o'-nine-tails would inflict on your lovely skin. And then there's keelhauling."

"And what might that be?" she asked in a more subdued voice.

"Your wrists would be bound, and you'd be tossed over the stern on a rope to be dragged from one side of the ship to the other . . . until you stopped struggling for air. You'd most likely be rubbed to a bloody pulp by the barnacles on the the ship's underside."

Her expression tightened. Then her gaze drifted to his waist. "It takes a resourceful man to acquire two ships and crews— and to be hired as an escort for Lord Havisham's daughters," she stated coyly. "You'll come up with something, captain."

Damned if she didn't burrow into his bed as though to claim it for herself. Damon strode toward the long lump under his bedclothes, ready to yank back the coverlet and haul her out of—

But that's exactly what she wanted, wasn't it? He'd fall prey to her charms the moment his skin touched hers . . . from the first brush of her lips against his ear as she whispered provocative suggestions.

Delacroix paused at the side of the bed to compose himself. Every word he said would be an invitation for Sofia to sidetrack him, to lure him into joining her between his clean sheets, which would smell like her perfume long after he sent her away.

"Sofia, if you won't willingly return to the *Lady Constance* I must bind your wrists and ankles and deliver you there myself. You have no choice."

No response. Just the slightest shift where her backside would be.

"Fine. I'm fetching the irons," he warned. "You leave me no recourse."

She uncovered her face to smile slyly. "You don't want me telling the Havisham girls they're only so much 'ballast' among the goods you intend to trade along the way," she informed him. "Just as you don't want me telling Lord Havisham's crew you plan to meet up with Blackbeard himself! To barter the dowries in exchange for keeping the brides alive, I'm guessing. You'll split the profits with him later. Won't you?"

Damon bit back a sigh. "Your imagination is every bit as keen as your tongue, eh? I'm tired of arguing for—"

"Ah, but what will you have to barter if Daphne and Beatrix order their ship turned around?" Sofia sat up, and when the coverlet fell past her mussed hair Delacroix again caught sight of her smooth, bare shoulders and breasts. What in God's name was he to do with this brazen woman? She knew too much and had no qualms about telling Havisham's crew of his intentions. If they turned around, he and O'Roark and their men would forfeit several weeks' wages—and he wanted no part of a mutiny. Didn't want to hire new men after these sailors walked out on him, either, dammit.

Control. He must take control . . . even if his cock so badly wanted to take something else.

He opened the large trunk at the foot of the bed. It grieved him to think of clapping irons around this delectable morsel and then parading her in front of his men, but she gave him no alternative.

"Captain Delacroix . . . Damon, if I may," she said in a tempting sing-song, "who will be the wiser if I simply remain here, in your quarters? I promise you, sir, I didn't stow away to make a nuisance of myself or to cause trouble among your men—"

Damon snorted in disbelief.

"—but once you reveal my presence, you must contend with their curiosity . . . their insistence on following the Code. Do you really want to die for having me aboard your ship, captain? I could be . . . your sweet little secret. For the entire trip to America."

Oh, she tempted him! For a brief and shining moment he envisioned the fantasy she'd spun with her alluring words. . . .

But a knock at the door brought reality crashing home. "Captain, sir, we need your opinion about our navigational bearings as we leave the harbor for the open—" His quartermaster, Quentin Thomas, scowled from the doorway. "Irons already, sir? I've never known you to constrain a sailor before the rum kegs were tapped."

What could he say? Damon glanced at the iron cuffs that dangled from his hand and knew he could keep no secrets, no matter how badly he wanted this woman all to himself. "The abigail who was to accompany Lord Havisham's daughters has stowed away in my quarters, Thomas," he confessed. "She refuses to return to her post—"

"Can't blame her, from what I've seen of the girls." He stifled a laugh as he glanced at the captain's bulging breeches.

"So I must confine her until we reach port, where I will sell her as a slave to the highest bidder," he continued in a loud, purposeful tone. "She will earn her meals by doing whatever Comstock demands in the galley. Tell the men I'll be on deck shortly with the stowaway in tow."

Quentin's expression held a hint of conspiracy. "Begging your pardon, captain, but if none of the men are the wiser . . ." Thomas's eyes widened, but he quickly refocused on Delacroix. "I—You could trust *me* to keep your secret, sir. You'll have nothing but trouble if you let *this* cat out of the bag."

Damon turned, exasperated. Why was he not surprised to see Sofia standing at his partition, wrapped in only a sheet? She'd followed their conversation with wide, dark eyes.

"After all the joy I've brought you, Captain Delacroix, how can you sell me, sir?" she spouted. "And why are you telling this man such a tale when you told me we'd play a little . . . slave game when you return from your duties on deck?"

Quentin snickered. "I'll set our usual course south and west, sir, until you have time to render your final decision on this most *pressing* matter."

"No! By God, I am the captain, and I have spoken!" Scowling at Sofia, he stalked out of his quarters behind Quentin Thomas. His mind was made up. He would have no more of her impertinence.

Never mind that he slammed the door on Sofia's laughter.

5

"Because Sophia Martine is aboard the ship illegally—and she's as wily as the slyest fox—anyone caught speaking to her will be marooned." Damon spoke from the quarterdeck beside the *Courtesan's* wheel, overlooking the curious crew gathered below. "She will follow orders from Comstock and myself, and under no circumstances are you to engage her attention or say one word to her. Is that clear?"

The sailors glanced at each other, but then they gazed at his prisoner: Sofia stood in shackles, cuffed to his arm. She wore her gray uniform, but with her ebony hair blowing around her dusky face, wearing a dejected expression, she looked alluringly helpless. Any man would volunteer to be marooned for the favor of a single caress. A single kiss.

"What's to become of her, sir?" one sailor piped up.

"She'll be sold as a slave—for more than any of us could afford in our lifetimes, I'll wager," he added to stem any interest in pooling their funds. "We've voted to uphold the Code, and for good reason, when one considers—"

"So where's she sleepin', sir?"

Damon searched the crowd for the upstart who'd made every-one snicker. "She will be confined to my quarters," he replied in his most commanding voice. "Who among you wants the re-sponsibility of Sofia's welfare? Comes a time we must fight to protect the common good, we can have no jealousy or distrac-tions. No sense that I favored any man above the others. I alone will bear the burden of her safety, understood?"

The sailors nodded, muttering among themselves.

"Back to your posts, then." Damon stood in front of Sofia to keep her from making eyes at those who favored her with a last, fond gaze as they dispersed. "You're more trouble than you're worth," he muttered over his shoulder.

"You had other options, captain. Your quartermaster would've kept me a secret."

"And we know what sort of payment he'd expect."

"Is that such a high price to ensure your own gratification during this *loooong* voyage, sir?" Her breath teased at his ear: once again he'd invited trouble by scolding her. "And why did you relegate me to the galley? Surely leaving me at Mr. Com-stock's mercy is inviting—"

"Jonas Comstock hasn't pleasured a woman since a cannon-ball took off his leg." Damon turned to glare sternly at her. "So don't think you'll tease your way out of—" Her kisses—one, two, three of them in rapid succession—left him gaping. "Have you no respect for—"

"None whatsoever."

"—my position as—"

"The position I like best," she teased, "involves lying face-down in your cozy bed while you ride me from behind and I squeeze you inside my—"

"Dammit, Sofia, you try my patience!"

She smiled, triumphant. "And if you'll try *my* attributes, captain, we'll both be so much happier. Won't we?"

The warmth of her breath . . . the waves of heat coming from her lush body, which undulated shamelessly against his . . . the caress of her hair in the breeze made Delacroix very aware of what he could be enjoying if he disappeared with his captive. She was now officially his slave. And a woman like Sofia Martine would leave him no peace—no sanity—until he shut her up.

His pulse quickened, and his cock nudged Sofia of its own accord. "You're coming with me. Let there be no mistake about whose authority will be served—and who will serve."

Grasping her bound wrists, Damon hurried toward his quarters at a pace that made Sofia scuffle along in her leg irons. He scowled fiercely as a warning to any sailor who might smirk at them. When they came to the stairway, Damon descended ahead of her. As he opened the door to his quarters, he watched Sofia hobble unevenly down the steps in her leg chains. "Perhaps, so you'll suffer for stowing away, I should make you navigate the longest stairways—"

With a little shriek, Sofia pitched forward.

Had she stumbled, or had the ship shifted? Damon rushed to catch her, again aware of her power to completely disarm him. Sofia landed against his shoulder, soft and light and voluptuous.

And she was laughing, dammit. Not one whit of fear or apology as his arms closed around her.

"What am I to do with you?" he muttered as he entered his cabin. He kicked the door shut behind them and set her unceremoniously on her feet. "You cannot continue to demand my attention—"

"So give in." She gazed pointedly at his bulging fly buttons. "Let me suck that long, lovely cock, and we'll both be happier, captain. I've tried to tell you this, but you won't listen."

He closed his eyes, determined not to succumb. "Who's giving the orders on this ship, wench?"

"Why, you, sir."

"Damn right. Enough of your cheeky challenges! On your knees!"

Sofia squatted and awkwardly folded her legs beneath her. When she gazed up at him, Damon felt a thrill sizzle through his body, although her demure expression didn't fool him anymore. "You know what to do," he rasped.

Sofia nipped her lip. Then she fumbled with his fly buttons as though half afraid of what might spring out at her. "I would so love to lie back, sir, spreading my thighs in invitation. But wearing these manacles limits my—"

"Who said you were getting any pleasure? This is your punishment for defying me."

Her brow flickered as she scooped his member out of his pants. Demurely she licked her lips, contemplating the swollen shaft that pointed like a flushed sword. Somehow Sofia managed to look penitent, like a novitiate in a convent kneeling to pray, even as she opened her mouth to suck him. Her raven hair drifted forward as her warm lips closed around him, and Damon grasped both sides of her face.

"Ohhhhhhhh," he moaned. "Most women have no idea how heavenly this feels. How much a man enjoys . . ."

"Mmm," she replied. Up and back she stroked him, dragging her moist lips over his inflamed flesh. When she tipped her face slightly, Sofia appeared to be savoring this pleasure as much as he was . . . up and back as her tongue swirled around him.

Damon sighed languidly and grabbed the nearest chair to keep his balance. He didn't want anything to interrupt this fine, fine sucking . . . a working-over like he'd never before received, even from the most experienced trollop.

"Oh, Sofia . . . don't stop. My God, don't you dare quit licking and—" Damon rocked forward, curbing the urge to shoot down her throat. She deserved to do without, just as he'd threatened, yet as he accelerated toward a climax, Damon could think of more satisfying ways to fulfill his need.

"Get up," he whispered. "Sit on the edge of the bed and rock backward."

"Yes, captain. Whatever you say, sir."

Her deference wouldn't last, but Damon was too needy to tease her about it. The chain between her feet scraped the plank floor . . . such a chafing weight it must be . . . yet his pity remained unexpressed as Sofia followed his order.

Down she sat, and back she fell, raising her legs so her skirts slithered around them. Once again she wore nothing for nickers. Anytime she bent over in the galley, she might expose herself to Comstock.

The thought crazed him. Damon imagined the cook's randy thoughts, the way old Jonas would itch to get inside this young, lovely woman, and he grabbed Sofia's ankles. He slipped his fingers inside the iron leg cuffs to keep them from cutting into her tender skin, and then he lunged.

Sofia gasped and rose to meet him. They thrust against each other, and as he raised her legs as high as the irons allowed, Sofia writhed. Her desperate expression drove him on, and as his need crested, Damon prayed neither of them would cry out . . . alert the crew that he'd slipped away with her before they'd reached the open sea.

He shot his seed with a force that left him breathless. The minx beneath him rose to take in his full length, grimacing at the brink of climax.

"Damon, please—slap yourself against me and—"

Her wish was his command. He bucked against her hips, making a randy, wet sound as their bodies shuddered in opposing thrusts. Her muscles clenched, and he held her tightly against his thighs to bring her to completion.

Where had he ever met a woman who loved this give-and-take as much as he did? Even from a submissive position, Sofia gave and gave, making it seem like he couldn't take enough.

Making him realize he was as much her slave as her captor. A dangerous idea, indeed.

Damon eased out of her. Sprawled on his sheets, with her dark hair splayed about her face and a look of utter contentment, Sofia Martine was the most fetching thing he'd ever seen.

But he couldn't send her to her galley chores smelling of spunk. Even old Comstock had his limits. The cook might think of ways to bait Sofia if he caught a whiff of what she'd been doing, even if he couldn't consummate his fantasies.

Damon went to his washbowl and dipped an end of his towel into the water. Each gentle stroke made his lover's body quake with aftershocks as he cleansed her. So responsive she was, he felt his need flaring again.

He wiped himself and buttoned his fly. Still Sofia lay with her legs raised and her feet dangling, so the chains rested on her bare backside. Her eyes closed as though she intended to nap, awaiting his return later in the day.

And wasn't *that* a fine fantasy?

"Off to the galley with you now," he murmured, but it hardly sounded like an order. "And if we don't eat the most delicious dinner my crew has ever consumed, you'll tell them why. Lord Havisham mentioned that you assisted your mother in his kitchen, so don't pretend otherwise."

It took six days—six days!—to convince the captain he must raid the supply of spices aboard the *Lady Constance* if he wanted tastier meals. Jonas Comstock, set in his ways about how to cook for rough-and-tumble sailors, refused Sophia's advice about using a bit of cinnamon on the dried apples or a sprinkling of herbs in his tasteless stew—until *she* had refused

Damon Delacroix the spice he craved in his bed. The quickest way to a man's heart might be through his stomach, but making him change required pain where he'd hurt the most.

The captain had never really enjoyed Comstock's cooking, so after he and Quentin Thomas swung aboard Lord Havisham's ship for a chat with Captain Cavendish, Delacroix returned with a generous tin of the seasonings Sofia had requested.

The results were immediate. As she peeped from the hole in the galley wall to where the sailors bent intently over their tin plates, their smiles and sighs of satisfaction made her grin. Conversation was forbidden during meals, to prevent arguments while the crew was packed into such close quarters, but the utter enjoyment on their faces spoke volumes.

An uneven *thunk . . . ka-thunk* announced Comstock's return from the table. His plate clattered into the dish tub as he stopped behind her. "Well, the squeaky wheel gets the oil," he muttered, "so it seems you'll not be peeling potatoes or washing dishes anymore, missy. If you weren't the captain's . . . *courtesan*, I'd have something different to say about that."

The captain's courtesan. The phrase had a nice ring to it, even if Jonas had basically called her a whore. Sofia looked through the peephole again, hiding a smile. When Damon Delacroix spoke, everyone aboard his ship listened or faced the consequences.

"It was never my intention to upstage you, Mr. Comstock," Sophia said quietly. "I was doing the job I was given, and I used the resources at hand. You can't tell me you didn't enjoy that mutton stew more for the rosemary and thyme I put in it. You wiped your plate with my fresh bread and then took more. Twice!"

"Hard-tack biscuits is plenty good enough," he muttered. "We'll see how the men likes it when we runs short of supplies halfway across the Atlantic! We'll see how happy you makes the captain *then*, when he's got a shipful o' empty bellies and short tempers!" He barked at Billy and Gasper, the two lads who assisted him, and they scurried to fetch water for the mountain of tin plates and cups that awaited them.

Why was it wrong to feed these hardworking men good food? Did sailors willingly endure stale, overbaked biscuits and bowls of greasy swill for long voyages and short pay? These first days at sea had been enlightening: the cramped hammocks hanging below deck and the secretive skittering of rats there made service at the Havisham house look like a party by comparison. And when she thought about Daphne and Beatrix—the whining and sea sickness her mother must be tolerating—conditions aboard the *Courtesan* seemed rosy indeed.

Thank goodness her captor hadn't confined her in a cage in the dark, dank hold of his ship. The stench of unwashed bodies and live animals kept for slaughter would only get worse as the voyage went on. She appreciated her good fortune as Captain Delacroix's slave and intended to work her magic on him whenever he wanted her.

And for her next trick, she'd make her manacles disappear.

6

"You seem melancholy this morning, Sofia."

She continued to stare out the captain's porthole window partly for effect—because her chained stance suggested her despondent mood—but also to keep the *Lady Constance* in sight. At this hour, before dawn broke fully, she liked to think about what her mother would be doing. Magdalena Martine had served the Havisham family since before their daughters were born, had devoted her best years to keeping their household in order.

Had Mama convinced Daphne to quit sniveling? Had she caught Beatrix kissing a sailor yet?

Is she angry because I disrupted her life without a moment's notice? And that my chasing after Damon Delacroix has uprooted her forever?

Sofia sighed wistfully. "Do you ever miss your mother, captain?"

He looked up from lathering his face. In the flickering light from his oil lamp, the masculine shadow along his jaw called to her . . . such an alluring contrast between the white froth and that dark male stubble. As she recalled how his chin had chafed her when he'd put his head between her legs last night, his eyes blazed with blue fire.

"My mother's not the type a man misses." He laid his brush aside to pick up his straight razor. "She nagged at my father until he left us when I was ten. Had a knack for wearing everyone out with her chiding and criticism, unfortunately."

"That's why you left home for the sea?" she asked in a faraway voice. "I've always shared a wonderful love with Mama, even though I was born into service. She knows her place—her work—and she taught me to take pride in it, too."

"She certainly passed along her talent for cooking." He pulled his face taut to shave around one side of his nose. "You greatly improved Comstock's stew last night, Sofia, and I appreciate your demanding those spices. I admire a woman who insists on change that benefits the common good."

Sofia gazed across the room at him. Naked, half crouched to peer into his small shaving mirror, Damon Delacroix looked tigerlike and wiry. Predatory and very strong.

"Thank you. Mr. Comstock doesn't see things that way."

"Jonas is green. The entire crew adores you, and he can't compete."

The razor sang an enticing song as he cleared his face . . . revealed fresh, swarthy skin Sofia's fingers longed to stroke. She sighed and gazed out the window toward the *Lady Constance* again. "He claims my extravagance will cost us later on. Says we'll run short of food halfway across the Atlantic."

"He should let the quartermaster—and me—worry about that." Delacroix quirked an eyebrow. "Besides, it sounds like the perfect reason to veer south so we'll reach a port sooner."

What did he mean by that? Was he ready to sell her, even though her lovemaking drove him wild? Even though he enjoyed her cooking and a companionship that went beyond her sexual favors?

It wouldn't be good strategy to ask, so she changed the subject. "My mother filled in for me as the girls' abigail without having any choice," she said softly. "I'm feeling guilty even though I've always dreamed of a new life in America—and now she can join me. She's all I have, so I didn't really want to leave her behind at Lady Havisham's say-so."

Sofia glanced sideways to catch his reaction, but Damon was gazing into his small glass, intent on finishing his shave. He looked corded and strong, his muscles tensed to hold himself absolutely still as he focused on his poor excuse for a mirror.

"Know what else I've always dreamed of?" she ventured softly.

"Mmm?" He held his nose to the other side to scrape his cheek with short, quick strokes.

"If I ever get out of these irons," Sofia said dreamily, "I'll wrap my legs and arms around you when we're . . . fucking, Damon. I'll squeeze your ass between my knees and—"

"Dammit to—bloody *hell* that hurt!"

A red rivulet of blood seeped between his fingers, and Sofia nearly fell over her leg chains when she scrambled to help him. "Press against the wound! We must find—" She grabbed the bottle of brandy on his desk to soak a corner of his towel with the liquor. "Hold this against it while I—"

"This is your fault, dammit! Talking about wrapping your legs around—"

"I didn't mean to—"

"Yes, you did!" He glowered at her, clamping his hand around hers as she pressed the wet, pungent towel to his cheek. "And now you're wasting my best brandy—"

"We must cleanse the wound to prevent—"

"—and you lured me into this! Timed your brazen remark about legs and fucking for when I'd be—"

Sofia's mouth fell open. "Damon, I—surely you can't believe I'd deliberately hurt you! I'd have escaped you days ago if I hated you that badly!"

His crystalline eyes widened, mere inches from hers, but his anger still bubbled beneath his flushed face.

Or was that fear she saw? Was he afraid of the powerful attraction between them—so attuned to her that in his imagination, he'd followed where her naughty thoughts led? And then he'd shown his anger rather than any sign he cared for her.

When she finally dropped his gaze, Sofia gasped and grabbed the dripping towel. "You're badly cut, sir," she murmured. "I'll be needing a needle and—"

"It's not that serious! Not like I've never cut myself shaving or—"

"Damon."

His mouth clapped shut. He pressed her hand harder against his cheek, cursing to himself. Sofia was helping him even though he'd spewed accusations at her—even though it was his own damn fault he'd lost his concentration at the mention of her lovely legs wrapped around him.

When had any woman looked so concerned for his welfare? When had anyone fallen all over herself to come to his aid? Truth be told, the idea of being stitched up bothered him even more than how red and soggy the towel had become with his blood. And if his men saw his eyes swimming this way, like crazed fish, they'd know a secret he'd concealed for years.

And Blackbeard, bastard that he was, would capitalize on this weakness. Not that he would mention that notorious pirate to Sofia in her present state.

Her eyes took up half her face. The vein in her pale, slender neck throbbed, a grim reminder of his own lifeblood pulsing . . . precious moments passing as she awaited his answer. Sofia carefully took the razor from his hand and laid it on the wash stand.

"Damon—Captain Delacroix," she whispered. "If you'd rather I didn't sew you up, I'll summon whoever—"

"No. I—" He blinked away the first wave of dizziness. "I

was concerned that you'd not have the stomach—nor the steady hand—for—"

"I stitched Lord Havisham's leg after a nasty fox-hunting accident," she replied quietly. "You didn't notice him limping, did you? Now where will I find a needle and thread? And bandages? This is foolishness, and you know it."

He closed his eyes to savor the warmth in her voice . . . the tingle of strong, healing power in her hands, if he'd allow it to flow into him. His mother would be squawking about how stupid and easily distracted he was; how he deserved to bear the scars of his licentious thoughts.

Thank God it was Sofia Martine tending him. Her leg chain scraped the floor as she stepped back, glancing around for what she needed.

"The medicine chest is in my armoire," he said with a sigh.

"And the key to these irons? I can't make tiny, invisible stitches with my wrists bound, Captain Delacroix."

So it was "Captain Delacroix" again? He swallowed back another wave of dizziness and the coppery tang of fear that invaded his mouth. Somehow her return to his formal title cut more deeply than his damn razor had.

"Top desk drawer. Center."

She nodded, disappointed that a fine moment between them had passed.

And so was he. When she pressed his own hand against the sodden towel and the gash, Damon felt bereft at the absence of her touch, even though she remained in his sight.

How dangerous was that? When had he become so enamored of the little troublemaker who'd stolen onto his ship—and stolen his heart?

No, that can't happen! Keep your thoughts straight! The loss of blood is making you weak for her.

He blinked against a wave of nausea and then realized Sofia

stood solemnly before him, holding a short iron key. Delacroix took it in his left hand, bungling as he fit its tip into the narrow lock of the handcuff. She held it against her chest to steady it for him.

At the snick of the first cuff, Sofia snatched the key and unfastened her other wrist. She leaned over to unlock her ankles and kicked the offending irons aside.

"*Now* we can get down to it," she murmured. She yanked the chair from his desk and sat him down on it in one smooth, powerful move. "Better be gulping some of that brandy, captain, while I fetch the needle. I'm the finest seamstress you ever laid unfocused eyes on, but I promise you this will hurt."

His eyes were unfocused? Damon forced his attention back to her . . . watched her gray uniform strain against the ample curve of her waist when she stood on tiptoe to fetch the medicine chest. Why was he fighting this attraction? Sofia was a fine-looking woman—

And she'll lead you down the primrose path every time. Just because she can.

Not that he could think of a reason not to follow her.

The long needle she lifted from the medicine chest made him turn away. Damon took a long chug from the brandy bottle, closing his eyes as the liquor's fire ran down his throat and into his stomach.

"Perhaps you should lie down on the bed—"

"I'll sit right here. I'm fine."

"—so I can reach the wound at a better angle," Sofia finished in a firmer tone. Then she chortled. "You don't really think I'll take advantage of your disadvantaged state—wrap my wicked legs around you and hump you—when you can't hump back? Do you?"

A weak laugh escaped him. "Point well taken."

She pulled a length of discolored thread from a wooden spool and snapped it quickly between her teeth. "We'll see who comes to a point—and who takes it—now that I'm a free woman, captain."

Damon coughed. "You could've used the razor to cut—"

"And why would I touch the vile blade that did this to your face?" she retorted. "You might consider a beard, captain. Deft as I am, I can't guarantee you won't scar. Now close your eyes and drink up. Cock your head this way and hold it steady . . . steady . . ."

He wasn't prepared for the searing pain when the point of the needle pierced his skin and then caught the other side of the wound. "Jesus, woman, you'll—"

"Suck down more liquor and hold still," she ordered in a low voice. "If you want a bullet to bite, tell me where to find one."

Her face swam before him, but there was no mistaking her intent: before he could argue, she nipped him again with the needle, and again.

To keep from blacking out, Damon gulped the fiery brandy. He concentrated on its sweet burn . . . thought about what style of beard might cover a scar . . . a constant reminder of how fast and far he'd fallen at her suggestion of sex. "Ouch, dammit," he muttered and then sucked in a shuddery breath.

"I'm so sorry, Damon, I know this has to hurt," she whispered. "Two more should do it."

Before he could protest, Sofia skillfully stitched the rest of his wound. She knotted the thread and this time used his razor to sever it. "Didn't want to pull out your stitches if I didn't bite right," she explained.

He nearly keeled over from the thought of that pain . . . of possibly having to endure a whole new set of stitches. The familiar room lurched around him despite how he fought the blackness that threatened to close in.

"Are . . . are we tossing in a storm?" he mumbled, glancing around.

"I don't recall any clouds warning us of . . ."

Sofia tucked his poor head against her shoulder. With a clean cloth, she gingerly dabbed the wet, sticky wound. "Another wiping with that brandy, and we'll be done," she crooned as if he were a scared little boy. "You did well, captain. You'd have finished stitching *me* on the floor, I'm afraid. I don't handle pain well."

Damon sighed languidly. After one more swig of the warm, sweet brandy, he let himself drift as he rested against the firm, solid warmth of her. "No, you're not afraid, Sofia," he murmured. "You're the bravest woman I know. And thank you for . . . having your way with me."

Sofia smiled against his soft, dark curls. The captain had finally passed out in his chair and was dead weight against her.

7

Damon awoke slowly, aware of a stale sweetness in his mouth and a pillow that felt extraordinarily soft and warm and . . . moved and had a pulse. His eyes drifted open, and he saw dusky, sweet skin. Skin that begged him to kiss it. So he did. "Sofia."

"Welcome back, captain. You sailed away for a bit, but you've returned to me."

When he tried to lift his head, a gentle hand held him firmly in place against her chest. "Easy, now. You've lost a lot of blood, but your stitches are holding nicely. Don't move too fast, or you'll fall off your chair."

Chair . . . stitches . . . pain alongside his chin that made it all come back: he'd cut himself with his razor because of a brazen remark she'd made. Had apparently survived her surgical attempts to fix him—such as he was—and yet his backside felt stiff from sitting on a hard chair.

He scowled. "You've been standing here this whole time? How long was I—asleep?"

Her soft laughter rumbled under his ear, enveloping him in a cozy happiness. "What matters is that you rested long enough to let the wound clot and to allow your color to return. You were out long enough for me to realize what a handsome devil you'll be if you grow that beard we talked about."

"How long was I out?" he insisted.

Again she chuckled, the little minx. "Minutes, Damon. But, then, our days and weeks are made of mere minutes, aren't they?"

He lifted his head faster than he should've, and her face swam before him. "Stop being so—I have a ship to run! I can't stay in my quarters for—"

She shrugged prettily, which formed a tempting crevice between her breasts. "I haven't felt a jolt or heard any nasty bumping noises, so your crew has been doing its job. Your quartermaster has taken charge. And isn't that why you hired them?"

Women! They never saw the real point, did they? They—

Damon's head turned ass-over-teakettle, and he damn near fell against her. "Fresh air. I need fresh air and cold water and—"

"Sit here by yourself while I fetch you some water, sir. Then we'll see about a stroll along the deck railing."

A stroll along . . . like some toothless old invalid being supported by a nursemaid as he clung to the railing? The image made Damon find the floor with his feet, and he immediately regretted it. He grabbed the back of the chair to keep from falling as he heard Sofia's exasperated sigh.

"Fight me, then," she teased as she held the cup to his lips. "I'll let you go upstairs and collapse in front of your men, if you insist. And when your head whacks the deck and your wound gushes blood, won't you make a fine, inspiring sight?"

He gulped the water greedily, wishing she weren't right. Why did this woman always have to be right, dammit?

"The water's making you stronger already," she murmured. Her voice teased at his ear . . . that voice that always sounded as though a laugh lurked just beneath the surface, yet a voice that wrapped around him so compassionately he didn't know how to grasp it. Why on God's Earth would she care about *him*?

"When you can keep your feet underneath you and walk as though *you* are escorting *me*," she continued with a grin, "I hope you'll show me how to use your spyglass, captain. Might we catch sight of my mother aboard the *Lady Constance*? Or perhaps spy on Daphne and Beatrix to see what sort of trouble they're causing her?"

Sofia's head cocked slightly, and her smile made him flutter inside. Damn, she was gorgeous. Why would he walk her up to the deck when they could sprawl on his bed and make mad, passionate love? Without those cuffs and leg irons, she could give herself as freely as she longed to . . . perhaps wrap those fine thighs around him, as she'd hinted when this whole mess had gotten started.

Damon blinked. Her gaze was sneaking to his crotch, as though she knew he was growing hard even before his cock thought of it.

"Is that a yes, captain?" she teased. "For a walk in the fresh air, that is?"

He gulped more water. "Probably a good idea to show myself soon, yes," he said gruffly. "What were *you* thinking I wanted?"

"Me."

Coyly she took the tin cup from his hand and returned it to the washstand. Testing him to see if he could stand up by himself. This had to be the most humiliating—most exasperating—experience he'd ever had with a woman.

Damon sucked a few deep breaths to clear the fluttering cobwebs from his head. Gazed at her to be sure his vision had cleared—at least enough that his men wouldn't suspect he'd passed out from the sight of his own blood and the pain from that blasted needle.

"And what shall we tell them when they ask about your stitches?" she inquired sweetly. Sofia linked her arm through his and started toward the door. "We need to have our story straight so—"

"Ah, but the rule still stands about my men not speaking to you or engaging your attention," he reminded her brusquely. "Releasing you from your irons didn't change that."

Her face fell, and he wanted to kick himself. After the way she'd stitched him up—would keep his secret about how blood-letting made him woozy—he was insulting her again. Had he spent his life at sea, away from potential mates, because he might mistreat them? Or because he didn't want to lose himself, lose control, in love? He wanted to believe in that dream when he looked at Sofia Martine, but the prospect scared him speech-less.

Damon sighed. Time to put such ponderings aside and take command again, wasn't it?

He smiled at the fine, fetching woman beside him. She returned his smile, feline that she was. Sofia had taken charge but was careful not to remind him of it. Clever wench.

And once on deck, with the brisk sea air caressing his face, Damon's strength returned. Quentin Thomas stood on the quarterdeck, at the large wooden wheel, gazing out toward the horizon . . . and then at the ship sailing about twenty yards to their left, and then at the *Odalisque*, which led their trio from the other side of Havisham's ship.

Their sails were pregnant with a brisk wind, and the Atlantic whisked them along them like a sea-green witch with her effortless, rolling magic. Although he would prefer having the *Courtesan* as the lead ship, all was as it should be, with his partner out in front. He hadn't missed a thing, nor had anything gone wrong in his brief absence. When they got closer to New Providence and went looking for Blackbeard, he would shift their position.

"Fine day for a sail, Thomas!" he exclaimed with a nod to his quartermaster. "I'll have a look at what's ahead of us, from the bow."

"Aye, sir." Quentin's gaze lingered on the spot near his chin—the stitches now throbbed like a dog was clawing him there—but Quentin said nothing. Merely smiled and glanced briefly at Miss Martine.

Damon took the spyglass from the wheel stand to stroll along the rail as though he felt perfectly fit. Sofia had assumed the air of his deferential slave once again, walking with her hands clasped and her eyes averted. When they reached the peak of the bow, he focused on the middle ship—twisted the end of the spyglass to correct the blur. All seemed calm aboard that vessel, as well.

"Here—you look." He handed the instrument to Sofia, who eagerly put it to her eye. "If you follow the railing of the *Lady Constance* to your left, you'll spot something of interest."

Damon watched the smooth flow of her movement . . . the slow parting of her lips as she gazed through the spyglass. Her ebony hair teased him in the breeze until he wanted to grab it and pull her close for a kiss.

"There she is! There's Mama!" Sofia gazed eagerly toward the bow of the middle ship, holding her breath to concentrate. "She's on the deck with the girls. Oh, Mama, it's so good to see you. . . . I hope you've forgiven me for following my own selfish inclinations . . . stowing away and leaving you to carry out my duties."

Damon listened, spellbound. That this vixen would be concerned about her mother's forgiveness took him by surprise. Was it because he'd seldom given a thought to his own mother's well-being—or to forgiveness, in general? Or because he'd so enjoyed Sofia Martine's impulsive decision to hide in his quarters?

"Just a thought," he murmured, "but perhaps you did your

mother a favor. Lord Havisham and Lady Constance might have put her out, once she reached an age where she could no longer serve. You've provided her the same fresh start you've made yourself."

Sofia took the spyglass from her eye. Her look was one of astute gratitude. "I hope New York will prove a hospitable place, for I suspect the girls' two grooms already have their own staff. Mama and I may well be on our own in a strange new country and—"

"A resourceful woman like yourself will want for nothing." Damon wasn't sure where that sentiment had come from. To be sure she didn't misinterpret his remark, he flashed her a fox-like grin. "And if mother is at all like daughter, she'll find her place, as well."

"Are you saying you have plans for us, Captain Delacroix?"

"No!" He chided himself for entertaining her fancy . . . leading her to believe she was anything other than a stowaway whose presence was forbidden. "America is a land of new opportunities. I'm expressing my confidence in your ability to capitalize on them."

"Ah. Which implies you won't sell me as a slave once we've detoured to that port you mentioned earlier." A grin lit her impish face. "Thank you, Damon!"

"I—don't go thinking . . ."

And wasn't that the whole trouble with this ebony-haired temptress—that she could *think*? Sofia had apparently remembered all he'd ever told her, and, dammit, he hadn't anticipated how good this made him feel. How good her body made him feel. . . .

"And is Miss Daphne still sick to her stomach?" he asked, to change this dangerous subject.

With a knowing smile, Sofia put the spyglass to her eye again. "She looks deathly pale and unsteady but resigned . . . at least until she meets her intended. And there's Trixie, admiring the sailors as they perform their tasks. From the time she was small, I saw those tendencies in her, a magnetism that will lead her into trouble."

"The pot's calling the kettle black, seems to me."

Sofia laughed aloud. "Are you complaining? What would you do if I was the type to fuss and fidget and bemoan my fate?"

"I'd return you to your two charges immediately. You'd pay penance for all the trouble you've caused me and your poor mother!"

Once again her direct gaze disarmed him: Sofia Martine had a knack for seeing right through him, for capitalizing on every verbal and physical opportunity he offered her. When she handed him the spyglass, Damon sensed he'd brought another fortuitous, happy moment to an end. Dammit.

"Mr. Comstock will be needing me in the galley. I hope your wound stops throbbing soon, Captain Delacroix."

Just that fast, she walked away, her gray uniform alive with the sway of her hips and the subtle flex of her waist. And just that fast, the gash began to throb like a son of a bitch.

How did she do it? How did Sofia twist everything to her own sly advantage yet leave him hungry for more of her company?

Damon exhaled harshly and put the spyglass to his eye again. They were a few days from land, so he saw nothing ahead but the open sea . . . yet the freedom it had always brought him, knowing he was in command of his own fate and his own fleet, felt strangely lacking now.

Nothing like a good fight with pirates to bring back the excitement! he reassured himself. *Nothing like being a man among men—and being the captain of them all!*

Was there? Well, *was* there?

8

"Nothing like a good fuck with a pirate to get me excited!" Sophia breathed in his ear. "Nothing like overcoming the captain himself—having my way with him until he succumbs!"

She grasped his hands and raised his arms above his head on the rumpled bedclothes. Damon laughed raggedly as she nailed him in place against the mattress: he loved this playacting as much as she did, and he looked deliciously nefarious with a red bandanna tied over his dark hair and an eye patch from his medicine chest. The stitches along his jaw rendered him downright devilish.

"Arrr!" he growled. Then he lifted his head to take a nipple between his teeth.

Sofia squealed and bucked against him, driving his cock deeper inside her. How she loved being on top, riding this rigid staff and the sinfully sexual man it belonged to. He thrust upward, watching her eyes widen, wiggled his hips in a quick rhythm as he rubbed that sensitive nubbin that would drive her wild with need.

When her breast slipped from his mouth, Sofia sat up and

gripped his hips between her knees. What a fine sight he made by lamplight, with his smooth muscles and skin slickened from their lovemaking. Lord, they'd been at it since he'd escorted her downstairs from supper! As his clock struck midnight, she remained in awe of his stamina—his ability to bring her to climax again and again, his willingness to pleasure her with his hands and mouth before he'd recovered from his previous climax . . . and the one before that.

It was sweet compensation for his unwitting little insults, wasn't it? A tongue up her slit made up for many a slip of his tongue.

Sofia smiled, feeling feline. Damon Delacroix didn't vex her on purpose. He was simply accustomed to being in charge of *everything*. Needed someone—her, namely—to teach him that receiving could be as good as giving and taking.

"You're wearing me out, lover," she murmured. Yet she couldn't resist arching her back to wiggle her breasts at him.

"Thank God you'll finally admit that!" he rasped. "I was wondering if you intended to sleep tonight. Not that *I'm* finished!"

She laughed as he wrestled her to the mattress to trap her beneath his powerful leg. "I don't see how you can possibly come again after—"

"Oh, ye of little faith." Damon's kiss took her from playfulness to need so fast her head spun—and then he rolled on top of her. "This time, however, it's *my* turn to ride, sweet creature. You're to lie absolutely still—no thrusting to meet my hips, no wriggling to speed things up. I have to please you one last time before we collapse, just to prove I can!"

Yes, it was the captain's almighty ego speaking, but who was she to argue? Sofia folded her hands beneath her head and settled deeper into his feather pillow. Morning—and galley duty—would come too soon, but for now she immersed herself in this fine, impassioned moment . . . in the crystalline glint in his eyes as he rocked against her hips . . . in the set of his jaw and the tightening of his chest as he increased his speed. The eye patch and that line of stitches on his stubbled cheek made him look so very dangerous. Bad to the bone and beyond redemption.

It was so difficult to lie there and just take it! And Damon knew that. In and out his member went, inciting fresh fires in flesh that had burned feverishly for hours now. She fought the urge to grip him with her inner muscles—he loved that! Her fingers itched to caress his smooth, damp skin—or to ruffle the coarse black curls framing his root. Or she could distance herself—could think of something else completely to make him labor in vain—but Sofia disliked such mental games. Far more exciting to play along—to feel the subtle thrum of her reawakening need.

"What a fine, feisty slave you are," Damon whispered. He closed his eyes, maintaining the slick in-and-out while pressing into her pubic bone. "The line between captor and captive sometimes blurs, but for now—for this pièce de résistance—you are mine, sweet Sofia. Here to do my bidding. Here to climax at my command."

Sofia followed his patter, allowing her body to flow with his. She would gladly become more than his slave, but it was too soon to fall for that fantasy, wasn't it? She must assume the captain would either deliver her to New York and then depart or sell her at a port before they reached America. But in her fantasies, Damon Delacroix wanted her for all time, wanted her in all the ways she longed for him.

She felt the first stirrings deep inside, answered his thrust with hips that couldn't hold still any longer. Her gasp echoed around his quarters like a wanton's call.

Damon growled low in his throat, a wild wolf summoning his mate. She grimaced, caught up in the impending wildfire. The ropes beneath the mattress creaked more insistently while the sounds of skin slapping damp skin goaded them on. His face tightened with the effort of holding back, waiting for her to fly high and fast with his release.

"I'm . . . so ready to . . . *explode*." He sucked air between his teeth, and his hips tucked inward. "But you've got to come along, my love. You've got to call my name and tell me when to—"

"Damon! Damon!" she panted. Sofia loosed her pent-up passion then: her mind spun into high, wild circles as she convulsed. Her head rose from the pillow, and the breath rushed from her lungs. "Please! Take me—shoot your cum up my—"

He gasped and poured forth. Again and again he drove himself inside her until she wrapped her arms around him and held him tightly against her breasts. Finally he collapsed. His breath tickled the hairs on her neck, slowing to normal over the next several minutes.

"Incredible. Absolutely . . . incredible," he breathed. And before he rolled off her, Damon snored softly.

Sofia smiled in the flickering lamplight. It was one of life's sweetest joys to cradle a sated lover . . . to know she'd satisfied him so thoroughly he had nothing left—not even the inclination for a sip of water before he fell asleep. His head found the crevice between her chin and shoulder, and he dozed peacefully.

Very carefully, Sofia reached beneath the spare pillow—the one she'd arranged against his bed head this afternoon. Ever so gently she tugged on the chain she'd hidden between the mattress and the post—didn't move another muscle as she slowly drew the handcuff across the untucked sheet. Damon had been accommodating enough to stretch his arm across her chest, and with one quick *click* she attached him to his bed.

He smacked his lips and mumbled something unintelligible. Then he resumed his soft snoring.

Sofia eased from beneath his body, again moving slowly,

alert to signs he'd awakened. When Damon was deep in sleep, she slipped to the foot of the feather mattress and gripped the leg iron she'd attached to the bed frame.

This would be trickier. She maneuvered the wide iron cuff around his ankle by pressing its opening into the soft mattress until it came up on the other side of his leg. The bedclothes muffled its *click*, and Sofia almost laughed aloud. Her lover was so exhausted he had no idea what had just happened to him.

Captain Delacroix was now *her* slave, held hostage in his own manacles!

She took a moment to admire his bare backside in the lamplight and the dip of his spine as it flowed into a strong back and broad shoulders that spanned the width of the pillow.

"Sleep tight, my love," she whispered. And out the door she went.

9

Sofia . . . Sofia, I long to see you. Are you doing well? Being treated well?

Sofia stood at the ship's railing as the mist rose around them before daybreak. What had drawn her to this post, with spyglass in hand? Inner voices had persuaded her to peer toward the *Lady Constance*, which bobbed languidly in the gray waters awaiting the wind. Thoughts of Mama made her gaze along the railing of the Havisham ship—

Was that an arm waving at *her?*

Sofia strained forward, holding her breath. Mama had always risen while it was still dark, before the rest of the household, so perhaps this habit had led her to the deck, as well. Her mother had surely learned she was aboard the *Courtesan* when Damon had fetched those spices for her, so—

There it was again, a movement barely visible in the mist. Yet she swore her mother had hailed her.

Impulsively she waved back, alive with the idea that fate had led her here—that her mother had called silently to her from across the water! Magdalena Martine had often teased the Havisham girls about having such powers, had convinced them she knew everything they did and said even when she wasn't present. Daphne and Trix called it "witchiness," but at this moment Sofia considered it a sweet gift, heaven-sent.

A gust of wind cleared the mist, and the solitary figure became clearer. Sofia twisted the end of the spyglass, willing the image to be who she wanted.

Again she waved, her heart pounding, and again came the reply.

"Mama!" she called, although her voice couldn't possibly carry that far.

The figure stood straighter, and then it waved more vigorously! That was clearly a dark uniform sleeve coming from beneath a cloak Sofia recognized.

"Mama, I miss you! I *love* you!"

The figure raised *both* arms in a wide wave—and then blew her a kiss!

Sofia's heart thudded. The mist moistened her cheeks as she gazed at the woman—

Someone was approaching from behind. His tread was silent . . . secretive. She turned to see who'd discovered her here, where she didn't belong.

"Miss Martine? How lovely you look without your leg irons."

How should she respond to Quentin Thomas? The quartermaster stopped a few feet in front of her, a panther on the prowl. She smiled and then looked toward the *Lady Constance* again. Perhaps Damon's rule about not speaking to his men had merit, after all.

"Such a shy lass. Yet I heard the captain's bed rocking far into the night," he ventured, stepping closer. "We could barely sleep, suspended in our hammocks down in the hold. The racket was so . . . *suggestive.*"

Her eyes widened. Had every sailor aboard heard them cavorting, then? Every night since they'd set sail? No reason to look around, for no one else was on the mist-shrouded deck yet. And with Damon chained to his bed, he wouldn't rescue her from this trap, either.

As Quentin came closer, his features became clearly visible in the mist: the chiseled cheekbones and lines bracketing thin lips, nostrils that flared like a stallion's when a mare trotted past, clothing more fashionable than the other sailors wore. This man was young and strong, and he wore his brass-buttoned frock coat and snug breeches well.

Don't accept the offer in those prying eyes, her inner voice warned. Or was it Mama, guiding her from the other ship? No doubt this man would swear he could keep a little secret, but word of her indiscretion would reach Damon in no time! Then the rest of the crew would be expecting a go at her—and what might Captain Delacroix do? She was his uninvited guest, at the mercy of his hospitality and moods.

"I realize the captain has forbidden you to speak to us," Quentin crooned, "but for just a quick kiss—a scratching of a desperate man's itch—I could become a good friend and protector, were Delacroix ever . . . indisposed."

Her breath caught. Did Quentin Thomas know the captain was chained to his bed? Had he heard Damon crying out or cursing? Sofia kicked herself for pulling such a trick on him, thinking she could come outside alone for a breath of air without any repercussions. The quartermaster smiled engagingly as he backed her against the railing.

"Think about this, then. If the captain decides to sell you— probably in New Providence, before we reach America," Thomas continued in a low, conspiratorial voice, "you'll be at the mercy of every unsavory character on the island. It's a pirate hideaway, you see. Nefarious men like Black Bart and Calico Jack Rackham and Blackbeard hide—and sell—their booty there. Do you want the likes of them bidding on you? Buying you for God knows what sort of purpose?"

Quentin's face was only inches from hers. His words and persuasive expression confirmed her greatest fears. And if she didn't get back to the captain's quarters to free Damon be-fore—if anyone saw her conversing with this man in such a compromising position—her fate was sealed with those pirates on New Providence, wasn't it? Captain Delacroix suffered no fools—and she'd just gotten caught behaving like one.

"Please, sir, if you'll excuse me, I should already be in the galley," she rasped. "Comstock will be wondering where—"

"Comstock can wait. I spent the night in agony listening to your moans and games," he replied tightly. "I have your best interests in mind, dear lady, and I'm prepared to pay you hand-somely for—"

"I'm not for sale!"

"—your *favors* now and again," he continued insistently. His eyes riveted hers, and his breath warmed her face. "If you agree, I'll buy you—your freedom, that is—from the captain before he puts you on the auction block in New Providence. I have a grand estate awaiting me in England. I can promise you a finer life than you've ever known in service. Or in slavery."

Sofia sucked in her breath to give herself room to think. The quartermaster blocked her view of anyone else who might be on the deck, and as her heart pattered rapidly she ransacked her brain for ways to outmaneuver this cunning seaman. As quarter-master, he was in charge of discipline aboard this ship. Above punishment himself, he believed, but he had the authority to make her life miserable.

"What if I don't agree?" It was a futile ploy to buy time. "The captain has already assured me—"

Quentin's snicker accentuated the angular lines around his eyebrows and thin lips. "If you believe *him*, well . . . let's just say many a lady's reputation has suffered from his empty promises. And many an unclaimed bastard walks the streets of every port he's visited, dear Sofia."

She raised one eyebrow, assessing these claims. "What has that to do with me? Had I been concerned about my reputation, would I have stowed away on a ship run by lusty, sex-starved sailors?"

Quentin chortled and kissed her quickly. "All the more reason Delacroix won't be choosy, come time to sell you. I, on the other hand, would love to settle on my estate with a fine, feisty wife. Life aboard a pirate ship is an adventure for a while, but the tightening of international maritime regulations means privateers and pirates will soon be caught and executed for their misdeeds. We're a dying breed, no matter how you look at us."

So it was true, then? Damon Delacroix had presented himself as an honorable escort for the Havisham girls, yet he intended to profit from this voyage—from the vast quantities of English textiles, spices, and gems in the holds of these three ships—even more than Lord Havisham had encouraged? Was he as heartless as he was unscrupulous?

What—whom—should she believe?

She knew nothing about this man Thomas except that he was playing upon her circumstances—taking every advantage of this situation. Sofia squirmed to see beyond his broad shoulders, prepared to cry out for help. But the mist was drifting around them again, and when Quentin Thomas placed his knee between hers, she was pinned to the wall by her uniform skirt.

"Please, Mr. Thomas," she pleaded. "I'm expected in the galley. I have an obligation to Captain Delacroix to—"

"Sofia," he breathed. His eyes narrowed, and he inhaled raggedly. When he pressed against her thigh, his erection felt very hard. Ready to invade her in the time it took to lift her skirts and step between her legs.

She stood absolutely still. Anything she said or did fueled his need to possess her. To overpower her.

"If you won't agree to my generous offer, I'll have no recourse but to report this indiscretion to the captain," he whispered. His kiss was hard and greedy and fast. "You were wandering the deck like a wanton, and I nobly offered to protect you—your honor—and provide for your future. Only an ungrateful little bitch would turn me away."

Sofia held his gaze, assessing her options. She was damned if she gave in to Thomas and damned if she didn't: he was second in command to the captain. Quentin Thomas was in charge of steering the ship, and he had authority over all matters of deportment aboard the *Courtesan*—matters of life and death, in cases of extreme violations of the rules.

Rules he applies to everyone but himself.

The wind blew her hair in her face—which meant either the ship or the wind had changed directions, didn't it? And where were the sailors who should be clambering up the ropes to the yardarms, to position the huge sails? If she could bide her time, surely someone would interrupt this distasteful discussion, which smacked of blackmail.

"On the contrary, Mr. Thomas," she replied in a purposeful purr, "I find your offer generous and attractive—especially because I must consider the welfare of someone other than myself. You see, my mother is aboard the *Lady Constance*. I was waving to her when you found me here, and—"

The quartermaster's laugh was edged with sarcasm. "What sort of fool do you take me for? I didn't become the captain's lieutenant by believing every far-fetched story a pretty wench fed me, so—" He yanked her skirt to her knees. "What'll it be, Miss Martine? If you need more time to decide, perhaps the rats and roaches in the hold can assist with your decision."

10

Damon awakened with a start. His dream of Sofia had gone awry when a faceless stranger had stepped from the mists to lure her away from him. And when he'd tried to rise up against the intruder, he couldn't move!

"What the—?" Pain shot through his wrist when he tried to roll over, and then his knee-jerk reaction nearly broke his damn foot!

He groaned. He'd been so concerned about rescuing Sofia from the stranger in his dream, yet she'd chained him to the bed—with his own irons! The minx must've hidden the manacles before dinner . . . and while her trickery put him at a disadvantage, he was chuckling. She'd planned this little slave game—had worn him out last night to show him who really had control of their arrangement, which had grown even more sexually charged since he'd freed her from these chains.

He admired her for that. Sofia Martine was anything but boring.

But how the hell was he supposed to run his ship? The gray

light at his portholes announced an overcast dawn and a day aboard the *Courtesan* that had started without him.

"Sofia? If you're behind me laughing—"

But only the ticking of his desk clock broke the silence in his quarters. Last night's brandy soured his mouth. How long had she been gone?

What sort of trouble is she causing? Even if it's unintentional?

"Somebody? Anybody!" he cried hoarsely. "Ahoy, sailors! Your captain needs—"

But did he really want his men to find him this way? His eye patch had slipped to the pillow, and his bandanna felt askew on his rumpled hair— reminders of the costuming Sofia had coaxed him into. His limbs felt heavy from being driven by her insatiable *wanting*, her unspoken challenge to keep up with her need. Again and again.

Surely someone would notice his absence. Surely Quentin would come along soon, and by now Sofia would be busy in the kitchen under Comstock's watchful eye.

He should relax. No sense in thrashing about, possibly reopening the wound on his face. His men were perfectly capable of navigating and carrying out their duties until he appeared.

Yet as the minutes ticked by, marked by the four-note chiming of his clock at the quarter hour, Damon grew uneasy. Why did his gut tell him something was terribly amiss—just as in that dream in which he couldn't identify the man who'd seduced Sofia?

More important, where's the key to these handcuffs?

A secretive knocking interrupted his racing thoughts. At the quiet creaking of his door, Damon cleared his throat loudly. "Yes? How may I help you?" he demanded, hoping he sounded fit and ready to come around the room divider to greet his visitor.

"Captain, sir? I had a sneakin' suspicion—" *Thunk . . . ka-thunk . . .*

Damon closed his eyes, awaiting his cook's reaction. Better Jonas Comstock than some of his other men, but he could predict what the crotchety old salt would lecture him about.

"Well, now. Why'm I not surprised to find you 'indisposed,' captain? Things ain't been goin' right ever since that hoyden hid herself here," he remarked gruffly. "Gives credence to that superstition about females bein' unlucky on board."

Jonas approached the side of the bed so he could fully take in Damon's predicament and speak to his face rather than to his bare backside. He pursed his weathered lips and glanced around, presumably for the key.

Delacroix coughed awkwardly. "This was a little game Sophia— only a *joke* she played after—"

"I'd find it a lot funnier if you was in plain sight and Quentin Thomas was at the wheel, sir." Comstock fished in his pants pocket and then flicked open his knife. "Miss Martine's leadin' you both around by the . . . leg, captain. And which one do you s'pose bribed the crew to steer clear of starboard deck? Your quartermaster or your whore?"

As the cuff at his wrist popped open, Damon scowled. "Why? What's going on?"

Comstock lifted a shoulder in a disapproving shrug. *Thunk . . . ka-thunk.* He hobbled to the foot of the bed to slip the point of his knife into the keyhole of the leg iron. "Heard her voice on the deck, so's I stepped out to see what was keepin' 'er—and it was Quentin. Gettin' real . . . friendly with her, he was."

"How do you mean, friendly?" Damon rolled into sitting position, rubbing his sore wrist. "Where the hell were the men? Don't they feel how the wind's shifted? If a storm's blowing in and—"

Another cryptic shrug. A raised eyebrow furrowed Jonas's

old forehead. "Sounded like some sort o' proposition he was makin' her—"

"That bastard!" Delacroix hopped from the bed and searched for his pants, which Sophia had apparently hidden under his bed as another part of her joke.

"And from the look on her face, she weren't turnin' him down, neither. The woman's no good, I tell ya. New Providence ain't but a day or two away, and she needs to be offa this ship, sir," he insisted. "If ya don't mind me sayin' so."

Oh, he minded, but the cook would criticize him anyway. Damon yanked the bandanna from his head and stepped into his pants. "Get back to the deck, Jonas. But not a word about how you found me—or turned me loose. Understand?"

"Aye, sir."

"Roust the men back to their posts—including Mr. Thomas," he added pointedly. "I'll make my appearance after I've assessed the situation."

As Damon watched the cook adjust to the marked rolling of the ship, his thoughts swirled like the upcoming storm. What should he believe—and whom? Comstock gloried in reporting doom and gloom—and dirt. Worse than a gossipy old crone, Jonas was, when it came to tattling.

Damon glanced at the foggy shaving mirror, running a finger lightly over the line of his stitches. If Quentin Thomas had taken liberties with Sofia, the quartermaster would suffer more bodily harm than a needle could mend.

Damon clenched his fists. It required the vote of the entire crew to depose the *Courtesan's* second-in-command—and in the same way, the men could remove the captain from the helm of this ship. Several of them had helped Damon claim it as a prize from the Royal Navy's fleet during a skirmish last year, and their pride and proprietorship had kept them all loyal to each other.

But by God, if he got ousted when they arrived at New Providence, Sofia Martine would be at *his* side.

Wouldn't she?

He finished dressing and proceeded upstairs cautiously. Time to find out which way the wind was blowing—on the open sea and among his companions, as well.

11

Sofia closed her eyes to endure another forceful kiss from the quartermaster. His hand had slipped beneath her uniform to fondle her thigh, and when it roamed higher, she gasped, hoping she sounded impassioned rather than impatient. "Mr. Thomas, sir, perhaps if we went . . . This shifting of the wind will have sailors swarming the deck to—"

"Let me worry about that," he whispered hoarsely. "Open the barn door and set my stallion free! Quickly, or I'll have to secure you below deck until you see things my way."

Thoughts of rats and roaches that scurried across her in the darkness made Sofia swallow hard. She squeezed her eyes shut and felt for the bulge in his pants . . . fumbled with the top button . . .

"So *here* you are!" A gruff voice accosted them in the thinning fog, punctuated by a *thunk . . . ka-thunk* on the wooden deck. "You've shirked your duties, Miss Martine! And because I had to leave my kitchen to come lookin' fer ya, breakfast'll run late."

Jonas Comstock's sneer appeared in the mist then, only a

few feet away. "Can you fathom how *unhappy* the men—and the captain—will be when they hears *why* they's been made to wait?"

With a sly chuckle, Thomas backed away from her. "She was prowling the deck, Comstock. Had I not stopped her, she'd be stirring up trouble among the men."

"And where would we be without fine, upstandin' officers like yourself?" the cook said with a sarcastic laugh.

The quartermaster raised an eyebrow. "Shall I inform Captain Delacroix of this incident, or will you?"

"That'd be your job, I'm sure. I've got a galley to run and breakfast to serve up while the weather's still fit."

Thomas's laugh sounded as mirthless as the assessing gaze he leveled at Sofia. "If my morning meal is inedible, someone will be made to pay. Have I made myself clear, Sofia?"

"Oh, yes, Mr. Thomas," she replied with a hiss. "Perfectly clear."

Sofia trotted after the gimpy cook, relieved yet wary. Comstock had caught her at a moment when even the most understanding of witnesses would assume she was enjoying the quartermaster's attention as much as he had relished hers. Even in the mist, Jonas had seen what was going on between them and would no doubt report it to the captain.

And how would she free Damon from his chains if she went to the kitchen as she'd been ordered? Her stomach clenched at the consequences of her little game, and she tried to think up an excuse—the loosest of reasons—for returning to Delacroix's quarters. But when Jonas turned to be sure she was following, his expression held secrets: he knew more than he'd ever let on. So she'd better toe the line, considering what he'd caught her at.

She entered the galley wincing. Was Comstock fumigating the place, or was that *breakfast* she smelled?

Sofia glanced into the huge pots bubbling on the cookstove and swiveled her head to keep from gagging. Somewhere some farmer's hogs would be happy to devour such a hodgepodge of scraps, but she couldn't imagine sailors eating it. "Salmagundi *again*, Mr. Comstock?" she asked before she caught herself.

The old cook crossed the galley with a heavy *thunk . . . ka-thunk*. As he dumped chunks of salted raw fish and potato peelings from last night's supper into the open cauldrons, he sneered. "The likes o' *you*, comin' from the upper crust's kitchen—havin' your way with the men who runs things—has no idea about usin' every last scrap 'afore it rots. I can see yer delicate sensibilities is offended by such humble fare. Not that I care!"

His rude laughter brought a flush to her cheeks. Jonas had tolerated her well enough the first few weeks of the voyage when she was chained, but lately he'd grown more peevish—and was getting in his jabs now after catching her with the quartermaster. But by the saints, she would *not* be cowed by this self-righteous old buzzard!

Sofia grabbed a long-handled spoon. "For your information, Mr. Comstock, I was born into domestic service," she began in a tight voice. "And while we were punished severely for wasting food, we did not ask anyone to eat such swill as this! How can you expect hardworking sailors to—"

The *pop* of a cork shut her up. "Sailors don't hire on with Delacroix for the food, missy," he informed her as he emptied a bottle of red wine into the pot. "If they gots complaints, they can go elsewheres to work—where the meals and the sleepin' arrangements ain't nearly so *exquisite.*"

Sofia held her breath as he dumped in a pan of coarsely chopped, hard-cooked eggs. The wine, as vile as vinegar, combined with the odd chunks of edible debris in the pot, made her eyes water. The bile rose in her throat.

"Keep stirrin' so's nothin' sticks to the pot bottoms," he ordered. "I need to confer with the captain 'afore we starts this day."

The old sailor thumped out of the galley before she could protest. And what would she tell him anyway? He'd come to his own conclusions about finding her pinned to the wall beneath Quentin Thomas, so if he was itching to report this to Delacroix—and because he was in such a bad humor today—Comstock could just hunt all over the *Courtesan* until he found—

The thought of Damon spread facedown, naked, and chained to his magnificent bed made Sofia snicker even though she was in deep trouble. She held her nose and stirred the salmagundi, imagining her lover's chagrin when Comstock discovered him. What she wouldn't give to see Damon's face at that moment! After all, her little trick wasn't funny unless someone else discovered how she'd taken him hostage.

Sofia glanced around the shadowy galley, itching to slip over to the captain's quarters. But where were Billy and Gasper, Comstock's two young helpers? The cardinal rule was to watch the fire at all times; if sparks from the cranky old stoves ignited the kitchen, the *Courtesan*'s timbers and sails would be aflame in minutes—and she would be to blame. Captain Delacroix would never forgive her the loss of his ship, and she'd never forgive herself if any of these men died because of her carelessness.

So she stirred . . . and stirred . . . and then switched arms. What on earth was taking so long? Surely it was time for the men to congregate, awaiting their breakfast. . . .

"Alone again, Sofia? How . . . fortuitous."

The familiar voice made her stiffen at the stove. She kept her back turned.

"One would think, with the dozens of hot-blooded sailors aboard this ship, some would try to pick forbidden fruit," he continued in an oily voice. "Just my luck that they haven't, eh?"

Sofia's mouth went dry. She stood absolutely still despite the noxious fumes wafting from the salmagundi.

Quentin Thomas approached her slowly from behind until his thighs found the backs of hers. He bent at the knees, forcing her to do the same despite the nearness of the hot stove. "And what trouble are we stirring up now, sweet Sofia?" he murmured against her ear. "Lord knows you don't need the fire in this cookstove to set every man on board aflame."

She bit her lip to keep from crying out when his hands closed over her breasts. He pressed into her hips to be sure she felt his erection. "We're going to be . . . Any moment now, Comstock's lads—or the cook himself—will return," she said in a tight voice.

"Not until I tell them to. Not until I hear your apology for rejecting me earlier and you agree to the 'plan' we discussed for your future."

His hot breath made her neck prickle. Sofia's eyes narrowed at his talk of her "rejection"—as if she had initiated that contact on the deck earlier! Well, she was one for making plans, too, rather than following someone else's.

What would it take to overturn this pot of salmagundi? Could she splatter the lecherous quartermaster instead of herself?

It might be worth some scald wounds, though, to boil this man's sausage. If she wounded the Captain's second-in-command, Delacroix would surely sell her on New Providence. But, then, compared to Quentin Thomas's nasty little games, life on a pirate's island sounded like a tea party.

Quentin's lips brushed her jaw. "Why are you so averse to my advances? To life as my lady at my estate in Wales? What could the captain possibly promise you that I can't?"

Sofia braced the long wooden spoon against the bottom edge of the pot nearest her. If she swung herself around—threw her weight away from the hot cauldron while she pulled hard on the spoon—surely she could escape most of the boiling stuff that would splatter. . . .

"Miss Martine! We must talk immediately—"

Damon! Her heart jumped at the sound of his commanding voice, and somehow she caught the heavy pot before it dropped off the edge of the stove.

"—about a certain instance of insubordination on your part and—and *retribution* on mine!"

Quentin let out a crude laugh as he stepped away from her. "As though this crafty wench knows what you're talking about! All she understands is the baiting of your sailors, captain. Her wiles require nothing other than female legs open in invitation."

Thomas thought she was a creature of animal instinct rather than intellect, did he? Clenching her teeth, Sofia positioned the long spoon against the bottom of the pot again. By the saints, she would not let this crude quartermaster—

A dull *clunk* made her drop the spoon; the business end of a pistol had struck the outside of the pot, and the captain himself was gripping its inlaid handle. Delacroix's other hand closed around her upper arm, and his eyes bored into hers. "*Enough* of your connivery! Come with me!"

Her heart thudded weakly. She had no choice but to keep up as Damon escorted her unceremoniously from the stove. Their footsteps beat an uneven tattoo as he steered her toward the wooden stairs.

"I—If you'll hear *my* side of this story," she protested, scrambling to match his long strides.

"I've heard and seen all I need to, dammit." A final shove got them to the top of the stairs, where they were met by the curious stares of the entire crew, who lined the deck. The first face she focused on was Jonas Comstock's, and the cook's smirk made her want to spit.

He'd played her for such a fool! When he'd gone to find Damon, Comstock had alerted Thomas that she was alone again—needed to be put in her place!—while the men gathered to watch her fall from grace. Sofia jerked her arm, but the captain held her tight.

"Billy! Gasper!" Delacroix ordered, searching the crowd for the younger crewmen. "Fetch me the pen from the hold. The one where the sheep are kept."

The two boys, who looked like gangly, unkempt ruffians, stepped from the line to gaze quizzically at Delacroix. "And what'll we do with the sheep, sir?"

"Figure something out! Anything other than letting them wander loose on the deck," he added tersely. As the two scurried off to do his bidding, he addressed the rest of his men. "Word has gotten back to me about *someone* breaking my rules! Who has spoken to Miss Martine?"

Eyes widened, and heads swiveled. Sofia opened her mouth to name the culprit, but Damon's dangerous glare silenced her.

Why was he behaving as if she was at fault? With his own eyes he'd seen Quentin fondling her while she stood helpless, unable to move from his lecherous grasp.

"Shall we review the punishment for those who don't abide by the rules?" he asked in a more insistent voice. The breeze ruffled his dark hair, and his swarthy face hardened as he studied the silent crew. "Barkis! What say you? And by God, if any of you don't know this answer—if the culprit's too cowardly to confess—I won't tolerate his presence another day! It's over the side with him!"

Barkis, a barrel-chested man with auburn hair and freckles, swallowed so hard his Adam's apple bobbed. "We's to be tried in court. Right here on the deck, cap'n," he rasped.

"Precisely. And if found guilty by majority vote?"

Barkis cleared his throat. "Mr. Thomas, the quartermaster, he decides the fate of the accused."

Sofia stiffened in Damon's grasp. Quentin Thomas, the weasel, now stood above them on the quarterdeck, steering the ship as if he'd been at his post all along. If only she could tell them—if the captain would let her speak . . .

But here came Gasper, leading Billy as they awkwardly trundled a makeshift iron pen between them. It was made of three barred sides without a floor, so the men could reposition the live animals when their stench grew bothersome below—or stow the pen in the lower hold, once all the sheep had become mutton during the voyage.

And what had that contraption to do with her?

"Set it on the foredeck in clear view." Delacroix's tone made the two lads scurry to the opposite end of the ship while the rest of the crew shifted nervously. Did they know of some onerous punishment involving the pen? Or were they concerned about the captain's methods of extracting confessions from wrongdoers?

Damon held her in such a firm grip she could feel his pulse. The stubble on his face rendered him darker and more dangerous than before, and she saw a more potent storm brewing in his blue eyes than on the horizon.

In fact, now that the morning mist had cleared, the day appeared sunny. Breezy enough to be beneficial, with no dark clouds or signs of impending rain. Sofia frowned. More was going on here than anyone had let on.

"Go below and get your breakfast," Delacroix ordered. "When you return to swab the deck and tend the sails, we'll discuss my new . . . arrangement for Miss Martine's captivity. Comstock and his lads go first, of course," he reminded them, "so they can dish up the meal."

Whispering among themselves, with many a secretive glance at Sophia and the captain, the crew trundled down the stairs. Damon waited until most of them were below before he turned to her.

"And now, my little vixen," he muttered as he escorted her toward the foredeck, "you'll be dishing up a few things yourself. In you go."

Sofia stepped into the pen as he held a side open for her. The sides came to the top of her thighs—a barrier that would keep sheep but would never hold an unwilling woman. *Was* she unwilling? Would she cause problems during this entire voyage, or would she follow his lead?

Damon hooked the third barred side to complete the iron triangle, watching her reactions. It was difficult not to blurt out what he knew—what he'd heard from others and seen for himself to meld his impressions of this morning's situation. But he had to know exactly where Sofia Martine stood—besides inside this symbolic pen.

"What have you to say for yourself, Sofia?"

Her dark eyes drank him in. She stood straight and tall, her hands clasped calmly before her, with no sign of apology in her demeanor. The light in her expression—the pressing of her lips into a delectable, distracting line—told him she was considering her answers carefully. No fool, this beautiful creature.

"It was only a game, Damon," she began softly. "I'm sorry it got out of hand, but most of that was not my doing, sir."

Ah, but that *sir* rankled him! He longed to make her call out his name in passion and release again—but if that were to happen, this conversation had to establish who would lead and who would follow. "Start from where we left off last night," he murmured. "Start from the moment you slipped those manacles on me, little witch."

Her lips quirked. "I was only playing with you, Damon. You fell asleep immediately after our last climax, and I chained you to your bed—and you were smiling sweetly as I did that," she added with a saucy smile. "I went up on deck for some air then, intending to free you before I went in to help Comstock."

"And?"

Her gaze drifted over the bow of the *Courtesan*, toward the two other ships that now sailed quite a distance ahead of them. "Something led me to gaze toward the *Lady Constance*, and there stood Mama! I waved, and she waved back! I—I got so excited, I cried out that I loved her—"

"You're sure it was your mother? The mist was thick this morning and—"

"Damon, really! I've known her all my life! How would I mistake her for someone else?"

His mouth clapped shut. Why did he assume that others had experienced the same cold, empty home life he had? He touched her cheek and felt wetness—a tear she was too proud to wipe. "I'm sorry. Please go on."

Sofia raised her chin to that haughty level he'd come to adore. "I heard someone behind me. Mr. Thomas, it was, and he propositioned me—"

It was the very word Comstock had used. Damon's hands balled into fists.

"—about . . . scratching his itch in return for a secure future at his estate in Wales. Oh—and this was *after* he offered to pay me and I refused him."

Her rising pitch bore out her distaste for the quartermaster, and the picture she painted fit with Damon's own assumptions. "Comstock insinuated it was you who lured Quentin into this discussion by—"

"One man will lie, and his friend will swear to it," she remarked hoarsely. "I'm outnumbered several times over here, Damon. You'll believe what you want to, so if you've already passed judgment upon—"

"Not upon *you*, dear Sofia." He grabbed her hand, well aware that Sofia Martine wielded more power than all his men put together—and she was smart enough not to flaunt it. "After all, I stopped you from hauling that cauldron off the stove to boil him alive."

Her lip quivered like a little girl's. "And why did you draw your gun, captain? For a moment I thought you intended to use it on me."

He squeezed her soft hand within his. "I'm sorry I frightened you! I wanted to scorch the bastard myself when I saw he'd trapped you against the stove. Taking up where he'd left off, apparently?"

"Insinuating that he'd keep our . . . little secret," she said with a hiss, "if I'd service his need. But if I refused him, he'd tattle to you about my wanton ways, walking the deck unchaperoned among men so helpless against my wiles! I was so disgusted I wanted to—"

"Sofia," he whispered. "I never believed you invited Thomas's attentions. But I had to hear the story from you."

She sniffled endearingly, and he pulled a bandanna from his pocket. What a picture she made, dabbing at her face! Her smile was like the sun shining from behind the clouds. "So . . . so you're not angry about me chaining you to your bed—"

"I thought it was wickedly funny that you held me hostage in my own irons." He glanced around, noting the sailors who tended their duties at a discreet distance. "And when I felt the ship changing direction—yet saw no storm clouds through my windows—and then caught my men exchanging money—"

"Money?"

Her childlike tone softened him even more. He should maintain the stern demeanor of a captain in charge of his ship and his crew, but, dammit, she'd been taken advantage of in an unforgivable way, by a man who knew better. "The sailors were wagering as to whether our illustrious quartermaster would get what he wanted from you. Quentin had instructed them to stay away. He'd left the wheel—the entire vessel—unattended to pursue pleasures that were against the rules and that put the entire company at risk. That's why the *Courtesan* was turning in the current," he added in a coiled voice. He, too, looked out to sea, shielding his eyes. "And that's why the other two ships are now so far ahead of us. If this spoils our plan . . ."

Damon pulled himself back into the present moment to see if she was figuring things out. Her lip had curled. What woman wanted to hear she'd been the subject of such wagering—even if she'd won? It cheapened her, and Sofia Martine was not a cheap woman. Matter of fact, she was costing him more pride and personal peace than he cared to admit, because, unwittingly, she'd brought out the worst in men he'd trusted.

Sofia stood before him, contemplating what he'd just told her. Her shoulders relaxed. She made no effort or demand to be freed—simply tested things in her sharp mind. "Does . . . does Thomas have an estate that you know of?" she asked.

He smiled sadly. "He once told me he'd been disinherited for corrupt behavior that turned his father and brother against him. The sea is his home because he has nowhere else to hang his hat, apparently."

"And he told me you were a notorious rake with illegitimate children in every port," she muttered. "I—I didn't want to believe that, so—"

"And do you believe it, Sofia? For all the intimacies we've shared, you know precious little about me." Damon released her hand, wanting her unsolicited testimony on his behalf.

As the seconds ticked painfully by, he knew the anguish of being the victim of others' assumptions and rumors, just as Sofia had been. Because she was lush and lovely—had had enough pluck to stow away on his ship rather than endure the Havishams' petty dramas—she was assumed to be a woman of dubious character.

Which made them a well-matched pair, didn't it?

"No, Damon. I believe you're a man of honor and integrity— even as you've admitted you're a pirate," she stated quietly. "And I believe you'll protect me and punish Mr. Thomas for the way he compromised the safety of your ship this morning."

He wished it were that simple. Oh, how he wished it were that simple.

13

At the sounds of footsteps coming from the galley, Sofia watched the emotions at war on Damon's face. He looked heavy laden, burdened by choices he and his crew must make.

"Stand your ground, Sofia. Keep your temper and state the truth if you're questioned," he said quietly. He nodded to the sailors as they cast their curious glances and then looked away.

Sofia didn't like this one bit. Would there be a major choosing of sides? Would someone—perhaps she—be voted off the ship? Maybe before they reached land?

She sighed. None of this would've happened had she kept her post with the Havisham girls.

"The crew's verdict must be a clear majority," Damon was saying to her, "for they've entrusted their lives to Thomas and me, and we've both . . . bent the rules." He gazed at Sophia with relentless blue eyes. "No matter what happens, I will not forsake you, sweet Sofia. Will you trust me on that?"

Her throat closed over an answer. Love—or something like it—welled up inside her, and she longed to caress his handsome face. No one but Mama had ever expressed such a commitment to her. "But what if they—"

"Don't worry, sweetheart. Be your inimitable self, and the truth will come out. I dislike making you a sacrificial lamb," he added with a grin that twitched wryly. "My intent is to separate the sheep from the goats. Always remember that we are the sheep—even if we're just a little bit black."

Sofia bit back a giggle. Then she watched a remarkable transformation in the man standing beside her: Damon, her lover and protector, once again became Captain Delacroix, privateer and swashbuckler.

As he squared his shoulders, his loose linen shirt rippled in the breeze, and the lean cut of his pants accentuated his muscled thighs. His hand went to the pistol tucked at his waist, he was wearing it for all to see, for the first time since they'd set sail. Damon's hair shone like a raven's wings in the sunlight: his emerging beard hardened his look. Gave him an unconquerable air, while the line of stitches rendered him formidable rather than weak.

His gaze made Sofia tight with pride. And *wet*. She felt hot and damp and itchy—so she looked away to regain control of her thoughts.

Unfortunately Quentin Thomas came upstairs just then. "Do you recall our conversation about what would happen if you ruined breakfast?" he asked tersely. "That *slop* you concocted—"

"No, Mr. Thomas," she countered quietly, "I was here on the deck this morning—with you—while Jonas made the meal."

His hand flew back to slap her, and as Delacroix stepped forward, the captain's hand went to his weapon. "We're going to settle this matter right now, Quentin. Who do you appoint to steer the ship during the trial?"

"Trial? I've called no bloody trial to settle my . . . differences with Miss Martine," he spouted.

"No, but I shall. Name your sailor or I will." Damon stepped closer, his gaze relentless. "We'll have a decision before we reach New Providence. Or we'll circle the island until we do."

The younger man scowled. "It's not your place to—"

"I'm the captain. I navigate the sea and her complexities while we're aboard the *Courtesan*, just as you were appointed her quartermaster. And one of us hasn't been doing his job."

"*That* part's correct!" Thomas brayed. He eyed Sophia suspiciously and then turned to address the men who scattered around the deck to assume their duties. "Our illustrious captain has called for a trial!" Thomas cried over the whistling of the wind. "Barkis! Man the wheel while I preside over these proceedings!"

"Aye, sir!" came the redhead's reply.

"And, Gandolf, you and Tripplehorn and Reilly are to post the lookout and mind the mainsails."

The three lithe crew members sprang to the rope ladders, clambering to the crow's nest and the yardarms while the rest of the men gathered around the foredeck. "Who's on trial, cap'n?" one of them called out.

"An excellent question!" Thomas barked. "Judging from who's been confined, we're finally to bring Miss Martine to her reckoning! High time, I say! We've seen what havoc's been wreaked by the presence of a stowaway—a woman who's up to no good!"

Sophia's cheeks flared, but she held her tongue. She still stood inside the tiny pen on a level slightly higher than the sailors, with the captain and the quartermaster on either side of her. Tension bristled between the two men until she nearly suggested they square off to settle their differences—and leave her out of it.

"Beggin' yer pardon, sir, but we *likes* Miss Martine!" someone called out.

"Aye! She ain't been no trouble a-tall!"

A chorus of agreement buzzed around the deck, and some-one else said, "Sure, an' it'd suit me fine if she did all the cookin'! Yer a good fella, Comstock, but me guts're rumblin' from that odd brew you served up this mornin'!"

"Hear! Hear!"

"Order! Order, I say!" Thomas called out. He paced around the pen, his arms raised in a ceremonial gesture for silence.

It was then Sofia realized the quartermaster resembled a peacock: his bright blue frock coat and deep green breeches set off his aristocratic bearing—at least among this crowd—yet he was all for show. This little drama was affording him the atten-tion he craved, wasn't it?

"Because Captain Delacroix has requested this hearing, we shall let him speak," Quentin announced with a condescending smirk. "Our verdict rests upon your consensus and opinions, my friends, but we cannot proceed if you all express them at once! Is that clear?"

The men nodded, focusing eager eyes upon Delacroix, Thomas—and *her*. Sofia stood stock-still inside the pen, careful not to let her gaze linger on any one of them. She clasped her hands, hoping to appear demure and above reproach. It was best to let Damon command their attention so no one could blame her for influencing the trial's outcome with flirtatious gestures.

"I commend you sailors for respecting my orders about not talking to our captive and for respecting Miss Martine as the fine woman she is," Damon began with quiet fervor. "And while Jonas Comstock has worked miracles with precious few provi-sions on earlier voyages, we've savored the finer fare Miss Martine has prepared for us—"

"Aye, sir!"

"Fine woman, that one!" came their murmured replies.

"Shall we get to the point, captain?" Thomas stopped pacing

to plant a fist on one hip. "Our duties await us—while it remains a fact that the woman you extol is aboard this ship illegally and that you intend to sell her in New Providence! Why
are we wasting our time—"

"My point," Damon countered, aiming his finger toward
the far horizon, "is that while the *Odalisque* and the *Lady Constance* have made good progress this morning, the *Courtesan*
has fallen dangerously behind."

The captain stood in front of Quentin Thomas then, speaking loudly enough that all the men could hear him. "When I
awoke this morning, the ship was spinning as though caught in
a storm, when in fact no one was steering her! And the decks
were deserted!" he exclaimed. "Why is that, Mr. Thomas? We
were hired to escort Lord Havisham's ship, yet we've nearly
lost sight of her!"

The crowd around them grew deathly silent. Sofia shifted
from one foot to the other, wondering how the quartermaster
would respond.

Quentin's expression curdled. "And why did *you* not correct this situation, captain? Perhaps because you'd been chained
to your bed with your own manacles? By Miss Martine?"

The crew drew a collective gasp, and someone snickered.

"Some blokes gots all the luck," one sailor muttered, and
those around him chuckled.

"I won't deny that story, because you've told it," Delacroix
said darkly. "But my behavior put no one else at risk, did it?
You, sir, bribed the men to clear the decks—to take advantage
of Sofia's walking alone this morning. By the time I showed up,
you'd not only made improper advances, but you were holding
her captive between yourself and the hot cookstove!"

"You have no proof—"

"I saw you myself! And I have heard Sofia's story about—"

Quentin sneered. "So you'll believe the tales of a tart yet dis-
count my testimony—"

"What say *you*?" the captain queried his crew. He gazed fiercely around the crowded deck until every one of them focused on him. "Did Mr. Thomas pay you to make yourselves scarce? And because he's your quartermaster, you followed orders?"

Silence. A lot of nervous swallowing.

"See there?" Quentin crowed. "To a man, they deny your outrageous claims—"

"Aye, sir, that's the way it happened!" came a voice from the rear. "We was followin' orders—"

"And God's own truth, had we knowed he was lettin' the ship go astray—"

"And makin' unseemly advances!" another crewman sang out. "Shame on you, Mr. Thomas, sir!"

"She was talkin' to 'er mother, too!" the outcry continued. "Lord love 'er, she was seein' after her own dear mum!"

Pandemonium broke loose then, and while Sofia's heart swelled with the way these ragtag sailors had taken her side, the real conflict was just beginning. What would happen if the man responsible for steering the ship—and the ship's business—got voted out while they were still at sea?

And what would happen if Quentin Thomas sought retribution? His stormy expression bespoke trouble on several fronts . . . on hers, yes, but it was Captain Delacroix the quartermaster wished to depose. Thomas's nostrils flared, and his face became a mask forged by hatred and traitorous intent.

"And where is all this ill-advised sentiment getting us?" Thomas demanded. "The fact remains that Miss Martine's presence has been the catalyst for—"

"I say we puts the *quartermaster* in the pen!" someone piped up.

"Aye, that'll do! In plain sight, here on the deck," another man joined in. A chorus of vigorous nods followed.

"Is it true that he defiled ya, Miss Martine?" somebody demanded. "'Cause if he did, we'll *beat* on 'im 'afore he's in that pen—"

"Captain, sir! We's got trouble ahead!" Gandolf hollered from the crow's nest. "Another ship's just fired on *the Lady Constance!* And she's flyin' the Jolly Roger, sir!"

14

Pirates! Far sooner than he'd planned for. Damon's pulse galloped, and he set aside his aversion to the man who swore he'd done no wrong to Sofia nor neglected his duties. "Can you see the flag?" he called up to the lookout.

"Black, with a white devil thrustin' a spear into a red heart, sir."

"Blackbeard," Damon muttered, glaring at Quentin. "Were we flanking Havisham's ship, he'd have recognized the *Courtesan*'s colors and not fired! As you know, this has always been our arrangement, but *you* . . . Delacroix reigned in his fury, for too many lives were at stake in a game gone wrong. "Man the cannons!" he called out. "Prepare your weapons, men! Take up rowing and speed us toward our sister ships!"

"Aye, sir!" came the unanimous answer.

"Musicians! Set the tempo! Prepare us to fight!"

"Aye, sir!"

All around them the crew scrambled to follow orders—except here, where Sofia stood in the sheep pen with Thomas beside her. Damon had wanted their dilemma solved, but personal politics mattered little when the brides' lives—and his men's livelihoods—were at stake.

"Man your post, Mr. Thomas," Delacroix commanded. "And by God, if your negligence has endangered anyone, you'll answer to me and to Lord Havisham! Dismissed!"

The quartermaster stalked across to the quarterdeck, oblivious to the sailors who rushed below to prepare the *Courtesan*'s cannons. And while meeting up with the notorious Edward Teach would ordinarily stir Damon's blood and make pirating an incomparable adventure, he wished things were going according to plan, dammit! The *Lady Constance* would have to defend herself until O'Roark's ship could turn around and come to her aide.

Meanwhile, Damon had left his partner in the lurch. While he and Morgan had devised a safe, simple plan for Blackbeard to plunder the goods aboard Havisham's ship—and to excite the girls a little—Teach didn't know this! They'd had no chance to get word to him, so the New World's most bloodthirsty brigand assumed this was business as usual. The *Lady Constance* would be easy prey unless he and O'Roark arrived in time!

"Damon, what can I do?"

He blinked. Behind them, two pipers and a drummer tuned up while, below, men's voices echoed in the hold as they prepared the cannons for battle. Yet here stood Sofia, her eyes alight and her dark hair whipping in the wind.

"Do?" he demanded. "Get yourself down to my quarters to—"

"Don't be ridiculous! If you think I'll hide myself away while—"

He grabbed her arms, astounded that her pulse raced and she looked so damn ready to fight alongside his men. Fearless, she was! Feisty and fetching and all those other things that made his blood pound for another reason entirely. She'd probably enjoy the pirate's life, and her beauty would convince authorities to look the other way rather than convict her for her crimes.

"That's my mother aboard Havisham's ship!" she reminded him. "I can't sit idly by, knowing Mama must take charge of Daphne and Beatrix in my place!" She raised her skirts to step nimbly over the iron pen, her expression defiant.

"Where do you think you're going?"

One eyebrow arched, and Sofia looked wickedly resolute. "To the kitchen. It's my place, you know."

"Excellent idea!" he cried over the trilling of the pipes. "If you can prepare us something *edible* before we douse the stove's fire to go into battle, that would be—"

"I'll see what I can do, sir."

Off she hurried, her hips swaying to the beat the drummer had set for the oarsmen below. He smiled at her spirit, yet Damon suspected she'd do as she damn pleased.

Just as Blackbeard would.

Sofia marched down the stairs to the galley, muttering. Wasn't it just like a couple of overgrown boys to quarrel and challenge each other—and then presume she'd hide when things went awry? The dim, low-ceilinged galley still reeked of the salmagundi that remained in the cooking pots and in many of the men's unwashed bowls. Comstock had chided *her* for being wasteful, yet he'd tossed so many eggs and pounds of pickled fish—and bottles of wine!—into this rank concoction that . . . well, it looked like it had been eaten before.

Ignoring that nauseating thought, she searched the shelves and bins. Her foot tapped to the patriotic tune the pipers played while the drum drove her heartbeat. Here was a bin of hard-tack biscuits, made the first week of their voyage and now showing signs of weevils and certainly deserving of the name *hard tack*. While conditions undoubtedly deteriorated when supplies ran low, Sofia shuddered to think that men were expected to eat such unappetizing, paste-colored lumps and soup made from what passed for garbage in the Havisham home.

Yet surely this salmagundi could serve a purpose . . . and who would *miss* these vile old biscuits?

Sofia smiled slyly. As she took pitchers and pans from the galley shelves, she pictured herself confronting the infamous Blackbeard—who, by God, would be sorry if he harmed a hair on her mother's head! She would prove herself so fierce and resourceful and indispensable Captain Delacroix couldn't possibly sell her when they reached New Providence.

If they made it. As the *Courtesan* surged across the sea, she heard the distant thunder of cannons. Wondered how Mama was faring with the Havisham girls.

But this was no time for guilt. Holding her breath, Sofia ladled the rank salmagundi into her pots, determined that her fight with pirates would bring about a resounding victory . . . to show what she was made of, but also who she was made *for*.

"Hoist the Jolly Roger!" Damon cried.

The Havisham banner of blue dropped down the pole. As the crimson flag with a crossed saber and dagger fluttered up in its place, Damon allowed himself a moment of sheer joy. Was there anything so grand as commanding a ship in defiance of the Crown? For most privateers and pirates, the booty meant little compared to the sweetness of setting one's own destiny at sea.

As they raced toward the *Lady Constance*, Damon gazed through his spyglass. Even from a distance, he heard Blackbeard's crew and musicians making a racket to frighten Havisham's men into surrender—which wouldn't take much, considering that Captain Ned Cavendish and his sailors were long retired from the Royal Navy. The *Odalisque* was now positioned to sacrifice herself if the battle raged for real; Damon surmised that the wily Blackbeard had fired his ship's weapons only as a scare tactic, for Damon saw no damage to his fleet.

"Full speed!" he called out above his musicians' accelerating tempo. "Row like your lives depend on it!"

His loyal oarsmen responded with an increased speed that made his heart swell. Moments like these made him damn glad he'd quit the Royal Navy to be his own man—and to allow his crew their freedom, too. When all went as planned, pirating ranked as a rewarding life. Well worth the dangers of confronting unpredictable outlaws like Edward Teach.

He saw the infamous pirate now, standing at the bow of his *Queen Anne's Revenge*. There was no mistaking Blackbeard: broad and tall he stood, festooned in bright sashes of silk that hung from his shoulders like holsters to keep his three pairs of flintlocks at the ready. Cutlasses and daggers encircled his waist, but his dark, bushy beard had become his trademark weapon; black braids tied in colored ribbons hung to his chest and waved in disarray around his wild eyes. Fuses of hemp, soaked in saltpeter and lime water, dangled from his hat, and he was now lighting the damned things to scare the bejesus out of those aboard the *Lady Constance*.

With a tight wave, Damon silenced the pipers. "Easy now," he cautioned his crewmen below. "Let her drift but be at the ready!"

"Aye, sir!"

Damon gulped air, hoping this unrehearsed maneuver went well, hoping Morgan realized what he was trying to do. "Teach!" Damon cried out. "Hold your fire! We'll deal!"

The behemoth aboard the other ship lit his match and put it to the end of a hemp fuse as though he hadn't heard Delacroix's offer—or didn't care. The *Courtesan* had come close enough that he *had* to know she was within firing range and ready to fire back.

The rows of cannons protruding from the *Queen Anne's Revenge* convinced Damon to try again. While most pirates didn't fire on a prize, preferring to keep a ship intact and convert it into their flotilla, Blackbeard's disposition was as unpredictable as those Havisham girls Damon heard squealing in abject fear.

Teach heard them, too. He tossed his spent match aside and took up his spyglass to peruse the passengers aboard the *Lady Constance*.

"Teach! Edward Teach, you bully mongrel, answer me!"

This time Blackbeard turned, glancing up at the crimson flag with its cross of sword and dagger. "Delacroix? Go find your own prize!" he roared. "I smell virgin flesh!"

The hair on Damon's neck bristled. Teach was a notorious womanizer with a wife and child in London—which didn't stop him from snatching and wedding any other woman he wanted. "We've sailed here to make you a sweet deal!" he called out. "Come aboard the *Courtesan* and pick your prize!"

The *Queen Anne's Revenge* now floated close enough Damon could see puffs of smoke that appeared to be coming from the pirate's ears. Blackbeard seemed to be considering his motive for offering a deal.

"We'd hoped to meet you near New Providence." Damon called out in a more jovial voice. "And the fine English goods in our holds will prove to your liking. Extremely profitable, my friend!"

This time the brigand took the bait. Lithely wrapping a rope around one leg, the bearded pirate swung the brief distance between their ships and landed on the *Courtesan's* deck with a solid *whump*.

"Delacroix," he grunted, glancing around the decks at the wary sailors. "Up to a little skulduggery, are we? I'm not keen on your intrusion of my—" Blackbeard's manic eyes focused on something behind Damon's back. His smile waxed diabolical. "If the wench is part of the prize, I'm all ears, man. Two ears with a cock on the rise between them!"

15

Sofia clung to her pot of salmagundi, holding the legendary pirate's gaze. He spoke as though she were part of a bargain with the Devil himself and with *him!* Lord, but he looked like a shaggy beast from hell with those dark braids waving around his face and smoke pouring from beneath his black hat. She hadn't expected such a villain to display his pistols in colorful silk sashes worn over flamboyant, fashionable clothing.

But, then, every man had a weakness for something, didn't he?

Damon's expression warned her to keep silent! To let him do the dealing!

But she had a weakness for speaking her mind, didn't she? "Blackbeard, is it?" she challenged. "What an honor it is to meet you, sir!"

The pirate shook with laughter. "Let's leave *honor* out of it, for I certainly have none!" he crowed. "How about you? Are you concerned for your honor around the likes of me, missy?"

"Why should I fear a man who sets his hair afire?" she shot back. "You're all for show, I'm thinking!"

"Sofia, that's enough!" Damon snapped. "We've three ships hanging in the balance—"

"You think I'm mad, then? More lunatic than legend?" Blackbeard advanced toward her, sizing up her attributes. "Methinks the minx had better mind her wayward tongue—and I've got places to put that tongue, too!"

Sophia's hand crept over the lid of the pot she clutched. She'd probably gone too far, but she had a point to make. "My mother and my two charges are aboard the *Lady Constance*. So help me God, if you lay a hand on them—"

"Why would I do that?" The pirate stood close enough now that the smoke from his fuses wafted toward her like clutching phantom fingers. "From what I've seen, the two lasses and their chaperone won't supply me half the sport I require. Can *you* handle all I've got?"

"She's not part of the bargain!" Damon spouted as he grabbed the brigand's frock coat. "So you can just—"

Blackbeard swatted him off as if he were a pesky gnat. "I strike my own bargains, Delacroix. I see what I want, and I intend to have her!"

Sofia's heart thudded, and she took a step back, her eyes still riveted to Blackbeard's. If she glanced at his fly, he'd have those few precious seconds to take further advantage—not that she needed to *see* how his erection tented the front of his pants. Edward Teach was every inch the debaucher legend had set him up to be, and much of his magnetism lived in his frightening yet hypnotic eyes.

"What'll it be, Sofia?" Blackbeard's voice coiled around her like a cobra. "Shall I plunder *you*? Or commandeer all three of these fine ships as my prize? I already know what you want, vixen. I smell your heat."

So this dandy fancied himself her lover, did he? Sofia braced herself; dared herself to follow through on her original plan.

"Would you like a better whiff?" she teased in a low voice. "Come and get it!"

When Blackbeard laughed lustily and grabbed for her, Sofia tossed the potful of salmagundi in his face. She broke away, toward other pots and pitchers she'd stashed around the deck.

"Grab those buckets!" she hollered at the sailors who'd been watching cautiously. She pelted Blackbeard with hard tack biscuits, and the men took up her cause with a rowdy vengeance.

"No! No, this is not—"

But Damon's cry got drowned out by a maniacal howl. A very wet, smelly Edward Teach clamped his arms around Sophia's waist and hoisted her over his shoulder like a sack of potatoes. He wiped his face against her hip, muttering. The burly pirate batted away the men who came to her aid while stomping across the drenched, biscuit-littered deck. Sofia struggled and kicked, but all she heard in return was his mean laughter.

"You'll pay for this, feist!" he vowed as he wrapped his ship's rope around them. He scowled at Damon and the others who reached up to grab him. "If you expect me to agree to any damn *deals*, Delacroix, proceed to New Providence ahead of me. We'll see how willing I am to bargain after I settle my score with this bitch!"

Blackbeard launched them across the waves that churned between the two ships. As Sofia flew past the *Lady Constance*, she caught sight of the Havisham girls: Daphne, whose face blanched in terror, and Trix, who looked absolutely flabbergasted—and downright delighted with this spectacle.

There stood Mama, too. Her exasperated expression told Sofia she'd gone a bit overboard with the salmagundi and biscuits.

But hadn't she distracted Blackbeard away from *them*? Hadn't she bought Damon and Morgan O'Roark time to strategize a plan? Captain Delacroix and Lord Havisham still had their ships intact, too, and perhaps she could convince her new captor to leave them that way, to allow the girls and their dowries to sail for New York while *she* served as the marauding pirate's prize.

It was a noble gesture on her part—until Blackbeard landed on the deck of his *Queen Anne's Revenge*. "I've brought us back a nice ripe tart, laddies! But I'll be sharing none of her until I've gotten my fill!" he crowed above his men's exclamations. "You, Bensen! Take a handful of your randiest men aboard the *Lady Constance*. Inventory the hold and then bring back the two lasses and their abigail."

"Aye, sir!"

Sofia squawked and kicked. "They'll give you nothing but trouble! Leave them—"

"I don't humor women, missy," he replied gruffly. "Pipe down or I'll spread you right here on the deck while the men watch. And then they'll take their turns!"

Keeping his arm clamped tightly around her, the pirate captain hailed more of his men. "Hurley! McGalliger! Station crewmen aboard Delacroix's three ships to be sure they take the direct route to New Providence. On with it, now! We divide the spoils tonight when we arrive at the island!"

"That was not what you said aboard the *Courtesan*—"

Blackbeard set her feet on the deck so hard pain shot up through her ankles. "Before you threw that slop in my face, I was inclined to be lenient," he muttered. "Now, however, you'll wash me and my clothes, and you'll heed the 'guidance' I give you about proper behavior in the presence of a gentleman. Your mother must be appalled at all this—and she hasn't seen the half of it! Now, scoot!"

He shoved her forward. Sofia staggered to the stairs leading to the captain's quarters beneath the ship's bow, wondering what he had in mind. Poor Mama. By now Daphne would've passed out in a fit of the vapors while Beatrix was probably displaying her charms to best advantage, flirting with whichever pirate had captured her.

And once again, all this has happened because you aban-doned your post to follow your own impulsive urges. The last thing Sofia saw before she went below were pirates pirouetting in their ropes, hurling themselves over to Lord Havisham's ship with swords drawn and bloodthirsty cries.

"Cantrell!" Blackbeard called out. "Bring hot water to fill my tub!"

"Aye, sir!"

The moment she stepped inside Blackbeard's quarters, Sofia realized what she'd forfeited by tossing that soup on him: the furniture here had barely survived many a drunken brawl, and it wasn't so much arranged as strewn about the low-ceilinged room. What a dark, dingy cave this was. The man who occupied it seemed a Neanderthal, indeed, compared to Damon Delacroix.

Footsteps thundered down the stairs behind them. Cantrell and two other snaggletoothed sailors dumped buckets of steaming water into a trough near the cabin's only window. They eyed her with lewd curiosity before hurrying back to the galley for more water.

Blackbeard leered. He sloshed liquor from a bottle into a tankard and then tugged on the two fuses that still smoldered in his hair. They made an infernal *hisssss* when he dunked them. "We'll be removing these offensive garments now," he informed her as he slipped his pistols from their silken holsters. "Make yourself useful."

Sofia's insides clenched. While Edward Teach exuded an impressive presence with his height and those fancy clothes—not to mention that beastly wreath of black, braided hair—the pirate was no prize up close. He smelled of an unwashed body and harsh cigars. And then there were those wild, maniacal eyes that never stopped moving yet always remained focused on her. Little chunks of Comstock's stew clung to his braids and clothing, which did nothing to improve her opinion of him.

"Undress me! *Now!*" He stooped to bring those cold, shiny eyes to the same level as hers. "Don't tell me you're an innocent, Sofia! I've fucked and forgotten more whores like you than Delacroix will meet in three lifetimes!"

Such a remark was hardly a compliment to either of them, and it made her regret her brazen stupidity even more. Would Damon want her after Blackbeard left his mark? She'd had half a chance to convince Captain Delacroix he should keep her rather than sell her, but his expression had looked less than encouraging as she had sailed away on Blackbeard's shoulder.

"What were you doing aboard the *Courtesan*?" Teach grabbed her hands and placed them on the buttons of his smelly, saturated coat. "Delacroix knows better than to flaunt the likes of you in front of his men."

How should she answer that? No matter what she said, he'd twist it to his own advantage like a knife in her back.

"I'm his intended—his talisman!" she blurted. "Contrary to superstition, I've brought him great fortune and joy. He—he named his ship for me!"

"He keeps a courtesan aboard as a charm?" Blackbeard's lip curled in derision, and then he grabbed the vee of her neckline in both his powerful hands. "Seems Captain Delacroix's luck has just run out."

16

What the bloody hell went wrong? And so damn fast!

Damon stood fuming at the stern of the *Courtesan*, watching Blackbeard's ship swing into position behind the three vessels in his command. Like a trio of square-rigged sheep, they sailed ahead of the wolf who herded them into his lair. All because Sofia had taken charge before he could discuss his plan for Edward Teach to share their booty.

So now Quentin Thomas and the other two quartermasters steered toward New Providence while Blackbeard's minions held them at gunpoint. Other pirates from Blackbeard's ship patrolled the decks to keep the captive captains from signaling one another.

"Shoulda opened fire on 'em whilst we had the chance," Jonas Comstock muttered beside Delacroix. "Damn bastard's gonna do things his way, no matter what he's *said*."

"I was ready to attack! Full cannon fire!" Damon raised his spyglass to peer toward the *Queen Anne's Revenge*. "But I'd likely have hit the Havisham girls or Mrs. Martine. Or Sofia."

"No loss there, cap'n. She's been nothin' but trouble since—"

Delacroix sucked in his breath. Teach's quarters were beneath the fore, directly in front of him now. Through his lens, Damon peered into the captain's sanctum . . . saw Blackbeard rip the uniform from Sofia's body in one vengeful, bloodlusty move. No doubt she was egging him on *again*, playing her sultry games because she'd caught the fancy of the most notorious—

Then he saw her face.

Regret. Remorse. *Sheer terror.* Those were not the eyes of a temptress at play as the dull, careworn clothing fell from her body. She shrank away from her captor, trembling. Pleading for mercy.

Deep down, Sofia Martine was not the vixen she made herself out to be. It occurred to him then, dammit, that she'd thrown that salmagundi and those biscuits as distractions . . . to attract Blackbeard's attention away from him, so he could prepare to fight, if need be. She was concerned for her mother's safety, saying the Havisham sisters were troublesome—anything to keep the pirate from believing he wanted them.

But once the bastard saw Sofia, it was all over. *Two ears with a cock on the rise between them.* Teach had described himself perfectly, and as his frock coat came off and he ordered Sofia to strip him naked, that cock sprang out like the devil's pitchfork, deep red and ready.

Damon grabbed his pistol and shot at Blackbeard's window. Any fool knew it was too long a distance—just a way to relieve his frustration. . . .

"What the devil're you doin'? You're daft if ya think—"

The glass shattered with a gratifying tinkle. But when Blackbeard swore and glared out the high window of his quarters, Damon knew he'd made a grave mistake. Sofia pitched forward into her captor's naked embrace.

The rivulets of red trickling down her back made the bottom fall from Damon's stomach. An apology sprang to mind, but before it reached his lips Comstock gasped and slumped to the deck beside him. Then a pistol butt met Damon's skull, and he blacked out, as well.

"God dammit to hell, when I get my hands on that bastard Delacroix . . . Cantrell!" Blackbeard roared. "Help me, you son of a—bring her mother! I know damn well you're at the key-hole."

Sofia bit back a snicker. She remained utterly still, dead weight in the arms of the man who'd vowed to ravage her be-fore—and after—his bath. Her shoulder stung, and she felt the trickle of warm, sticky blood, but Damon had shot out the window! He'd been watching over her, even after Blackbeard commandeered his three ships! He'd saved her from being bru-talized, and she would—well, she'd love him forever for it.

Hurried footsteps . . . the sound of a struggle . . . and then a pitiful cry came through the doorway. "Sofia! What have you done to my—she's bleeding!"

"Not my fault, dammit!" Blackbeard snarled. "Put her on the cot while I go after the bastard who shot her!"

Sofia remained limp and boneless as Cantrell carried her across the room, muttering. Her breath rushed from her lungs when he dropped her on a hard canvas surface, but somehow she made him believe she was out cold. Soon to be further gone.

"Hot water's in the tub," Blackbeard growled from across the room. "And you're not to *stare*, dammit, while I change clothes. This is all your harlot daughter's fault!"

Mama hovered over her, whimpering softly, scared out of her mind about what Teach might do next. Sofia longed to hug her mother close and whisper reassurances, but for the moment her endangered state was her best weapon.

When boots clomped across the room and up the stairs, Mama let loose. "Sofia! Sofia, tell me you're not—"

"I'm fine, Mama, but keep wailing! Make everyone believe I'm not long for this world."

Two warm, trembling hands clasped her face. "You're talking!" she whispered.

Sofia opened her eyes, focused on Mama's strained face, and then winked. "Takes more than death to shut me up!" she quipped. "Damon's shot just grazed the skin. Use my shift for a bandage—"

"Shhh! Footsteps!"

Sofia went limp again and shut her eyes. Lord, but that wound was starting to throb! Yet she could subdue the pain by peering through the slit of one eye . . . to see that Cantrell had returned.

"I don't need your—don't you touch her!" her mother huffed. She was ripping the muslin shift into long strips, standing between the sailor and the cot, bristling like a rabid mongrel. "Go find someone to help you carry this cot to wherever you've hidden the Havisham sisters! I *will* watch over my girls! I'm a *witch*, mind you, so don't think you'll defy me!"

Sofia bit her lip to keep from laughing at the yellow-toothed pirate's dismay. When he trotted off, she opened her eyes again. "A witch, Mama? Why, if *I* had called you that, you'd—"

"Enough out of you, too, Sofia. Brace yourself for the sting of this whiskey."

Mama grabbed a decanter from Blackbeard's shabby shelf and tipped it. Liquid fire singed the wound on Sofia's shoulder, and she sucked air. It was sweet relief, however, to feel her mother's loving hands wiping the blood from her back . . . the pressure of her fingers stanching the flow . . . the quick competence with which she wrapped the strips of muslin tightly around the top of her arm.

"I'm going to cover you," Mama announced stiffly. "Why you've chosen to play with fire—and these pirates—is beyond me, but—"

"Mama." Sofia gritted her teeth against the pain when she shot out her arm, but she gripped her mother's wrist anyway. "Mama, I did a stupid, selfish thing, leaving you to watch over Daphne and Trix. I'm so sorry—"

"Shhh, they're coming again," her mother replied with a weary smile. "I was peeved about it at first, but when I realized you'd written me a ticket to America—that I wouldn't be losing you at Constance Havisham's whim—I adjusted myself to the circumstances. Even if Daphne is a royal pain in the arse with all her puking and passing out."

Sofia muffled her giggle against the smelly cot and closed her eyes again. Cantrell had returned with a cohort. Mama tucked the torn uniform around her bare body and warned the two men again that she was a witch ready to hex them if they touched her daughter.

She felt herself being lifted, trundled off to God knew where.

Anywhere but here, she mused as a pall of pain settled over her. *Thank you, Mama, for loving me in spite of all this.*

17

As they floated toward the harbor of New Providence at dusk, the island held no excitement for Damon; his head throbbed like a son of a bitch, and a knot had risen on it. As he looked toward the torch-lit streets teeming with gaudily dressed strumpets and the drunken sailors who chased after them, his usual sense of anticipation dimmed.

He'd shot Sofia. That much he recalled, although the balance of the journey remained a blur. He gripped the railing to keep himself upright as his men heaved the huge anchor overboard, lacking their usual enthusiasm, too. Blackbeard's sailors had kept close watch since he'd fired his pistol, and he couldn't predict what the mighty pirate might demand of them now that his pretty new playmate had been injured.

Why had he made such a stupid move? He'd endangered all of his crews, not to mention the Havisham girls and their dowries, with that spur-of-the-moment shot. By all rights, it shouldn't have hit the window, much less Sofia.

You were defending her from that brute Blackbeard. Any decent man would've done the same.

Small consolation, that.

You wanted her safe, and you'll never forgive yourself for not shooting the bastard when he first grabbed her.

Damon blinked. His heart raced crazily, and he searched the decks of the *Queen Anne's Revenge* for signs of her. At least he hadn't seen any bodies being slipped overboard—

But he'd been out cold. What if that heartless monster had dumped Sofia into the sea without giving Damon one last look at her lovely . . .

Is she dead or alive?

A sob caught him by surprise, and he glanced around to be sure no one else had heard it. His men were scurrying up to the yardarms like monkeys, securing the sails while Blackbeard's watchdogs looked on. He saw Captain Cavendish pacing the deck of the *Lady Constance* on one side of him, while Morgan O'Roark held an animated discussion with the brigands who'd taken over the *Odalisque*.

No, this was not their usual jovial landing at New Providence. It felt anything but providential.

"Delacroix! Bring your partner before I turn my sailors loose in your holds."

Blackbeard stood on the pier glaring up at him, his legs spread at a cocky angle, and his hands clasped behind his broad back. He'd changed his clothes, but those six flintlocks still rode prominently in fresh silken sashes.

Damon straightened, reminded himself to show no sign of pain or weakness, because Blackbeard probably didn't know he'd been knocked out. Every step down the gangplank made his head throb. His sight blurred in and out of focus, but he made it to the pier without stumbling.

Blackbeard studied him for a few moments while they waited for O'Roark. One hand snaked out, and a finger found the line of stitches along Damon's cheek. "A memento from that she-devil?" he teased. "Surely you knew better than to let Sofia shave—"

"What have you done with her? So help me God, if you've—"

The pirate's sarcastic laughter echoed around the waterfront. "Fine time to worry after you *shot* her, for Christ's sake! Any civilized man would be more careful where his *betrothed* was concerned. Most wouldn't aim at a *talisman*, much less fire at her."

Betrothed? Talisman? Damon almost blurted out a denial, but if Sofia had told her captor she was his fiancée, his good luck charm . . .

Or had Blackbeard made up this story as a trap?

"Any decent man would've shot you for grabbing her," Damon muttered, "but I foolishly assumed our previous deal-ings—ventures and prizes we've shared—would foster more respect for my woman. If you thought I'd allow you to rip off her—"

"If you thought I would wear the reeking coat and pants she ruined, you're a jackass, Delacroix. A crazy, cockless jackass."

The pirate was tormenting him into revelations he didn't care to make—at least until he learned of Sofia's condition. Damon cleared his throat, trying to think despite his throbbing head. "Had you given me the chance—had you not snatched Sofia before we could talk—you'd know my ships are escorting a nobleman's two daughters and their very generous dowries to New York. I'd planned to be a sporting sort—to share my good fortune without you having to lift a finger! But until I see Sofia—"

As Teach let out another rude laugh, a fluttering motion caught Damon's eye. A white dove, perhaps? What sort of omen would that be?

He turned as though to greet Morgan O'Roark, and when his gaze traveled to the railing of the *Queen Anne's Revenge*, he saw a small white handkerchief. Sofia's mother was waving it at him!

She was smiling. Like she knew a juicy secret.

Damon's pulse settled into a dull roar. He kept his face in a guarded mask, pondering his options. The moment Blackbeard swiveled his head, however, Mrs. Martine disappeared.

"O'Roark! Is everyone aboard the *Odalisque* behaving properly under the watchful eyes of this dragon Blackbeard?" Damon kept his tone playful, but he shot his partner a purposeful look.

Morgan removed his hat to smooth his hair while gazing up toward the tavern nearest the bay. "Aye," he responded tightly, "but we were none of us happy to have those uninvited 'guests' come aboard. Considering our fine cargo and the plan to *share* it with you, Teach, your commandeering of our ships was rude and—"

"I had no chance to tell him of our offer," Damon interrupted. "He absconded with my beloved fiancée, Sofia, and when I shot out his window to protect her honor, he used her as a shield! She took his bullet." Damon kept his expression somber, and his eyes wide in silent warning.

Morgan covered his confusion with genuine shock as he glared at Blackbeard. "Why the hell'd you do that? My God, man, have you no regard for the fairer sex—"

"Too much regard!" Delacroix countered hotly. "He snatched her for himself even after she pelted him with hard tack and tossed salmagundi in his ugly face!"

"Not only rude but stupid to ignore the lady's obvious dislike of him!" O'Roark remarked. "Not a man I'd trust for any exchanges of—"

"You two buffoons can natter all you want, but the fact remains I have captured your ships, and I'll damn well take what I want." Blackbeard's swarthy face hardened in a sneer—and then his head swiveled to look toward the railing of his ship again.

"Ha! So the sly tart has made a miracle recovery, has she? Cantrell!" he bellowed. "Chain her to the mast—and the other bitches with her! We'll let Captain Delacroix watch as we take our pleasure. Then she'll bring us a fine price on the auction block!"

Damon's pulse sang when he saw Sofia's foxlike smile. Her hair was arranged fetchingly about her dusky face, and she wore an alluring gown of purple that teased at her cleavage. When she was grabbed from behind, her shriek sent him into a rage. "She'd go willingly enough if . . . You don't have to treat her like—"

"Like the ripe and ready tart she is?" Blackbeard laughed again, gesturing toward the gangplank of the *Queen Anne's Revenge*. "Let's see how much your intended loves you—how much she's worth to you, Delacroix. Let's see if she's indeed your ship's talisman. Are you feeling lucky, captain?"

Sofia cried out when Cantrell jerked her arms behind her to chain her to the mast. Her wound broke open, and the blood would ruin the violet dress Beatrix had loaned her. It was a plain, dark gown the young blonde hadn't fancied on herself—one of the many new ones in her trousseau—but Sofia had felt well dressed for the first time in years. Eager to entice Damon with how pretty she looked in something besides her gray uniform.

"You needn't be such a beast about it! What have we done that calls for such crude treatment?" Sofia's mother rushed over to check her shoulder, but a trio of Blackbeard's bullies grabbed her, too, with manacles at the ready.

Cantrell flashed a nasty, gap-toothed grin as he snapped the irons on Sofia's ankles. "When you lovelies get wrestled to the auction block to be poked and prodded in all yer private places, we'll seem like titled gentlemen," he replied in an oily voice. "Even after we satisfies ourselves, we'll look like saints, compared to how the slave mongers treatcha."

Slave mongers. Sophia swallowed a sob. She'd come so close to escaping that fate, convincing Damon Delacroix she was worth more to him as a lover than as a commodity. Daphne's shriek pierced the evening air behind her, and then came Trixie's curses. The younger Havisham sister could've been a stevedore, the way she shot vile language at the sailors who bound her, and if her mother had been here . . .

But so many things had gone wrong since they'd left Lady Constance waving from the pier. Even Lord Havisham, with his sly suggestions about making a fortune on this voyage, would be appalled at this cruel turnaround in Damon Delacroix's plans.

And here came her captain now, looking angrier than she'd ever seen him. Yet beneath that fringe of dark, fledgling beard she noted a pallor, a haggard anxiety he was trying to hide. She'd wondered why he hadn't come to her aid sooner, but Sophia had never guessed that he, too, might have been mistreated. Was he beaten for shooting at Teach through his window?

"So, mates!" the swaggering blackguard cried as his sailors gathered on the deck. "It's the moment I've awaited! Had Delacroix not wounded this vixen, why, I'd have had my go at her and turned her over to you lads long ago. But the waiting only intensifies the wanting, eh?"

Randy laughter rang around them, and Sofia's stomach knotted. She wasn't a bit shy when it came to lying with a man, but the looks on these sailors' faces suggested a brutal sport she'd never endured—nothing like love or even mild happiness lit their eyes as they gazed at her. Like a pack of wild dogs, they licked their chops in anticipation of bringing down their prey. And this while poor Mama looked on.

"Ten pieces of eight!" Sophia called out. "Set my mother free, dammit!"

Silence. All eyes went from her to Blackbeard, whose lips quirked. "Your noble generosity moves my heart, but that's hardly enough to—"

"It's all I have! Please, sir, leave her out of this!" Sofia flexed her wrists behind her voluminous skirts, testing the cuffs that bound her to the mast. If she relaxed her hands . . . The manacles were designed for much bigger limbs than hers. . . .

Cantrell's eyes went wide when he realized the other sailors had shackled her mother. "That'n's a *witch*! I seen her workin' her spells—why, she nearly hexed me, sir!" He scurried over to unlock her mother's manacles and then jumped back as though Mama might curse him with her vicious glare.

Mama—now Magdalena Martine playing to a potential audience—stepped away from the chains. Her salt-and-pepper black hair had fallen loose in the uproar and blew around her slender, pale face. After a purposeful glance at Sofia and the Havisham girls, she held herself haughtily, flexing her fingers as if she were about to turn the sailors into toads or render them impotent.

Blackbeard stepped forward, bristling. "I've given no orders to release—"

"We'll not be sailin' with ye, sir, if the crone sets her black magic loose on yer ship!" another sailor chimed in.

"Ain'tcha seen the way that oldest girl twitches and heaves and the younger one bares her teeth at us?" another crewman called out. "They's under her spell, and we will be, too!"

Sofia suppressed a smile as, around the ship, Blackbeard's men were nodding cautiously as they considered their risks. Sailors were such a superstitious lot! If Mama's powers had grabbed their imaginations, playing along was Sophia's best weapon, wasn't it?

A glance at Delacroix suggested that he, too, was following this unexpected turn of events. And when his gaze met hers, the intensity of those crystal-blue eyes—the longing on that dear, grizzled face—sent a jolt through her. He *did* intend to rescue her! He *did* have feelings he hadn't expressed.

"Fifty gold doubloons! Plus the silks and spices aboard the *Lady Constance*!" Delacroix cried. "Set the girls free!"

Blackbeard pivoted with a sneer. "The wench's charms are worth far more than—"

"That's to free the *sisters*," Damon clarified. "Lord Havisham's connected to the Crown. He'll have the Royal Navy chasing down every last one of us if his girls don't arrive in New York."

"Then it'll be worth more than that to Lord Havisham to ensure their safety, won't it?" Blackbeard countered. "If your three ships are loaded with fortunes untold, why's your offer so skimpy, Delacroix?"

Morgan O'Roark stepped forward. "Fine, then! I don't want that witch hexing *my* ship! You can have the *Odalisque*—lock, stock, and barrel—as ransom for the Havisham lasses."

Dismay flashed across Damon's face until O'Roark's gaze prompted Sofia's mother to keep the hoax going. With a dramatic flourish, Mama raised both arms to encompass the entire crew of the *Queen Anne's Revenge*, and then she pivoted to face the sunset. The horizon glowed like hellfire, and the full moon rising in the fiery sky seemed a bad omen indeed.

"Moon of revenge and moon of sorrow," she chanted in a high whine, "Change these men to maidens tomorrow!"

With a cry of sheer terror, Cantrell fled the deck, and his companions followed. Down the ropes and off the decks they scurried, their eyes wide while Blackbeard's commands went unheeded.

"Fools!" the pirate captain hollered after them. "That woman's no more a witch than . . . You'll not be claiming your share of the prize if you—"

The thunder of boots drowned him out, which gave Delacroix and O'Roark a moment to exchange strategy. Sofia stood with her back against the mast, watching them, waiting. Her hands were free, and by slipping off the kid slippers that matched Trixie's dress, she could wiggle her feet from the leg irons as well.

But it wasn't smart to flee with the crowd if she was to be used as the next bargaining point. That had to be Damon's reason for not including her in his offer . . . didn't it?

O'Roark's grin bolstered her spirits. Mama still stood with her arms raised and her hair blowing about her face; at the captain's slight nod, she faced the *Odalisque.*

"Fie upon thee and thy decks!" she cried. "Haunts with hands around thy necks!"

O'Roark rushed to the helm to holler at his crew. "Abandon ship, men! We've been cursed! Abandon ship!"

And with that, he joined the last of Blackbeard's fleeing pirates while Damon went to the opposite rail to signal his own crew. "Thomas and Comstock, abandon ship!" he cried. "Captain Cavendish! Flee for your lives! We've a witch in our midst!"

Sofia wanted so badly to laugh, but Mama had turned toward her to point at the mast where she was chained.

"Manacles, fall away!" she shrieked.

With a flourish, Sofia raised her arms. The handcuffs landed on the deck, and then she hopped from the leg irons as well.

Blackbeard's face fell; if only for a moment, he seemed worried.

This gave Damon time to rush to the Havisham sisters with a small knife. The two girls, however, had already slipped their irons, so they sprang from their poles with triumphant cries and hurried off the ship. Mama then pointed a witchy finger at Blackbeard and held it there like a pistol while she steered Sofia toward the gangplank.

The last thing Sophia saw was Damon's handsome grin, rendered more brazen by that rugged line of stitches along his whiskered chin.

"Best of luck unloading the *Odalisque*—or finding a new crew," Captain Delacroix crowed. "Word of Magdalena's witchcraft will spread around the island like wildfire. There won't be a stevedore or sailor to hire for days!"

18

Teach was no fool, so Damon hurried down the gangplank, the last in a long parade of crewmen headed toward the pubs of New Providence. No doubt Damon's ships would be empty by the end of the evening, once Blackbeard paid locals to unload them, but at least his passengers were safe. So safe, in fact, that as he quickly searched the streets he saw no sign of Sofia, her mother, or the girls.

He ducked down an alley he knew well and into the tavern his partner had designated as their rendezvous point. Behind the noisy room, where kohl-eyed women in parrot colors propositioned him at every turn, Damon found the open court-yard and the crews of his three ships. His sailors lifted pints and guffawed with each other while sloe-eyed wenches circulated with trays of smoked meats, pickled eggs, and fresh tropical fruits the crews hadn't seen since their last visit.

"Delacroix! You made it out alive!" His partner hailed him from across the crowded space, waving a tankard above the crewmen's heads. "Any repercussions?"

Damon squeezed between rowdy sailors, who clapped him

happily on the back, and then accepted a fresh tankard from one of them. "Can't argue that meeting like this was a stroke of genius, with a little help from witchcraft. But Magdalena's hex will wear off once Blackbeard pays some locals to unload—or even sail away with—our ships."

"I've taken care of that." O'Roark looked as smug as Damon had ever seen him. "I whisked Sofia and the other ladies into the innkeeper's care and then assured Blackbeard's men the hex wouldn't harm them if they returned to their captain—*unless* they allowed him to commandeer our ships."

"And you bought them with . . . ?"

O'Roark shrugged. "Lord Havisham didn't load his holds with silks and spices for nothing. We pirates honor our commitments to each other, so," Morgan quaffed the rest of his pint and then wiped his mouth on his shirt sleeve, "I was simply upholding our promise to Blackbeard by allowing his *crew* the spoils we'd budgeted for him."

The younger captain snatched a pair of hard-cooked eggs from a tray, held them to his chest, and wiggled them provocatively at the serving girl. She laughed and playfully slapped his cheek. "That's comin' to ye later, O'Roark," she teased. "Don't forget me, now!"

"Not on your life, sweetheart!" He popped an egg into his mouth and washed it down with a fresh tankard of rum punch. "A bevy of beauties have been paid to escort Blackbeard's crew to cribs all around the island to keep them too skunked—and too scattered—to sail for him tonight or even tomorrow," he said with a grin. "Our men, meanwhile, plan to slip back to the harbor after nightfall and set sail for America. If that's fine by you, of course."

"Damn fine. Thanks for overseeing those details while I was detained." Damon raised the tangy-sweet liquor to his lips; it felt good to see his men gathered here as a crew with their glasses raised in salute. Even Ned Cavendish, older and more refined, as befitted the captain of a nobleman's ship, came up and clinked his tankard to Damon's.

"Sheer genius, having the abigail conjure up a hex!" Cavendish said with a grin that was getting lopsided. "You can be sure Lord Havisham will hear of your recovery efforts and quick thinking! But we wondered why the *Courtesan* lagged so far behind—"

"Gentlemen! Crewmen aboard Captain Delacroix's ship!" a voice rose above the crowd's noise. "We may have ducked from under Blackbeard's thumb, but we left an important matter unsettled, did we not?"

Damon looked toward the far wall, where Quentin Thomas was stepping up to a tabletop. "Our quartermaster became . . . distracted and left his post—left the wheel untended—while I was indisposed," Damon replied to Cavendish. "Damn sorry we're airing our dirty linens here, but my crew deserves to sail for the man they trust. Please excuse me."

The sailors cleared a path for him as Damon strode forward to join his accuser. This impromptu hearing would be easier to endure if he himself had tucked Sofia out of harm's way . . . and if he knew her inclinations. It was best, however, that his men settled this matter where witches and pretty women wouldn't sway the vote.

"Yes, gentlemen, we were discussing whether Mr. Thomas's neglect of his duties—his ruthless pursuit of Miss Martine—are grounds for his dismissal, or whether I should bow out for allowing Sofia to remain aboard in the first place." Damon hoisted himself on a tall stool beside the table, thinking the depleted trays of food near Quentin's feet looked risky.

"But without a quartermaster, the *Courtesan* is a ship without a rudder!" Quentin raised his tankard to launch into his argument. "Who has so competently minded the accounts? And who would—"

"But she's the captain's own ship!" a crewman near the front piped up.

"Aye! Hear! Hear!" came the unanimous response.

"We could choose to sail for another captain," a different sailor spoke up, "but it suits me to elect Comstock as the quartermaster—"

"Aye! He rations out the rum, anyways!"

"—and have Miss Martine take over the galley!"

The pounding of tankards on tables was nearly as deafening as the sailors' outburst in favor of this arrangement. Damon smiled and sipped his rum punch: Thomas had just stepped on some sliced fruit, but he was too agitated to notice.

"What're you saying?" Quentin demanded above the uproar. "It was Sofia who got us into this mess! And because Delacroix refused to set her off—because he's been partaking of her 'favors'—"

"At least the captain's been a gentleman about it!"

"And he weren't payin' us off, expectin' us to look t'other way!"

"Silence!" a voice thundered from the other side of the courtyard. "Silence, I say! I've heard enough!"

All heads turned toward Captain Cavendish. Two of his men had hoisted him to their shoulders, and he sat as regally as a king surveying his subjects. "As Lord Havisham's representative, I shall act as arbitrator," he announced sternly, "because the two men in charge are those on trial. The crewmen of the *Odalisque* and the *Lady Constance* shall step back to allow the *Courtesan*'s sailors to step forward and vote in plain sight."

After a stunned silence, the men followed his directions.

"Thank you, sir," Damon said calmly. "All here may vote without concern for repercussions, and any wishing to leave my employ shall be paid his fair wages. I apologize for the way this unfortunate situation has affected us all."

"Gentleman, you must vote only once, either in support of Captain Delacroix," Cavendish intoned, "or for the retention of Mr. Thomas. I shall see that the vacancy is filled immediately.

Expedience is our our best defense against Blackbeard's treachery."

He straightened his thick shoulders, looking much like a bulldog in uniform, but every sailor present respectfully awaited his pronouncement.

"All those in favor of Mr. Thomas, please raise your hands."

Quentin clenched his fists, glaring at the men gathered around him—sailors he'd shared many a mug and meal with. When the only response was the shifting of feet and clearing of throats, he thrust up his hand to vote for himself. "I've been the finest administrator—the best damn—"

His foot slid forward on the moist fruit. As his frustrated cry rang around the courtyard walls, Thomas landed against Damon's outstretched hands, and several sailors helped him find the ground with his feet.

"I hereby declare Damon Delacroix the winner by unanimous accord!" Cavendish declared. "We shall follow Captain O'Roark's excellent suggestion and reboard the ships without further ado!"

A gratifying cheer filled the courtyard. Damon gripped the hands extended toward him, but the man he wanted to reconcile with scuttled angrily through the crowd. "Quentin!" he called above the din. "Quentin, at least accept your pay!"

Thomas flashed him an odd grimace and then swung open the high wooden door in the courtyard's wall. As the sailors from the three ships surged around him, his laughter rang with a defiant tone. "*This* is the only pay I'll be wanting, captain!" he cried. "I've delivered your beloved to the Devil himself!"

Scowling, Damon shoved between the crewman. "What's this all about?" he demanded of O'Roark. "You assured me Sofia and her mother were—"

But Sofia stood on a low, makeshift dais between two torches—an auction block, it was. She was surrounded by notable pirates and traders from around the island who looked her over with intense interest—probably because she was tightly wrapped in a rope, which cut into her arms and made her breasts jut lewdly between its cruel stripes.

Beside her, Blackbeard stood in his usual cocky stance, feet planted firmly and hands clasped behind his back. His braided beard shook with his laughter when he found Damon in the stunned, silent crowd.

"What am I bid for this fair beauty, gentlemen?" he crooned with a wicked laugh. "Who'll start us off with a nice, high offer?"

19

The abject terror in Sofia's eyes made something inside Damon snap. He grabbed the dagger from his boot and let out a wild cry as he ran toward the dais. *"Sofiaaaa!"*

All he saw was his lover in trouble because he himself hadn't ensured her safety. Why hadn't he anticipated Thomas's duplicity? Why had he assumed his quartermaster would wage a fair fight here, when he'd played his captain and his crew so dirty aboard the *Courtesan?*

"Sofiaaaaa!" All he knew was he had to have her, had to save her from the treachery that threatened to undo them both. Vaguely aware that his men had taken up his cry—that all around him, knives and pistols flashed in the flickering torchlight—Damon rushed toward the woman he was suddenly ready to lose his life for.

Blackbeard, the bastard, stood beside her appearing haughtily invincible even though he was so outnumbered. He drew a flintlock from its silken holster and fired a shot into the air. "Stop where you are!" he cried. "You intended to sell her all along, and I'm merely—"

The traders and privateers fled in every direction. Sailors stormed the dais so fast Blackbeard didn't know what hit him—and Damon didn't care. He snatched Sofia on the run and kept moving—slung her over his shoulder as he pointed his blade at whoever dared get in his way. "Hang on, love," he panted as he ran toward the harbor. "Hang on and trust me to—"

"I knew you'd come! Oh, Damon, that damnable Thomas." Her breath rushed against his ear, sending warm, electric sensations through him as he kept his focus on the *Courtesan*. "But I don't know what he's done with Mama! Or with the girls! Please—we've got to help them!"

He kept running, clutching his woman . . . knowing full well how close he'd come to losing her. "It'll all work out, Sofia," he panted.

How could he promise her that when he had no idea what she expected of him? Or what he had to offer her? They'd made love—and, yes, they'd fucked themselves oblivious—many times, yet he'd looked no further than her face and her fine, ripe body. Hadn't Sofia Martine been the insatiable, flirtatious woman who wanted a tumble without any strings? Yet here he was, suddenly faced with the way he *felt* about her . . . and the way he wanted to feel her.

Up the gangplank he trundled, tossing his dagger aboard so he could steady her bound, inflexible body with both arms. When he reached the deck, Damon set her gently on her feet. Then, not so gently, he kissed her.

Oh, lord, how that woman launched into him with lips that promised a *yes*, no matter what he asked her! He pressed Sofia against the wall with his entire body, drawing his breath from hers as he poured his relief into one kiss and then another and another. When he released her to look into her wide violet eyes, he saw himself mirrored in those dark pools of mischief and mystique.

And he liked what he saw. And he liked it that Sophia had apparently spotted herself, as well.

"They say the eyes are the windows of the soul," she murmured, maintaining her gaze. "So if I'm reflected there, in eyes that sparkle like a crystal stream in this moonlight, or like diamonds tossed into the sky—"

"You have a jewel of an imagination," he quipped. But he was smiling, brushing the loose raven waves from her flushed face. "What do you see in me, Sofia? I have to know."

She went still. But just as he was chiding himself for asking such a presumptuous question, her eyebrow quirked. "You first, captain. Unless, of course, you'd rather untie me."

He laughed and dashed for his knife. Torches moved along the street leading to the piers, and he recognized faces and voices, heard triumph in their laughter, and then spotted Magdalena and the Havisham girls being escorted aboard the *Lady Constance* by Captain Cavendish himself.

Damon smiled slyly. Did it really matter what they'd done with Blackbeard? Or what had happened to Quentin Thomas? All was well: the chicks were being returned to their nest, and the sailors who escorted them strutted aboard their respective ships like proud roosters. Which meant Damon had precious little time for what truly needed doing.

"I'd rather not," he murmured as he hoisted her over his shoulder again. "It's time I took you captive in a whole new way."

Sofia squealed and struggled within the rope that bound her arms against her body—not that she fought very hard. With Damon Delacroix's strong arms wrapped around her, she felt safe and playful again. Ready to enjoy whatever he had in mind . . . for he had a mind every bit as adventurous as her own! She'd seen how his gaze had lingered on the parts of her body so bawdily accentuated by Blackbeard's rope, and now that he'd rescued her from that brigand's clutches, Sofia was set on celebrating!

"What're you going to do to me?" she rasped. It wasn't a good imitation of fear or shock in her voice, but it made Damon chuckle. And she so loved it when he laughed.

"I'm claiming you for my own lewd and lascivious intent," he said, growling against her midsection. "Taking you hostage before anyone can stop me!"

"Should I fear for my maiden's honor? My . . ."

Damon bounded down the steps and into his quarters, slamming the door behind him. He set her down and then held her head between his broad, strong hands. "Sofia," he whispered hoarsely, "you should fear for much, much more than your honor. When I get through loving you, you'll wonder if you have any sanity left. Or any compunction to leave my clutches, much less cast your eyes on any other man, ever again."

Her heartbeat faltered and then sped up. He'd locked the door and lit the lamp. Buttons pinged to the floor in his haste to remove his shirt. Sofia rested against the wall, watching as his bare skin glimmered in the moonlight that filtered through his porthole. What a fine, broad chest he had, with a distinct vee of black hair that narrowed below his waist, as if his upper body had been expressly designed to call attention to the cock that rose tall and proud between his muscled legs. His beard brought his face to a provocative point, nearly covering his wound.

"I should remove your stitches—"

"All the more reason to keep your arms bound at your sides." Damon stepped out of his pants, eyeing her mischievously. "Pulling out the threads would hurt like a son of a bitch, and I'm not in the mood for—"

"Maybe these ropes hurt, too. I feel burn marks where the rough hemp has rubbed my skin raw."

As she'd hoped, Damon's expression—his whole attitude—

changed immediately. "Sofia, I'm so—how inexcusable of me not to consider . . ."

When he grabbed his dagger again, Sofia sucked in her breath: Damon Delacroix, man of action—naked—was truly a sight to behold. He deftly slipped his blade under the coils that bound her and slashed them with bold, decisive flicks of his wrist. What sweet relief when those bindings sprang away from her.

"Thank you!" She threw her arms around his neck. "I've been your willing captive since you caught my eye in Lord Havisham's mirror, you know. No need for leg irons or hand-cuffs or—"

His breath escaped him. He held her against his unclothed body, burying his face against her neck. "I've been a beast. A heartless, cruel—"

"Oh, never heartless, Damon! You may be a pirate, but you've the heart of a lion—a fierce protector!" Sofia stopped gushing to gaze at him, sneaking her hand down to what it longed to grasp. "While I wasn't really worried you'd sell me—"

"That was never my true intention, Sofia. From the start, you . . . captivated me." His grin went boyishly crooked when her fingers wrapped around his cock. "I recognized a like-minded soul, and I was suddenly ready to sail the seas with you and . . . share your bed forever and—"

"Forever?" Sofia's heart pounded wildly. This was Damon Delacroix, swashbuckler, talking. She'd never expected him to admit his feelings so freely or to have the deep, immediate need for her she'd felt for him.

Overhead, boots clomped loudly on the deck. Crewmen called to each other as they prepared the *Courtesan* to sail; Comstock's voice carried above the rest. The ship shifted when a crowd of men labored at pulling up anchor.

"Come with me." With a conspiratorial wink, Damon grabbed her hand. They trotted behind the partial wall that separated his sleeping area from the main cabin, and when he shoved against the bed's frame, it revealed a sliding panel door behind the massive mahogany bed head. "This is where I store our most valuable cargo, along with my share of the plunder. Not even the men know where to look for it. Sometimes the captain keeps a few secrets, you see."

Sofia stepped inside the low-ceilinged closet . . . heard the scraping of a flint until a spark caught and lit a candle just inside. When Damon lowered the globe over it, she could distinguish shelves and crates and armoires, all neatly arranged around an interior room about half the size of Miss Daphne's at home. Indeed, had she known about this cozy hideaway, she would've stowed away here!

Unlike the hold, this sanctum smelled of dried herbs and the fresh matting of the woven rushes that covered the floor. Damon's smile looked downright devilish as the lamplight made his beard glimmer. The shadow of his erection, enlarged against the opposite wall, made them both snicker.

"High time some of this treasure saw the light," he murmured as he pulled open a drawer. He tossed a folded bundle at her—plush, crimson velvet, it was. "Over the years, I've amassed some choice booty, and while it's all beautiful and highly valuable . . . well, it's not of much use without someone who'll do it justice."

"Oh, Damon, this is so gorgeous," she breathed. "Even the Havishams have nothing fashioned from such—"

"Spread it on the floor, Sofia. I want to see you sprawling on it naked."

Her cheeks went hot with his command, with visions of what he intended to do to her. As she bunched fistfuls of the fabric to form a deep cushion, Sofia heard the secretive, silken whisper of delicate chains. Jewelry, perhaps? Her hands were shaking so hard she could barely finish her task without demanding what he was doing.

"Give me the pleasure of unfastening this dress," he murmured behind her. His hands deftly separated the voluminous sleeves from her bodice, and then he bared her back. "You looked lovely on the deck, dressed in this dark gown with your hair pulled up. Not that I don't fancy you even more this way."

In one fluid move Damon swept the violet dress down the length of her. She turned, feeling almost shy, like a bride on her wedding night.

He was holding a pendant that caught the lamplight in its million facets; the two side strands sparkled richly with cubes and orbs along their length, and a fabulous heart-shaped stone hung from the center. Sofia's fingers fluttered to her throat. "I've never seen anything like—"

"Good. It suits you perfectly, my love. It's brilliant and brazenly flamboyant—and priceless." He looped the pendant around her neck, his expression tight. "Lift your hair, Sofia. Let me array you like the queen you are."

When she did as he'd asked, his eyes riveted hers. "Will you wear this as a token of my love—as a sign that you'll be my woman . . . my wife someday?"

Her jaw dropped. "I—oh, Damon! Yes! *Yes!*"

"Promise you're not saying that just because I'm draping you in diamonds."

Sofia swallowed hard. While Lord Havisham had bestowed Lady Constance with many fine pieces—most of them peace offerings or gifts to assuage his own guilt—Sofia had never seen anything half so grand as this. And because she'd dreamily fastened a few of those pieces around her neck after cleaning them, she realized just how many diamonds graced this grand, weighty pendant. "Damon, I wanted you—wanted to be yours—when the only prize I knew about was that piece between your legs. I risked *everything* to be here with you."

His close-cropped beard glistened when he smiled. "Yes, I suppose you did. So you understand what a . . . monumental risk this is for me, as well?"

"Nothing ventured, nothing gained," she whispered. Again she lifted her hair from her neck so Damon could admire the sparkle of the gems he'd just bestowed upon her—even if he was really watching her breasts move. "Now, what was it you wanted? Something like this, perhaps?"

She slowly lowered herself to the pallet of rich, red velvet. When she stretched out, Sofia dropped her dark hair so it fell in the soft disarray of waves her man loved to weave his fingers through. Languidly, like a contented cat, she stretched her legs and arms.

His eyes glimmered with wanting. He stood tall and proud with a member that jutted toward her as though it couldn't wait to bury itself in her velvet depths. She opened herself to him, grinning. "While I love these diamonds, dear man, just *imagine* what a serving girl like me might do with a string of pearls."

His snicker filled the little room. He reached into the open drawer again and drew out a lovely length of pearls, glossy little globes of cream in the lamplight. "Don't think you get to have *all* the glory while I stand idly by," he said in a husky whisper. "I know of one particular pearl—a sensitive, wet, pink one—just waiting for the smooth yet bumpy attention I'm about to give it."

He knew her thoughts, knew precisely what she'd had in mind—to titillate herself while he watched her squirm. Damon knelt between her knees, holding the pearls taut between his hands. He positioned the strand lengthwise along her belly with the bottom pearl at the top of her slit, watching her reaction . . . holding his breath along with her as he began the slow, delicious torture she begged him for with her wide, violet eyes.

One pearl, two . . . Sofia fought the urge to convulse with the smooth, cool sensation of the beads abrading her sensitive flesh.

Three pearls, four . . . spanning her slit tightly enough that she felt Damon's pulse as he pressed them into her moist crevice.

Five pearls, six . . . She shut her eyes against a little flash of light inside, and when Damon's thumb rotated the beads around that pearl he'd inflamed just by mentioning it, Sofia's breath rushed out in a wild cry. "Damon! Don't—I have to have you inside me—"

"Not until you've surrendered to me this way," he whispered. "Not until I feel your body quiver and writhe and thrum with a need you can't suppress."

Damn, but he was obstinate! She glared at him, but then he pulled the string upward and tugged it down over her clit and crevice again! Her protest sounded wanton as it echoed around them in the small room, and as the ship surged away from the pier—as the men above them cheered and stomped with the victory of escaping Blackbeard's diabolical wiles—Sofia cried out with the first curlings of her climax.

Relentless he was, rubbing and then teasing her flesh with quick flickers of the pearls until she clutched the velvet in her fists and gave in. The tremors overtook her—and then he ducked his head to goad her on with his tongue! Sofia's upper body shot up from the floor, and her inner spasms became so intense she wondered if she'd lose her sanity along with her will. She was every inch Damon Delacroix's willing victim—his slave, wrapped in velvet and draped with diamonds.

"I'm coming in," he rasped.

She wanted to wait, wanted to come down from this dizzy height before . . . But this pirate would plunder her as he chose, wouldn't he? He knew all her most sensitive areas, knew how she loved it when he buried himself to the hilt and then rubbed high, against her bone.

And when he did, she screamed—so he muffled the outburst with a ravenous kiss. "Can't have those randy sailors coming to see how I'm torturing you, can we?" he breathed against her ear. "They'll all want a piece of my prize, and I'm not sharing you! I went berserk, watching Blackbeard rip your gown, and, well, we'll have no more of that!"

Damon's body quivered with the emotion Sofia heard in his voice—the rage and frustration and *fear*. Fear for her safety. Fear because the situation had gotten out of hand—even though *she* had provoked it. Captain Delacroix had suffered almost as badly as she had when Edward Teach snatched her away, and Damon had forgiven her in the heartbeat it took for their fragile new romance to be threatened.

Sofia felt warm and cherished and protected when she realized this. And who had ever made her feel that way—except Mama?

Damon balanced on his elbows, gazing down at her as he slowly thrust and pulled up, thrust and pulled up. His lips parted, but it was his expectant silence that left her hanging suspended between blessed release and the faint stirrings of another climax.

"You're a beast," she muttered. "A ruthless, wicked devil of a Delacroix—and I love you for it."

His face softened. His blue eyes shone with so much of that same love, Sofia knew she'd never forget this moment—and never regret being the first to say that phrase outright.

"Sofia, my sweet, you're just beginning to fathom the meaning of that word," he whispered. Then he kissed her softly. "Can you tame me? Mold me into the loving husband who'll do your bidding?"

"Of course I can! Look how far I've brought you already!" With that, Sofia thrust upward and clenched his cock. When she wrapped her legs around his hips, the strand of pearls created a delicious friction between them—only this time it was Damon who grew desperate.

He grabbed her backside to control her so he'd last longer,

but she was having none of it! Squeeze, release, squeeze, release—the secret weapon she used to drive him wild worked every time.

For what would she do with a *tame* Damon Delacroix? What good was a loving, biddable husband when she wanted to be constantly surprised and delighted—needed a man who could put her in her place?

He laughed, a sound that started with a low rumble in his belly and sent them both into a quivering, aching frenzy of thrusting. She felt him tensing, saw the stitches along his jaw tighten as his need passed the point of no return.

Sofia held him tightly, rocking with him, singing out his name when his climax triggered hers. Spent, she relaxed into the makeshift pallet that cushioned them. With the cool weight of the diamond pendant on her chest and Damon's heavy warmth pressing her into the rich velvet, she felt like quite a queen indeed.

Sofia smiled. She did know her place; she was in it now. And she'd be forever enamored of the pirate who'd put her there.

Ties that Bind

Donna Grant

1

Kingdom of Hesione
Outskirts of the Quantra Province

If there was one thing Queen Jarina hated, it was when her uncle tried to control her. She was queen, after all, though he seemed to forget it at every turn.

"Ampyx, hold your tongue," Jarina said between clenched teeth.

Her uncle disregarded her order and spun toward the small group of nobles gathered in the chamber. "She must marry. No woman should rule alone. Each of you know what type of damage a woman can get us into," he all but shouted as he swung around and pointed to Jarina. "She's young and doesn't yet know her true position."

Jarina had heard enough. She rose on shaking legs and glared at the uncle she had come to despise. He was the only family she had left, but there were times she could have cheerfully called for his beheading. And this was one of those times.

"You overstep your bounds, Ampyx," Jarina said, her voice

loud and carrying well in the high-ceilinged chamber. "Though you may be family, you do not rule. I do."

"I know that all too well," he mumbled.

But loud enough that Jarina heard him. There was no mistaking the hate radiating from his gaze. She would have to be careful with her uncle. She couldn't throw him out—he had too much power with the nobles—but she would make sure that power began to decline. Immediately.

"If you know who rules, how do you dare tell me I should marry? Do you forget Queen Neffi, who ruled alone her entire life? She had no man at her side, she *needed* no man at her side, and she kept us out of war. Something you *men* can't seem to do." Jarina turned to the nobles. "Turg, was it not your people who disobeyed my father's direct order to stand down against the Pereths?"

Turg had the good grace to lower his gaze. "Aye, your highness, that we did."

Jarina whirled back to her uncle. "I will get us out of this war that has all but brought us to our knees, and it will not be by marriage, Ampyx. Understand that now, for I will not hear another word on the subject."

She held her uncle's gaze until he looked away and bowed, but not before she saw the malice lurking in his cold blue eyes. It was no secret her uncle wanted the throne. He had tried many times to convince her father to turn over the crown to him. Her father had been a good man, a soft-spoken, quiet man, but he had ruled with dignity, honesty, and fairness. The people had loved him as much as they had loved her mother.

Jarina waved the nobles from the throne room as memories of her parents flooded her. She sank onto her throne and rested her head in her hands. How she missed her parents. They had been loving and supportive. Since the day of her birth, her parents had tutored and readied her for her role as queen of Hesione.

She was ready to be queen, and she knew she could rule as well as her parents had—if her uncle weren't around to stir up the nobles and make them think she wasn't a capable queen.

"As if marriage to some pompous man would stop this infernal war," she grumbled to herself.

She still couldn't believe Ampyx wanted her to marry the king of Pereth, the very man who had started the war that had taken her parents.

"Never," she vowed.

After a deep breath, Jarina rose and looked around the chamber, vacant now of everyone except her personal guards and herself.

"Tyrus."

"Aye, your highness," the head guard said and stepped toward her. "What is your pleasure?"

Pleasure. She wanted nothing more than to experience pleasure, but that would have to wait. She blinked and smiled at her head guard. He was tall and broad of chest, with thick arms and a steely gaze that brought his men under control. From what Jarina had heard from her maids, Tyrus was quite the man in bed. It wouldn't be unheard of to bring him to her bed, but something held her back.

She swallowed and raised her gaze to Tyrus's dark eyes. "I think I will take my dinner in my chamber tonight."

"I'll see to it, your highness," he said and bowed his dark head as she walked past.

Just as Jarina reached the tall double doors of the chamber, the guards on either side opened them. She didn't need to look behind her to know that Tyrus and his two guards followed her.

There was no doubt she was lonely, and she wanted a king beside her, but not to help her rule. She wanted a love match as her parents had had, a man that would stand beside her and help her make decisions but not rule in her stead. Did such a man even exist?

By the time she reached her private chambers, Jarina wanted nothing more than to sink into her large marble tub and let the hot water wash away the day's events. She didn't wait for her maids as she began to unlace the front of her silver gown. She pushed it off her shoulders and let it pool at her feet before stepping out of it. She kicked off her soft-soled slippers and pulled down the stockings that covered her legs to her thighs.

As she stood wearing only a thin chemise, she saw the appreciative looks of her guards. Aye, she could most certainly lure one into her bed. If she so desired. There was no doubt to that desire within her—she just didn't desire any of the men who surrounded her.

Jarina turned and pulled off the chemise as she walked into the large bathing chambers adjacent to her chamber. She tossed the chemise aside, stepped into the tub, and sighed as hot water surrounded her.

Jarina didn't know how long she'd stayed in the tub, when her maid woke her for her meal. She quickly dried off and pulled on a robe of thick, dark red material as she sat at the small table on her balcony that overlooked the city of Hesione. Her city.

After a few bites of the foul, she motioned for her maid. "I think there is something wrong with the meat, Merda. Please tell Cook to have a look at it."

"At once, your highness."

Jarina pushed aside the foul and dipped her bread in the rich, creamy sauce that covered the meal. She drank deeply from her goblet full of the kingdom's best wine. She blinked as her eyes went in and out of focus; she didn't think much about this, because she had gotten little sleep over the past few weeks, thanks to her uncle. It was then she found it difficult to breathe.

Jarina blinked several times as her vision clouded. The chamber began to spin around her as she tried to grab hold of the table to steady herself. She missed the table and fell with a thud to the floor. Sleep pulled at her, but she fought it as she looked for her guards and then tried to cry out when she saw all three lying motionless on the floor.

And then the sleep claimed her.

2

Kyros ran a hand down his face and sighed. He wasn't sure Boreas's idea was a good one. Though Boreas was as close to Kyros as a brother, Boreas was known to get them into trouble on occasion. Which was fine before Kyros had become king of Pereth.

"Stop frowning," Boreas said with a grin. "Trust me."

"I trust you with my life, but that's not the point. Just tell me where we're going."

Boreas stopped walking amid the crowded streets of Pereth and faced his friend. They had both dressed as peasants so as not to attract attention. "I know you don't want to marry—especially to the hellcat of Hesione—so I thought of a plan."

"To get me out of the marriage?" It wasn't that Kyros didn't wish to marry—he just didn't wish to marry someone he didn't know. Though, if he was honest with himself, he'd do whatever it took to bring his kingdom out of the war with Hesione, and if it meant denying himself his future happiness, then so be it.

Boreas rolled his eyes. "I dearly wish, brother. Nay, I have something else in mind," he said with a smile as he turned on his heel to continue through the streets.

Kyros had no alternative but to follow his friend through the winding, crowded streets before Boreas was swallowed by the sheer number of people. Kyros kept his head ducked in case someone recognized him. He was just about to stop Boreas when he noticed they were in the slave market.

Intrigued, he continued to follow Boreas until they came to the sex-slave section of the market. Kyros smiled at his friend.

"I told you to trust me," Boreas said with a smirk. "Now, pick out a woman who will satisfy your lustful nature—because your wife won't be able to."

Hours went by as Kyros looked over every candidate. There were a few who drew his interest but none enough to purchase.

"I see nothing this day," Kyros said, disappointment heavy in his voice. "We'll return later."

They were turning away when the auctioneer called out, "And for the jewel of this auction."

Kyros looked over his shoulder to see a woman being carried onstage. She was bound with her arms over her head and her legs spread wide on the stand. Her eyes were covered and her mouth gagged. Though her curves would make a saint stand up and take notice, it was her wealth of dark, auburn hair falling in waves to her waist that captivated Kyros.

"I guess we're staying," Boreas said as he slapped Kyros on the back.

"I want her. I don't care how much she costs." He looked at Boreas. "Get her. Quickly."

Boreas smiled and walked to the head of the crowd. Kyros held his breath as the bidding began. The woman had elicited quite a fervor, and Kyros began to worry that Boreas wouldn't bid quickly enough to win her. Her price grew higher and higher with each call of the crowd.

Kyros's gaze shifted; the woman was moving as if just waking. He realized then that she must have been drugged before the auction.

A smile pulled at Kyros's mouth. She must be a feisty one. His rod grew thick and hard just thinking about how he would take her. Her breasts were large—plenty to fill his big hands. He couldn't wait to taste her flesh and feel her nipples harden in his mouth as he suckled her.

"Sold!" the auctioneer shouted.

Kyros jerked his gaze to Boreas to see his friend paying for the woman. Kyros breathed a sigh of relief, not realizing just how much he had wanted the woman until then.

He nodded to Boreas and turned to leave the market. He needed to prepare for his new slave.

Jarina tried to control the racing of her heart as she heard the man beside her yelling out figures. She tried to shake away the fuzz in her brain as she struggled to determine where she was.

When she found her hands and feet bound, her mouth gagged and blindfolded, she knew something was dreadfully wrong.

The feel of the cool air on her bare skin told her the absolute worst had happened. Somehow her uncle had managed to sell her to the sex-slave market. Jarina wanted to rage against her bonds, to demand her uncle's head on a platter, but she knew her cries would fall on deaf ears.

She was a queen, after all. She would figure out a way to escape her new prison and return to Hesione before her uncle did too much damage.

"Here she is, sir," she heard a deep voice say beside her. "I've never had a slave go for so much before."

A hand touched her cheek before moving down her neck to cup a breast and tweak a nipple. Jarina was at once outraged and curious at her response to the touch.

"Aye, she is certainly a prize. Where did you get her?" The man's voice was smooth and deep. Friendly almost.

"Ah . . . I cannot divulge where I get my merchandise," the other man stammered. "You, of course, understand, sir?"

"Of course," the friendly man said softly. Too softly. "You stole her."

"Never!"

"No need to get irate. I don't plan to investigate further."

Jarina felt tears threaten. She hadn't cried since her parents' death six months earlier, and she refused to do so now. She didn't want her new owner to think her weak.

Her hands were lowered from over her head. Her ankles were released also. She prayed that her gag and blindfold would come off as well, but she should have known better.

She used her hearing to decipher what was going on. She heard something rustle near her, and then she felt cloth against her skin.

"I cannot take you through the streets naked, my prize. I'd be gutted in an instant," the man whispered in her ear just before he lifted her in his arms.

Kyros was impatient to reach his chamber. Boreas had returned with his new slave a few hours ago, and Kyros was eager to slake his lust with her.

He entered his chamber to see the woman tied much as she had been at the market—her arms over her head and her legs spread wide. Boreas had used the two great columns near Kyros's bed to tie her. He had also left her blindfolded and gagged.

Kyros's gaze roamed over her beauty. She was tall for a woman, with long, lean legs, wide hips, narrow waist, and full breasts. Her skin was bronzed by the sun, and her nipples were a dark, dusky pink. The hair hiding her sex was the same dark auburn as the hair on her head, and he was ready to part her folds and seek the moisture of her sex.

Somehow Kyros held himself in check. She was awake, her

body held still as she waited for him to touch her. He walked around her, letting his fingers caress her stomach and then around her hip to her rounded bottom. Back to her stomach.

"Very nice," he whispered in her ear.

She jerked away from him in surprise.

"I won't hurt you," he assured her. "I'm your new master, and we will share many nights of pleasure." He cupped her breasts and watched as her nipples grew taut before his eyes. "You do like pleasure, don't you?"

When she didn't respond, he lightly pinched her nipples and heard her sharp intake of breath.

"A simple nod will do," he prodded. "Now, answer me. You do like pleasure, don't you?"

She gave one small nod.

"Were you bathed?"

Another small nod.

"Good." Kyros hurriedly pulled off his boots, his pants, and his tunic.

His rod ached to be buried in her softness, but again he held back. He wasn't sure why, but he wanted to go slow with the woman. He moved around her again and ran his hands down her back to her bottom and up. Her skin was petal soft, almost satiny. He moved against her until her back was molded to him. Then he let his hands wander over her body.

He cupped her breasts, plucking at her nipples before moving down to her hips and then between her legs to graze her sex lightly. Her breathing had become ragged, and he rubbed his straining rod against her bottom.

"Can you feel how much I want you?"

She didn't answer, which caused him to slap her bottom. Her entire body jerked.

"I asked you a question, slave."

Hesitantly she nodded.

"You'd do good to remember who is master here. I will do

as I please to your body, and you will do what I ask without question or complaint."

This time she gave a curt nod of acknowledgement.

"I'm glad you understand."

Kyros moved to stand in front of her and leaned down to take a nipple in his mouth. He swirled his tongue around the tiny bud before he began to suckle. A smile pulled at his lips when his slave gave a small whimper. Good. He wanted her to crave him as much as he craved her.

He kept his mouth at her breast while his finger ran back and forth over the other nipple, keeping it hard and straining. When her body began to shake, he moved his hand from her breast and lightly caressed the skin over her stomach. Her hips moved against him, seeking contact.

Kyros smiled against her plump breast as his hand dipped between her legs and parted her woman's lips. He groaned when he felt her moisture against his fingers. His rod pulsed with need, eager to seek the slave's tight sheath.

Yet he was more than surprised when he delved into her heat to find a barrier. It had never occurred to him that the slave might be untouched. The auctioneer had not known of it or her price would have tripled.

"You've not been touched before," he said as his fingers moved slowly in and out of her.

She shook her head and whimpered when his fingers grazed her swollen pearl.

"A gift I wasn't expecting."

He said no more as he sat between her legs and used both hands to part her sex. He leaned up and ran his tongue along her swollen flesh before he circled her pearl and began to tease it mercilessly.

Jarina's body jerked as pleasure consumed her. She had waited a long time to have someone touch her as the man now did. And she was fortunate because he caressed her as though he knew what he was doing.

Her breasts were full and her nipples hard. She hadn't realized it would feel so . . . delicious to have someone suckle at her breasts. She enjoyed it immensely and couldn't wait for the man's mouth and hands to return.

Yet they had moved between her legs, sinking into her core and causing waves of desire to drown out everything but the man, her master. With each thrust of his finger and swirl of his tongue against some hidden gem she hadn't known she had, she found herself building toward something. It both terrified her and thrilled her.

There was no stopping the feelings within herself, and she wasn't sure she wanted to stop them.

Her hips moved against the man's mouth, and he slapped at her bottom. Jarina gasped against her gag. That was the third time he had struck her. No one had ever dared do such a thing. She didn't like being at the mercy of this man's will, tied, gagged, and blindfolded, not knowing where she was or who the man was.

"Don't move," he growled as his mouth once again claimed that sweet spot on her sex that caused her legs to shake and an ache to start deep within her.

The urge to move against him was great, but she had no desire to be struck again. Granted, he hadn't hit her hard, but that wasn't the point. She was a queen, and queens were never struck.

All thoughts of her spankings were lost as the man added another finger inside her. The friction was intense, the pleasure enormous. When she felt his other hand move between her legs, she waited with baited breath for what he would do to her body next. When he dipped a finger into her to join his other hand, she moaned and sagged against her bonds. Her legs could no longer hold her.

And just when she thought it was all she could take, he

moved one hand from her sex to her bottom and pressed the finger against her opening. He kept the pressure firm but didn't push forward.

It sent Jarina over the edge.

She screamed into her gag as her first climax claimed her. She rode wave after wave of pleasure as the man continued to work his fingers in and out of her.

Slowly she again became aware of her surroundings, but it was difficult with the man's fingers still inside her. She wanted to lie down, to remove the blindfold and see just who had brought her such magnificent pleasure.

"Did you enjoy that?"

She nodded, eager to experience more.

"I want you. I want to bury my rod deep inside and pump in and out of you until we both scream our pleasure."

Then do it, Jarina wanted to bellow. Instead, she stood quietly, waiting to hear what he would say next.

"But I won't until your maidenhead has been broken."

With that, he removed his hands.

Jarina instantly felt his loss and wanted to call him back to her. Desire still throbbed within her, and she didn't want it to end yet.

Suddenly she felt a presence lean close to her. The scent of sandalwood, sex, and man invaded her senses.

"Until later," he whispered before he kissed her neck just below her ear.

3

Kyros had never wanted a woman as he wanted his slave. He didn't know what it was about her that tempted him as no one else had. The urge to return to her and pleasure her again was great, but he couldn't allow her to see just how strong his need for her was.

"Done already?" Boreas asked as he met Kyros in the white corridor of Pereth Palace.

Kyros rolled his eyes. "Not by far. The slave is untouched."

Boreas whistled as he fell in step with his king. "How did the auctioneer not know that?"

"My bet is that whoever sold the woman wanted her gone quickly, not giving the auctioneer time to do a thorough exam of her."

"Well, it has ended up being your benefit, my brother."

Odd, but Kyros didn't see it that way. It was the first time in his life he found he had a distaste for the slaves being sold. Pereth law stated that the people sold came freely, willingly to be auctioned, especially the sex slaves. It was known far and wide that the citizens of Pereth took excellent care of their slaves.

"Didn't you find it odd that she was gagged and blind-folded?" he asked Boreas.

His friend shrugged as he ran a hand through his blond hair. "In truth, Kyros, I don't go to the slave market that often. I've never had need of a sex slave, so I don't know how it is they treat them."

"She was the only one gagged and blindfolded today." He stopped walking and crossed his arms over his chest as he turned and faced Boreas. "I want you to set up a group of men and have them watch the market."

"Kyros," Boreas said as he lowered his voice and stepped closer to him, "our laws are strict about the slaves. Not to mention, Dugu is in charge of the slave market. He isn't someone you want as an enemy."

"Am I not the king? Do I not have more powers than some store owner who wants to have favor with me?"

Boreas sighed and took a step back. "You know you do. That isn't my point. Dugu has been in charge of the slave market since your father was king."

"Aye, and that just might be the problem. There is corruption there. I feel it in my gut."

"Then I will do your bidding," Boreas said with a bow of his head. He raised his gaze to Kyros and smiled. "So what will you do with your slave? Will you deflower her yourself?"

"By the skies, nay," Kyros said more harshly than he intended. He dropped his arms and blew out a breath. "I have no desire to have her first time with me be painful. I will bring in Seta and let her work her magic on the slave."

"Seta?" Boreas repeated. "You are taking great care with this slave."

Kyros grinned and slapped his friend on the back. "I paid a hefty price for her. I must make sure she is treated properly."

Boreas chuckled. "Oh, I'm sure you'll treat her properly quite regularly. Nightly, as a matter of fact."

And Kyros was already looking forward to it.

* * *

Jarina's body still pulsed with need. She wanted the man to return and touch her again, but more than that, she wanted to touch him, explore him as he had done her. She yearned to feast her eyes upon his rod, to run her hands along its steely length before he entered her.

But she feared he'd keep the gag and blindfold in place forever.

The opening of a door alerted her that she was no longer alone. Had he returned already? She wanted to smile, but the gag stopped her. Footfalls, light and quick, told her it was a woman, not a man, who had entered the room.

The soft scent of flowers reached her a moment before a gentle, warm hand cupped her breast.

"I was told you were quite beautiful," said a husky, unusual voice in Jarina's ear. "They didn't lie. Beauty such as yours is rare to find."

The hand that cupped her breast squeezed slightly before moving her fingers to Jarina's nipple. Jarina's breath hitched as a tide of desire washed over her. Then the hand moved to bury in Jarina's thick hair.

"This hair—it is glorious. The color, the length, the texture. Only nobles have hair such as this, and they usually pay handsomely to achieve it."

Jarina wanted to roll her eyes, for she did pay handsomely for the care of her hair.

The woman moved behind Jarina and molded herself against her. "I'm going to have fun with you." The woman chuckled as her hands moved down Jarina's curves slowly. "Though I am a slave, I outrank you. Which means what I say goes."

Jarina's mind raced at the woman's words. Just what did they have in store for her? No sooner had that thought entered her mind than the blindfold came off.

Bright light flooded the room. She blinked several times as

her eyes grew accustomed and focused on the room. It was a large room decorated with pale yellows, white, gold, and vibrant purple. The combination was softened by the many and various plants.

She looked down to see a white rug, handwoven and thick, which translated into costly. Her gaze swept the room again, this time noting the details such as the gold painting accenting the huge columns and doors. Whoever they were, the owners were rich.

"If you promise not to scream, I will remove your gag."

Jarina jumped, having forgotten the woman. She hastily nodded, and the woman removed her gag. Jarina attempted several times to swallow, but her mouth was too dry.

A woman with long, golden blond hair and vivid blue eyes stepped in front of her and held out a cup of water. "Try this."

Jarina drank deeply, with help from the woman, and sighed her pleasure when the cup was emptied.

"I am Seta." The name combined with the accent told Jarina the slave wasn't from here.

"My name is—"

"It doesn't matter," Seta interrupted her. "The only name you have is Slave until your master names you."

Anger flared in Jarina, but she realized it just might be for the best. If she could convince her master she was no threat, he wouldn't tie her, which would mean she could escape soon.

"What kingdom am I in?"

"Pereth."

Jarina blinked, unable to believe she was in the very city she had never hoped to see.

Seta cocked her hands on her hips. A simple white gown was tied at her waist with a belt that accentuated her figure. A slow smile spread over her heart-shaped face. "Let's begin."

Jarina wanted to ask exactly what they were going to start, but when Seta began to untie her, she kept her mouth closed.

There would be time enough later for questions. When her arms were untied, she rubbed the feeling back into them while Seta removed the bonds from her feet.

Seta then stood and took her hand to lead her to the giant bed. Jarina looked at the bed and then back at Seta.

"Climb atop the towel. Make sure you lie on the towel at all times."

Jarina was more confused than ever, but she did as Seta asked. The huge windows next to the bed were open, and a soft breeze blew into the room and across her bare skin, puckering her nipples.

Seta had moved to the foot of the bed. "Open your legs."

Jarina swallowed past the lump in her throat and spread her legs.

"Wider."

She looked up at the ceiling as she spread her legs as wide as they would go and stared at the painting of an ancient battle.

The rustle of fabric drew her attention, and she glanced down in time to see Seta push her gown off her shoulders. Jarina held her breath when Seta climbed onto the bed and sat between her legs. Seta then reached into a bowl Jarina hadn't noticed and squeezed out a small towel before she began to wipe Jarina's sex with soft, small strokes.

Jarina sighed and let Seta clean her. Her eyes drifted closed as she relaxed fully for the first time since she had awoken in the slave market. She didn't even flinch when she felt Seta open her woman's lips, exposing her. It wasn't until she heard the change in Seta's breathing that she opened her eyes to see Seta staring at her.

"Beautiful," Seta whispered before she tossed aside the towel. Seta moved so she reclined back and bent her legs until her feet rested on the bed. Her legs fell open, exposing herself to Jarina. Seta was completely shaved.

Jarina had never seen a woman's sex before, and, curious as

she was, she quickly rose for a closer look. She wanted to see just what made her knees weak when the man—her "master," as Seta called him—touched her. Her gaze moved to Seta's face to see the slave's eyes nearly closed and her lips parted.

"I prefer to be shaved, but your master was most adamant that I not shave you. He wants you just as you are."

Jarina's gaze returned to Seta's bare sex, her pink lips swollen and open.

"Touch me," Seta commanded. "My breasts. Fondle my breasts."

Jarina, having never touched another woman's breasts, wasn't sure what to do. Recalling the feel of both her master's and Seta's hands on her breasts, she cupped Seta's small breast and gently massaged it. Seta sighed, and her eyes drifted shut.

Curious as ever, Jarina used her other hand to pinch Seta's nipple. The slave gasped, and her head feel back. Jarina then grew bolder and began to use both her hands on Seta's breasts, squeezing, pinching, tweaking until Seta's gasps turned to moans.

"Use your mouth," Seta said between moans.

Jarina wasn't given much choice as Seta pulled Jarina's head down to her breast. The first taste of a woman's nipple in her mouth was . . . different but not unpleasant. Jarina used her tongue to swirl around the tiny nub before she began to suckle as Master had done to her.

Seta was quick to move her from one breast to another, where Jarina repeated her actions; all the while Seta was moving her hips against Jarina's leg. The desire that had never fully died in Jarina sprung to life again.

She pulled away from Seta's breasts and looked at the slave. Seta's breasts were flushed, her nipples hard, and her moans grew louder with each moment. She raised her head and looked at Jarina.

"No one has made me feel this way. Not even them," she said with a nod of her head.

Jarina followed her nod and saw two men standing at the bed she hadn't seen earlier. They watched eagerly but didn't move. She quickly scanned the room and saw two more men guarding a doorway.

"Have you ever touched a woman before?"

Jarina shook her head. "I've not felt another's touch before today."

Seta laughed. "It comes naturally to you. That is what your master saw in you. Passion. It will make your union with him most pleasing."

Just the thought of her master touching her brought a spasm of desire from her sex.

"Look," Seta said as she put a hand between her legs and dipped a finger inside herself. "I'm wet for you. No one has made me wet just from kissing my breasts."

Jarina looked down at Seta's sex and felt her own grow wet. Where was the spot her master had touched that had buckled her knees? She wanted to know how he knew where to touch her and how to touch her.

She ran her hands along Seta's thighs until they reached her sex. Jarina's fingers smoothed over the bare flesh before spreading Seta's lips as Seta had done to Jarina. The sight of Seta's sex swollen with desire made Jarina want to touch her. She ran a finger all along Seta's sex until she encountered one spot that made Seta cry out.

"You've found my nubbin," she said softly. "It brings great pleasure when fondled correctly."

Curious, Jarina moved her finger back and forth over the nub, slow at first, but increasing the tempo until Seta cried out again. Jarina then moved down Seta's sex and dipped a finger inside.

She was hot and wet. Was this what she had felt like to her master? Hot and wet? She squeezed her legs together and felt a jolt of pleasure.

"There was a place that he touched inside me," Jarina said.

Seta laughed. "Your pleasure point. I will show you where it is. First, put two more fingers inside me and move your hand in and out."

Jarina did as instructed and began to move her hand, it wasn't long before Seta was moaning and gasping loudly. And then Jarina felt something. She rubbed her finger over a raised spot and Seta cried out again.

"I see you found it yourself," Seta panted.

Jarina continued to stroke the spot as she watched pleasure play out over Seta's face. Suddenly Seta screamed, and her body began to convulse around Jarina's fingers. Jarina continued to move her hands as Seta's orgasm washed over her.

When Seta quit moving, Jarina removed her hand and sat back to look at the slave.

Seta smiled at her. "I've never climaxed that way before. You have a very special touch." She rose and pushed her long blond hair back from her face. "Now, lie back and center yourself on the towel."

"What are you going to do?"

"I'm going to rid you of your maidenhead so your master can take you properly."

4

Jarina stared openmouthed at Seta. Surely the woman was wrong. Jarina might not know much about coupling, but she did know it was the man who breached the woman, not another woman.

Seta smiled again. "Soon you will be crying out your pleasure," she said before she bent over and took a nipple in her mouth.

Jarina gasped at the sensation. Her hands dug into the covers as the desire grew. Movement caught her eye, and she spotted the two men on either side of the bed near her head.

"Boys," Seta said as she sat back.

Jarina didn't have time to blink before the men, now naked, climbed onto the bed on either side of her. Each one took a leg and brought it up to her chest, holding her immobile.

"Seta," she whispered, fear of what they might do dampening her growing desire.

"Shhh," Seta said as she lay down between Jarina's legs and dipped a finger inside her. "So tight."

Unable to fight the desire, Jarina sighed as Seta's finger moved slowly in and out of her, going deeper with each thrust.

"Ah, there it is," Seta said. "The barrier your master wants gone before tonight."

Jarina barely heard her. Desire had her in its hold, and all she wanted was to feel pleasure wrap around her body and find her release. Dimly she felt something rub each of her legs and she looked down to see both men's organs swollen and hard as they watched Seta between her legs.

Seta reached up and pulled gently at one of Jarina's nipples, causing her to cry out first in pain and then in pleasure. Her hips moved of their own accord, and she heard Seta laugh just before Seta's tongue touched her pearl.

Had the men not been holding her, Jarina would have jumped from the bed. A cry of pure pleasure tore from her throat. Seta's tongue worked back and forth over her pearl while her fingers worked in and out of her sheath. Desire spiked, and Jarina felt herself quickly rise to the pinnacle.

Just when she was about to reach her climax, Seta pulled back.

"Not yet," was all she said before her fingers began to trace her sex.

Jarina thrashed her head from side to side. She wanted her release. Her sex throbbed with need, but Seta didn't seem to care as she ran her hands along Jarina's bottom and then to her breasts.

Seta leaned over her and began to suckle on her already sensitive breasts. Jarina longed to rub her hips against her, but she was being held by the men and couldn't move. Finally Seta lifted her face and gave her a wink before she lowered herself between Jarina's legs once again.

This time when Seta slipped a finger inside her, Jarina felt something else as well. It was probably no thicker than a finger, but it felt wonderful to her. Seta was an expert and knew just how to move the device to bring about the most pleasure. Her thrusts grew faster, deeper as her tongue moved back and forth over Jarina's pearl.

The climax came fast and hard when it hit. Jarina screamed as the pleasure consumed her, and that's when she felt the slightest twinge of pain. She was slow to come down from the orgasm, and by the look in Seta's eyes, she was ready for another of her own.

She kissed Jarina's stomach. "Don't move," she said as she removed something from between Jarina's legs and jumped off the bed. "Boys," she called.

Instantly the men released Jarina and moved to Seta. Jarina watched in amazement as Seta kneeled on the bench at the foot of the bed and one man entered her with one thrust from the front. Seta's head fell back as she gripped the man's shoulders. He began to thrust slow and hard. All the while, the other man was smoothing something on his swollen rod. He moved behind Seta and rubbed the same oil in the cleft of her bottom opening.

Jarina's mouth went dry as she realized what the man was about to do. When he positioned his rod at the opening of Seta's bottom, the front man stopped moving. The back man pushed slowly inside Seta's bottom, her moans of pleasure echoing around the room.

Once the back man was fully sheathed, both began to thrust in and out of Seta. Her moans soon turned to soft cries as the men's tempos increased. Their hands moved over her breasts, giving more pleasure as they thrust hard and fast inside her. It wasn't long before Seta gave a shout and her mouth opened on a silent scream as she climaxed. The man in front followed and slowly pulled out of her, but the man in back continued his thrusting, bending her over the bench until she was on her elbows.

He reached around and began to fondle her nubbin, which caused another rapid orgasm, her screams loud as she held on to the bench while he gripped her hips and thrust deep and long inside her; then the man climaxed.

Jarina's sex clenched, seeking more fulfillment. After what she had just seen, she wanted to feel a man's rod inside her, to feel his seed as he climaxed. She moved her hand toward her sex, only to have a someone stop her. She opened her eyes to find Seta beside her.

"No. It's time to wash."

Jarina didn't understand until one of the men lifted her from the bed and she saw the towel spotted with her blood, her virgin's blood. The man lowered her into a tub of steaming water. When he stood, his rod was even with her face. Though he was growing flaccid with each passing moment, she wanted to touch him, to know what brought him pleasure.

"My master will take me tonight?" she asked as Seta came to sit beside her. The slave was still naked, and one of her men ran his hands over Seta's bottom, kissing her back and the swell of her hips.

Seta laughed and took the soap and began to lather Jarina. "Aye, he will take you tonight. Many times, I think."

"How do I please him?"

Seta stopped washing Jarina and moved her big blue gaze to meet Jarina's. "I could show you, but I'm not sure if I should."

"Why?" Jarina was more confused than ever. Why wouldn't Seta want to show her how to please her master? Shite, she hated that word. No one was master to her—at least no one before now.

"Your master likes your innocence. He may want to show you himself."

Jarina nodded. "I understand. Could you at least tell me something he might like?"

Seta looked at her men and laughed. "Their organs rule them. Fondle him, suck him, lick him, and he'll be pleasured beyond his wildest dreams. Right, boys?"

The men nodded, smiles on their dark, handsome faces.

Jarina sat back and enjoyed Seta's steady, smooth strokes as her body was washed from head to toe.

5

Kyros couldn't get to his chamber fast enough. He had made sure he was occupied the rest of the day to give Seta enough time to breach his new slave's maidenhead, but with each moment that passed, Kyros found himself wanting to go to her.

She was just a slave, or so he kept telling himself, but it didn't stop him from thinking of her all afternoon. His mind wandered from the many ways he wanted to take her to wondering what color her eyes were and if she would scream again as her climax washed over her.

He'd had women in the past who had claimed his interest before, but it had never lasted longer than the first time he'd taken them. Somehow he knew it would be different with this slave.

As he approached the room in which he had decided to keep his slave, the door opened and Seta walked out with her two male companions. Seta had earned her place in his palace, and though she was a slave herself, she was master to the two men. They had been a gift from Kyros for her loyalty and service.

The smile on Seta's face was wide as she approached him.

"Sire," she said as she stopped in front of him and bowed her blond head.

Kyros crossed his arms over his chest. "By the look of satisfaction on your face, I assume things went well."

"Absolutely." She raised her head and sighed. "She is . . . very passionate and curious, sire. I think you will be more than pleased."

"And only you touched her?"

"Aye."

Kyros let out a pent-up breath and dropped his arms. "Return to your quarters, Seta. I will reward you later."

Once she and her two slaves passed him, Kyros stared at the set of double doors. It had been a long time since he had felt such lust for a woman. Even now, his rod ached. He gripped his swollen organ and shifted it in his tight pants.

He reached for the handle and silently opened the door. He looked at first one guard and then the other stationed by the exit. With a quick jerk of his head, they moved to stand outside. Kyros wanted his beauty all to himself.

His gaze searched the large, open chamber and found her standing near the double doors leading to the balcony. The doors were opened, and a breeze whipped around her, molding her long, thin gown to her curves and lifting her hair from her shoulders.

For a moment, all Kyros could do was stare at her. She stood regally with her back straight and shoulders back. Even her chin was tilted upward as if defying the gods that she was a slave. Her glorious auburn tresses hung down her back in soft waves, still slightly damp from her recent bath.

Slowly he walked until he was able to view her profile. Her arms were crossed over her chest, and her gaze drank in the sight of his city. Kyros was proud of Pereth. Despite the years of war with Hesione, his people still saw the good in life and walked around with smiles on their faces.

He leaned against one of the many pillars in the room and wondered what his new slave thought of Pereth. Was it as beautiful to her as it was to him, with the lush plant life and tall trees that swayed gently in the wind? Did she see the grand architecture of the buildings and homes, the intricate designs of their gods and goddesses on the buildings?

"What do you think?"

Her head swiveled to him, and he forgot to breathe. Her face was the epitome of beauty and grace, with her full lips, wide, expressive eyes, and high forehead. Yet it was the extraordinary amber color of her eyes that held him captive.

One auburn brow lifted regally. "A master cares what a slave thinks?"

Kyros chuckled. "I do."

She glanced back out the open doors before she said, "It is beautiful."

"You say that as though you're surprised."

"Because I am. I don't know what I expected Pereth to look like, but it wasn't this," she said.

Pride welled inside him. "Pereth has many hidden gems."

"Ravages of war haven't reached your city."

Kyros stiffened and pushed away from the column. "The war has touched everyone that lives in Pereth. Why does it concern you?"

She shrugged and dropped her arms. "It doesn't. Word of the war between Pereth and Hesione has spread everywhere."

With a sigh Kyros moved to sit on the edge of the bed. "Too many years war has ravaged both kingdoms."

"Does your king not wish to end it?"

"Not wish . . ." Kyros could only stare at the slave blankly. "What kind of king do you think Kyros is?" he finally asked.

Suddenly she took a deep breath, and her lips relaxed into a smile. "I wouldn't know. I take it you are my new master."

Kyros shook his head in bewilderment. He had thought for

sure the slave was aiming for an argument about the way he ruled Pereth and the war, and what he couldn't understand was that he wanted to know her opinion. Instead, she had changed subjects to one he was most ready to delve into.

"Aye, I am your master. The only name you will know me by is Master. Do you know the rules of being a sex slave?"

She shook her head, her mass of auburn hair gliding delicately over the exposed skin of her arm.

"As with any slave, you do as you are instructed. You were purchased for one thing: my fulfillment. There will be other slaves who will come to see to your bath and dressing you, for I will want you dressed in certain ways. And you are never to leave this room unless I take you from it."

Her amber eyes snapped fire. He knew she wanted to say something, but she held back.

"Seta began as a sex slave and worked her way up to be in charge of all slaves. You will obey her as you obey me. The guards stationed at the doors are here to ensure no one disturbs you."

"And to make sure I don't leave."

He smiled at her. "Exactly."

"May I ask a question?"

He nodded.

"Why did you purchase me? You are handsome enough and rich enough to get any number of women into your bed."

He wasn't sure why her statement of his handsomeness pleased him so, but it did. "I bought you because I am about to be married to a woman I've no wish to spend the rest of my life with. You are going to be my diversion, the one thing who keeps me from going insane."

A small smile pulled at her plump lips. "How do you know your intended is so awful? Have you seen her? Spoken with her?"

"Nay. I know of her, which is enough."

The slave began to slowly walked around the room. "Ah, so she is not kind or beautiful?"

The last thing Kyros wanted to speak of was Queen Jarina. He would wed her to end the war between their kingdoms so his people could have peace, but he knew better than to hope for some kind of happiness with her.

"Enough of my intended. Let's speak more of you. Seta breached your maidenhead."

"She did." The slave glanced at him over her shoulder as she traced a long finger along a column.

Kyros sank onto the bed, hoping to ease some of the discomfort from his swollen rod. "Did she hurt you?"

The slave laughed, the sound like many bells tinkling in the breeze. "I barely felt anything, the pleasure was so great."

He turned and lay on his stomach to watch her. She was the most graceful creature he had ever seen, and though he wanted to slake his lust with her, he was content to watch her for the moment.

"Had you never been with a woman before?"

She stopped and turned to face him. The material of her sleeveless gown was thin, and the rays of the setting sun allowed him to see her dark nipples and patch of hair between her legs. He had seen her naked, but the simple gown sashed at the waist gave him a rush of desire that would have brought him to his knees, had he been standing.

"I had never felt another hand pleasuring me before you, female or not."

"Did you enjoy it?" He wasn't sure why he was torturing himself so—maybe it was his curiosity, which he usually held in check.

Her eyes briefly lowered to the floor before she raised them again to meet his. There was no fear in her amber depths, only resignation for what she now was. "I did. Seta's hands and mouth knew where to touch me. Just as yours did."

"The two men with her—did they touch you?"

She moved closer to the bed and shook her head. "They only held my legs as Seta broke through my maidenhead. I watched as they both coupled with her at the same time. I never knew a woman could take a man from behind."

"There are many ways to couple. You enjoyed watching them, didn't you?"

She smiled slowly. "I never knew what it could do to me to watch others. Ever since I saw the men put their rods in Seta, I've eagerly awaited your return. I want to feel you inside me."

Kyros growled as he got onto his knees on the bed. Seta was right: the slave was passionate. And eager.

"Come here," he ordered. He heard the gruffness in his voice, but there was no stopping the pure lust that consumed him.

She walked to the bed and waited.

Kyros balled his hands into fists to keep them at his side. He didn't want to touch her yet, for if he did, he'd take her right then, and she wasn't ready for that.

"Take off your gown."

Despite her words earlier, he noticed her hands shake as she untied her belt. The belt fell to the floor, and with just a twist of her shoulders, the gown pooled at her feet. His gaze moved from her feet, to her long, lean legs, to her flared hips and narrow waist, to her full breasts and then to her face. Her eyes had darkened with desire.

He held out his hand and waited for her to put her small hand in his. Her toned, sun-kissed skin glistened in the afternoon light as he gently pushed her down on the bed and held himself over her. His rod ached to be loosened from his pants, causing Kyros to rub his swollen organ against her sex.

Her gasp and then soft moan nearly did him in. He bent his head and pulled a nipple into his mouth to suckle greedily before twirling it around his tongue. Her hands gripped his tunic, and her hips rose to meet his, seeking fulfillment.

"Not yet," he whispered as he moved from one breast to another.

Her nipples were sensitive, and he could tell the slightest pressure caused her great pleasure. He could stay and feast on her full breasts all day, but his need to feel her sheath surround him was too great to ignore much longer.

He again kissed her nipple and then placed small kisses and licks to the valley between her breasts down her stomach to her hips. As he neared her legs, she opened for him. A smile pulled at his lips as his tongue flicked over her pearl. She jerked and moaned as her hips lifted, seeking his mouth once more.

Kyros loved watching the look of pleasure pass over her face, so he bent down and let his tongue tease her pearl until her breath was coming in great gasps. He gripped her hips in a desperate attempt to get control of his own desire. When he once again was in control, he moved from the bed and began to take off his clothes.

The slave began to rise, but he stopped her with a hand. "I didn't say, 'Move.' "

"I want to touch you," she said.

"Later. Right now, my desire is too high to allow that."

When she had resumed her position, he jerked off the rest of his clothes and kneeled before the bed. He gripped her ankles and pulled her toward the end of the bed until her sex was inches from his face. He placed her feet on the bed and kissed the inside of each thigh before he turned to her sex.

She was swollen and slick with her own juices. Kyros's rod jumped, eager to thrust inside her. Instead he pushed two fingers into her wetness. She moved her hips against him, seeking more pleasure.

"Don't move."

"I have to!" she cried.

"Move again and I'll take a lash to your bottom."

For a moment he thought she might argue, yet when he

moved his fingers inside her, her hips were still. He watched her face and knew it was difficult for her to keep still.

With his thumb, he rubbed her pearl while his fingers continued to move inside her. Soft moans slipped past her parted lips as she fought to keep from moving. When Kyros could take it no more, he rose up and positioned his rod at her opening.

Her gaze was locked with his as she waited. He pushed past her opening and stopped. Her eyes rolled back in her head, and her fingers dug into the blankets on the bed. It was all Kyros could do not to plunge inside her. Inch by slow inch, he entered her, and then he pulled out and rubbed the head of his rod on her pearl to tease her.

She was close to climaxing. He could see it in the way she moved. Once again he filled her, this time pressing deeper until he was fully seated. The feel of her hot, wet sheath nearly made him spill right then.

He lifted her legs and wrapped them around his waist. Slowly at first, he began to move within her. He reached and pinched her nipples. She gave a soft cry right before her body stiffened; she began to clench around him as her orgasm hit.

Kyros gripped her hips and slammed in and out of her. As the last waves of her orgasm drained, he threw back his head as his own climax claimed him. When the last of his seed left his rod, he looked down to find his new slave staring up at him curiously.

He pulled out of her and then lowered her feet to the bed before he crawled on the bed. She reached up and pinched one of her nipples, and a moan tore from her throat.

Instantly Kyros was hard again. He couldn't tear his gaze from her as she played with her breasts.

"Do all women's breasts feel this way?" she panted.

Kyros swallowed. "I don't know." He leaned over and took a nipple in his mouth. He suckled hard and then softly, ran his teeth over the nipple and then laved it with his tongue. No matter what he did, she cried out her pleasure, writhing on the bed.

"I wanted to give you some time to adjust to your new occupation. . . ."

"I cannot help what my body wants," she moaned.

Just as she moved her hand toward her sex, Kyros stopped her. "You aren't allowed to touch yourself without my permission."

She whimpered but did as he commanded. "May I touch you now?"

Kyros lay back on the bed and wondered if Seta had given his new slave one of their potions that could make a couple last all night. His new slave was everything he had hoped for and more.

6

Jarina couldn't believe how amazing it felt to have Master's rod inside her. Even if he was strict and wouldn't allow her to move or to touch herself at times, what he did to her was too wonderful to stop.

She'd finally been granted permission to touch him. As she ran her hands over his tall, muscled body, she had to admit she was more than pleased. He was incredibly handsome, with his chiseled looks, thick muscles, and browned skin. Her gaze feasted on his masculine face. Thick, light brown hair fell to his shoulders in waves that made her want to run her fingers through them as his hooded black eyes watched her.

Her hands moved over his rigid stomach to his trim hips. His rod, not as full as before, but swelling with each breath, was near her hands. She reached for the organ and wrapped her hand gently around him. A gasp left her lips as he hardened instantly, straining in her hand.

His rod mesmerized her. How could something so hard feel so silky and hot at the same time? Her curiosity was great, and she let her hands wander up and down his thick length, cupping his balls in the process. She could have played with him the rest of the night, she was so enthralled.

She glanced at him before she leaned down to flick her tongue on the swollen head. His gasp and moan made her smile. Seta had been right: her master was easily pleased as long as she played with his rod. The next time she licked him, she tasted herself on him. While her tongue danced around his head, her hand moved up and down his shaft.

"Take me in your mouth," Master said with a groan.

Jarina stopped for a brief instant before she took him in her mouth. His low moan of pleasure told her she had done something right. His rod bucked in her mouth as she took him deeper.

She enjoyed the taste of him but most especially the feel of him in her hands and mouth. He had brought her pleasure; now she wanted to give him the same in return. The more she moved her mouth and hand over him, the louder his moans became until he suddenly pulled out of her mouth.

In a blink he had her on her hands and knees in front of him, his rod pressing against her bottom. Jarina closed her eyes as his hands reached around and began to play with her nipples. She pushed back against him, eager to have him fill her once more. But instead he pinched her nipples more.

"Be still before I tie you again."

Jarina wanted to cry, her need was so great. She couldn't get enough of this man, whoever he was. With her body shaking, with a growing need that frightened her, she stilled and waited as her master ran his hands over her back, hips, and bottom. He ran the tip of his finger from the base of her neck down her spine to the crease that separated her bottom cheeks.

Jarina bit her tongue to keep from crying out as his finger came close to dipping inside her. She had never feared a man in her life, and she didn't so much fear this man who claimed to master her so much as she feared she would disappoint him somehow. It was a new feeling for her, one she didn't particularly like.

Her back arched, and a startled gasp was torn from her when he nipped her shoulder.

"I think I might have to tie you again," he whispered in her ear, all the while rubbing his rod in the crease of her bottom.

"No," she choked out. She wanted the freedom to run her hands over him, yet she couldn't deny the thrill of being tied and having him pleasure her in ways that brought her to ecstasy and beyond.

He licked the spot he had nipped. "Then be still."

"I cannot."

"You will," he ordered just heartbeats before he plunged his rod into her.

A cry tore from Jarina's throat. Not one of pain but of pleasure. She tried her best to keep still, but her body had a mind of its own.

He pulled out of her and slapped her bottom. "I told you to keep still."

Anger infused Jarina. "You ask the impossible," she barked as she turned to watch him.

As soon as she saw the silken ties, she knew what he was about.

"Lie on your stomach," he commanded.

A thrill of delight ran through Jarina as she rolled onto her stomach. She didn't fight as he pulled first one leg and then the other and tied them to the thick wooden bed frame so she was spread for him. What she didn't expect was for him to do the same to her hands. She almost said something but bit it back in time.

The knowing looking in his black eyes told her he knew exactly what she was feeling. Though she tried to tell her body not to respond, it didn't listen. With the slightest touch from Master, she was on fire for him again.

"I've never known a woman as passionate as you. You surpass even Seta, who is known for her passion," he said softly as he kissed her shoulders. "I don't know if I'll ever get enough of you."

Jarina heard the surprise in his tone, as though he often grew tired of women. The thought of never having him fill her again was disturbing. But he didn't let her linger on such thoughts as his fingers once again found her sex and opened her lips to play with her aching pearl.

He had tied her so she had limited movement, keeping her as still as he wanted her. She wanted to lift her hips, to rock back against him, but she couldn't. And he knew it.

His fingers teased her sex and her pearl, giving just enough to make her beg for more but not enough to satisfy. Jarina sucked in a breath as his hand cupped her sex and pushed against her slightly, at the same time, he pressed his rod against her bottom, his head grazing the slit between her cheeks.

"I will take you there soon," he said. "But not today."

Her breath came in great heaves as his rod pressed against her again. She gave a low moan when he grasped her pearl between two fingers and began to rub it between them. The friction nearly sent her over the edge, it felt so good. He stopped just short of her climaxing.

Jarina buried her face in the covers as tears of frustration blinded her. The more he touched her, the more she wanted him.

He didn't allow her to suffer for long as he once again filled her. He braced his hands on either side of her face as he loomed over her and began to thrust, slowly at first. She was shocked at the difference his rod felt when entering from behind her. It touched spots that left her shaking and seeking more.

Suddenly he stopped and put a finger on her lips. "Lick it," he said gruffly. His voice was thick with desire, which made heat flood her sex, knowing he was as aroused as she.

Jarina sucked his finger into her mouth much as she had

done his rod. Her tongue swirled around his finger. She used her head to move up and down on his finger before he pulled it from her mouth.

She anxiously waited to see what he would do next. She didn't have long to wait as he leaned back on his knees and put that same finger on her bottom hole. He began to move his rod within her again while he pushed through her tight hole with his finger. A feeling of fullness overcame her the deeper his finger went. She rotated her hips in answer to his finger moving back and forth.

One moment she was enjoying the pleasure, and the next an explosive orgasm ripped through her. She screamed as her body convulsed and he plunged deeper and faster into her. White lights burst around her as Jarina succumbed.

She felt him stiffen over her as he roared his own climax. A smile pulled at her lips when he fell to the side and put an arm over her.

Kyros woke in the middle of the night famished—but not for food. He rose quietly from the bed and quickly ran hot water in the bath. Once the bath was full, he padded softly to the bed and stared down at his slave.

Her mouth was parted slightly as she slumbered. Her beauty would forever be etched in his memory. For the first time since he'd bought her, he wished to know her name. It was the custom in Pereth to call new slaves Slave until they adapted to their lives. Then the master would rename them. Yet he didn't want to rename his new slave nor call her Slave. He wanted to know her true name.

He had seen the fire in her eyes. She had never been a slave before. If he had to guess, he'd say she used to be of the upper class. But it was a crime to sell the upper class to slavery unless they put themselves up for auction. The few who *had* been put to auction by others were soon set free once it was discovered who they were. His slave had made no mention of this, and he wondered if she'd admit it if he asked.

Of course, if she did admit it, he'd have to set her free, and he simply refused to do that.

Shaking his head loose from such dour thoughts, Kyros rolled her over and scooped her in his arms. She opened her eyes and gave him a sleepy smile before laying her head on his shoulder. He had always been good to his slaves, but the trust this one put in him humbled him.

He stepped into the tub and lowered both of them into the hot water. She sighed softly as he moved her so she lay back against his chest. Water lapped at her full breasts, making her nipples harden.

To his surprise, Kyros felt himself harden as well. Not since he was a young lad had he had so much coupling in one day.

He didn't stop her when she reached around and grasped him. A chuckle escaped him as he cupped both breasts. "I brought us here to wash, not to couple again."

"Yet we both wish to couple again."

"You're sore."

"I'm not complaining," she said with a laugh as she turned to face him. She straddled him and laced her hands behind his head. "Did I need to ask your permission first?"

"Aye," he said with a smile. "I'm a lenient master, though."

"Really?"

He laughed and leaned up to kiss her neck. The urge to take her lips in a real kiss, not something done to slaves, startled him. The smile dropped from his face. "What is your name?"

She stilled. "Slave."

"You're real name. The name you were born with."

"I lost that name the moment I was put up to auction. Besides, you wouldn't believe me if I told you."

There was something in her tone that told him it was very important he not ask again. It wasn't in his nature to give up on something, but he also knew if he gave his slave a little more time, she'd open up to him and trust him fully. With all her secrets.

"Tell me this, then. Did you put yourself up for auction?"

She lifted a cloth and began to lather it with the soap. "Does it matter?"

He watched her nonchalant attitude carefully. She was hiding something, but what? "It does."

"It shouldn't." She began to wash his chest as if she didn't have a care in the world.

"Who are you protecting?" His voice was more gruff than he intended, but the thought that some other man waited for her soured his stomach.

She raised her eyes coyly to his. "Just because I won't give answers to my past doesn't mean I'm protecting someone."

"It most certainly does. We've laws."

She laughed and began to wash his rod with slow, sure strokes. "Your laws cannot help me."

He opened his mouth to ask her what she meant, but she cupped his sacs and massaged them. Kyros closed his eyes and leaned his head back on the tub. "I thought I'd be tired of you by now," he confessed.

"Is that how you usually feel toward women?"

"Unfortunately, aye. Usually after coupling with them once, I no longer want them."

"What does that say about me then?" she teased.

Kyros sighed as he opened his eyes to watch her. "I don't know."

If he didn't know better, he'd say she'd bewitched him. He put his hands on either side of her face, stilling her hands, and looked deep into her amber eyes. "You aren't from Pereth."

"Nay."

She wouldn't know of Pereth's laws that slaves weren't

kissed. He brought her face closer to his and ran his thumbs over her cheekbones. "You're very beautiful."

Her eyes lowered briefly as though she was embarrassed. "I am a slave. There is no need to try to flatter me."

"I'm being honest. I've seen many beautiful women, but you outshine them all. How is it that some man didn't snatch you up and claim you for his wife?"

"I guess it was my inability to take authority," she said with a smile.

Kyros couldn't stop the smile that tugged at his lips. She braced her hands on his chest and moved against him, her sex rubbing against his rod. Kyros sucked in a breath and watched as her eyes darkened.

He raised his head until their lips met. The first contact was like a jolt running through him. He heard her sigh just before she wound her arms around his neck, and Kyros knew he was lost.

A moan left his lips as he moved them gently over hers, coaxing them to open for him. As soon as they did, he slipped his tongue inside her mouth. Desire swept through him like the ocean, drowning him in all that was his slave. Their bodies slid seductively against each other as he molded her to his chest and turned over in the tub so he lay on top of her. The kiss became deeper, their breaths mixing, their tongues mating.

It was a kiss unlike anything Kyros had ever experienced. It rocked him all the way to his very soul, and just for an instant, he thought his slave's soul had been laid bare as well. But just as quickly, she retreated.

Kyros broke the kiss and gazed down at her, determined now, more than ever, to discover who she really was.

"I need to feel you inside me," she said softly, her face flushed in the moonlight.

Kyros didn't need to be asked twice. He sat back and pulled

her with him. Then he situated her over his rod, the tip of him at the entrance of her sex.

"This position allows the woman to have control. I'm giving you this," he said as he wiped a strand of wet hair from her face.

With her hands braced on either side of the tub, she lowered herself on him until she was fully impaled. She smoothed his hair away from his face and leaned forward to kiss him.

"I know what it means for you to give this to me. Thank you."

Unable to speak, Kyros nodded and watched as she began to rotate her hips, the water gently moving in the tub. It didn't take her long to figure out just what kind of control she had as she experimented with different ways to move her hips. In return, Kyros reached up and tweaked her breasts, gently rolling her nipples between his fingers as she rode him.

His climax built quickly, too quickly. Afraid he would attain it before her, he reached between their bodies and stroked her pearl. Her movements became wilder as her desire built. Yet still she didn't come.

Kyros was on the verge and refused to have an orgasm before his slave. He gripped her pearl between two fingers and began to rub it the same time he found her bottom hole and pushed past her tight barrier.

That's all it took to send her over the edge. A scream tore from her throat as she clenched around him. Kyros gripped her hips and thrust once, twice inside her before he climaxed.

They each came down slowly, neither wanting to shatter what had transpired.

Yet fate had other plans.

7

Kyros didn't wish to leave the chamber, but dawn was streaking the sky, and he had things to see to. With one last kiss on his slave's brow, he tugged on his tunic and walked from the room.

As he closed the door gently behind him, he turned to the guards. "Do not disturb her. When you hear movement, have her meal sent in."

He hurried to his chamber to change and found Boreas waiting for him. He friend grinned as he bit into an apple.

"Ah, the sign of a satisfied man," Boreas said around a mouthful of apple. "Was she worth it?"

Kyros threw his clothes into a pile and laughed. "Worth every last coin."

"Good."

There was something in his tone that told him that Boreas had discovered something. Kyros pulled out a new tunic of dark purple and soft leather pants. As he pulled on his fresh clothes, he regarded Boreas. "What did you find?"

"You were right. Dugu has been in charge of the slave market for too long."

"Nothing new there. He'll need to be replaced immediately," he said as he swept his hands through his tousled hair. "Did you find much corruption?"

The lengthy silence from his closest friend made fear snake down his spine. He turned to Boreas. "What did you discover?"

"The very worst, Kyros. Hesione alone didn't start the war."

Kyros's legs nearly gave out. He walked to the table near the window and slowly sank into the chair. "Explain."

Boreas raked a hand through his hair. "It didn't take much digging to discover just what Dugu had done. I haven't yet discovered who, but someone in Hesione, along with Dugu, ambushed our soldiers."

"I want Dugu arrested."

"Already done."

Kyros nodded. "You're a good friend, Boreas. Thank you."

"No need to thank me. There is no telling what we'll discover, now that Dugu doesn't have his hold over the slave market."

"Halt all auctions," Kyros said suddenly. "I have a feeling my slave wasn't the only one sold without her consent."

"As you wish," Boreas said and made for the door.

"Boreas?"

"Aye?"

Kyros rose and looked out his window to his beloved kingdom. "I need to know who at Hesione did this to us. Their soldiers were killed as well."

"My men are already trying to get the name from Dugu. We'll have it before the day is out."

Jarina woke with a smile on her face. Something she hadn't expected had happened last night: it was almost as if their souls had touched. She wasn't fool enough to believe that anything could come of their union—she was queen of Hesione and needed to return as soon as she could. Which meant leaving her new master.

She rolled onto her back and sat up. Muscles in her legs protested when she moved, making her chuckle as she recalled the many times she and her master had coupled.

It had surprised her when he'd asked her name. Part of her had wanted to tell him the truth, to see what he would do, but another part had cautioned her.

She rose from the bed, hastily washed, and put back on the simple white gown she had worn the day before. She tied the belt loosely around her waist and then sat at the small table and mirror and began to brush her hair. It was knotted terribly from their lovemaking, but she didn't mind.

The door suddenly opened, and Jarina whirled around, hoping it was her master. Instead Seta came in bearing a tray laden with food. Her footsteps were hurried and her face pinched with worry.

"Seta? What is it?"

"I'm not sure. Something is going on, though. Dugu, the old lord who was in charge of the slave market, has been brought to the palace and is being questioned. It is rumored that someone will replace him as controller of the slave market, but, until then, all auctions have been halted."

Jarina could only stare openmouthed at Seta as she hurried from the room. She blinked and looked down at the food Seta had brought. A moment ago she had been starving, but now all she could think of was that her opportunity to return to Hesione might very well come this day.

"Kyros!"

Boreas's shouts thundered through the palace as he called for his king.

"Here!" Kyros bellowed as he rushed from his throne room to the hallway to meet his friend. "What is it?"

"Our troops need to be assembled. We might have moved too slowly in bringing Dugu here."

Kyros gripped Boreas's arm. "Calm down. What are you talking about?"

"The person at Hesione that was conspiring with Dugu is Queen Jarina. She and her army are headed here now to take over your kingdom."

Kyros's stomach fell to his feet like lead. He knew just how weakened and devastated his army was. They didn't stand a chance against Hesione's army. "Gather what men you can," he said. "Meet me in the courtyard in half an hour."

As Boreas ran to get the troops, Kyros turned to retrieve his armor, only to skid to a halt. If he left the palace, his slave could very well be killed if the city was attacked. Yet he couldn't take her with him.

"Guards!" he hollered as he rushed to his chamber.

The two men followed, eager to do his bidding. "I have a new slave in the east wing. Take her out of the kingdom and hide her in my country manor. Make sure she's safe."

"Aye, sire," they said in unison before pivoting to find the slave.

Kyros knew she'd be safe out of the kingdom. If she got out in time. He pushed aside thoughts of her as he hurried to strap on his sword and daggers. By the time he reached the courtyard, Boreas had already assembled the men, who now waited for Kyros outside the gates of the kingdom.

"Ready?" Boreas asked.

"To think I thought the queen had been duped like I was. What a fool I've been."

Boreas clapped him on the back once Kyros was mounted on his horse. "You cannot see everything, my brother. Let's finish this today."

"Aye. It's time for peace."

The ground rumbled like thunder as Kyros rode through the gates and set his army toward Hesione.

* * *

Jarina watched from her balcony at who she could only imagine was the king riding through the gates of the kingdom, where he met up with the entire Pereth army. Her stomach twisted in knots as she realized the man she had come to care for was out there somewhere and might never return.

She didn't want to think about never seeing him again, but there was nothing for it. Her hands gripped the rail of the balcony as the army began to move, the ground shaking in their wake.

The door to her chamber flew open. Jarina whirled around to see four guards fill the room.

"What is this about?" she demanded.

"We've been instructed to get you out of here," the tallest of them said. His voice was deep and his shoulders wide.

Jarina shook her head. "Why?"

"We're at war," another stated. "There isn't time. We must leave now."

At his words, the first guard tossed her another gown. "Change into that so we won't be stopped. We cannot leave with you dressed as a slave."

The other two guards who had been standing at her door since she'd arrived turned on their heels and hurried away. Through the door she could see other servants and more guards rushing around the corridors.

She gripped the gown to her chest. "Give me but a moment and I will be ready."

They nodded and left the chamber. As the door closed and she began to untie her belt, she couldn't help but offer up a prayer for her new master. Their time had been short, but it had been the best time of her life, and she didn't wish to see him hurt in any way.

After she stepped out of her slave gown, she put on the dark purple gown that hung sensuously against her skin, making her think of her master. She smoothed down the sleeveless gown and then tied the silk-braided belt around her waist. After a deep breath, she walked to the doors and opened them.

"I'm ready."

The guards nodded, and she followed them down a maze of corridors until they reached the outside. Standing in the courtyard were three horses. One guard quickly helped her mount, and before she had barely taken the reins in her hands, they were off.

Chaos ensued as Pereth readied for the worst, and deep in the pit of her stomach, Jarina feared that Hesione might be attacking, that her uncle was attacking. She had to reach Hesione before her uncle did something she couldn't undo.

Wind whipped at her face as she followed one guard through the streets and the other rode behind her. Images of her night with the man she called Master continued to flash in her mind, making it more and more difficult to leave Pereth without saying good-bye to him. But she had no choice.

She was Queen Jarina of Hesione, and with that title came responsibilities. Her happiness came second to the welfare of her people. As they passed the gates of the kingdom, she pulled up on her reins.

The guards faced her, their helmets obstructing her view of most of their faces. "What's wrong?" one asked sharply.

She took a deep breath and raised her chin. "Do you know who I am?"

"Nay," the second guard all but shouted. "We were told to get you out of the palace and to safety. And that's what we're going to do."

"What you're going to do is take me home."

Both guards stared at her silently for a moment, giving her time to continue.

"I am Queen Jarina of Hesione, and I must return to my kingdom at once."

The first guard started laughing as he took off his helm. "That's a nice try, but you forget I saw you dressed as a slave."

Jarina expected his response. "I was dressed that way so no one would know who I was. I was visiting King Kyros in an attempt to make peace between our kingdoms," she lied smoothly.

"I don't believe you," the first guard said, looking to the second.

The second guard looked as though he didn't know what to believe.

"You have two choices: take me back to Hesione and be well rewarded by me and your king, or keep me away and die when both kingdoms realize what you have done."

"Hesione is attacking us!" the first guard shouted.

"My uncle is attacking, you idiot. Now take me back to Hesione or stay here."

The guard sneered at her. "I'm taking you where I was ordered to take you."

Jarina nudged her mount forward until she and the guard were facing each other. "You won't take me to my people?"

"Nay."

In a blink she threw her elbow into his ribs. He grunted and doubled over with a moan. She lifted her knee the same time his face moved downward, and she kneed him in the face, knocking him unconscious. She pushed the guard off his horse, where he fell with a thud to the ground.

She then turned to the other guard. "I will go alone if I must, but I will return to Hesione."

After a moment the guard nodded. "I'll take you. I just pray you're telling the truth."

8

Kyros had never been so furious in his life. He couldn't wait to get his hands on Queen Jarina so he could wring her neck for her treachery.

Gaining entrance into her kingdom had been far easier than he had expected. He and Boreas only had taken ten soldiers with them as they'd entered the kingdom, while the rest of the army hid in the nearby forest. It would just take a blow from their horn to send the army descending on Hesione.

Kyros raised his hand to halt his men before he dismounted. The city was eerily quiet, as if it were deserted. His eyes scanned the nearby buildings, but he saw nothing.

"What is it?" Boreas whispered.

"I don't know. Leave two here with the horses. We need to get into the palace."

The men kept to the shadows as they slowly made their way to the palace. They encountered no one until they reached the palace of Queen Jarina. Two men guarded the front entrance and another two a side entrance. Just as Kyros was about to send his men to kill the guards at the side entrance, a door opened and a maid ran outside and into the trees, her skirts held high as she laughed.

Kyros and his men watched and waited as a man followed her outside; Hesione guards quickly disappeared into the palace. By the man's dress, he was a noble, and by the look on his face and the swell in his pants, he and the girl would be occupied for a while.

Kyros motioned his men inside the doorway after the couple wandered off. As soon as they entered, they found themselves in the kitchen staring at a portly woman who looked as though she had lost her entire family.

She raised her solemn gray eyes to Kyros and leaned back in her chair. "What do you want?"

"I've come looking for the queen," Kyros said. "Tell me where I can find her."

"I'll tell you where you can find her uncle. He'll tell you where she's gone," the woman answered tartly, fire lighting her eyes for a moment. She sighed loudly and pointed to a stairway. "Take those stairs. They will lead you to a long corridor. You'll find her uncle in the throne room. It's the sixth door on the right."

Kyros glanced at the stairway. "You need to come with us."

"Why?" she asked. "I'm not about to sound an alarm."

"I can't take that chance," he said as he took her by the arm and pulled her up. She barely reached his chest and met his gaze with more courage than he expected.

Her lack of interest in why he was at the castle puzzled him. As he pulled her toward the stairway, she pushed behind her ear a strand of gray hair.

"Why are you leading me to her uncle so willingly?" he asked her.

She shrugged her shoulders. "I don't care for the man. No one does."

"But you care for your queen?"

"I do."

He laughed as they stepped into the dimly lit corridor with soaring ceilings and many doors. "Yet you lead me to the very man that will hand her over to me. I don't think you like you queen very much at all."

She harrumphed. "I don't give a wart's ass what you think."

"Watch how you speak to my king," Boreas hissed from behind her.

She looked over her shoulder at Boreas and then glanced at Kyros. "He's not my king, so I'll talk to him however I please."

Kyros raised a hand to stop Boreas from chiding the woman further. He didn't care how this woman talked to him as long as he could capture Jarina and end the war before more blood was shed.

"There," the woman said as she stopped in front of huge double doors. "He's in there. He's always in there." She had such hatred in her voice it made Kyros pause.

He nodded to his men, who threw open the doors as he shoved the woman inside. She gasped as she stumbled into the throne room, giving Kyros and his men the diversion they needed to assess the occupants and take control.

Only four guards and two men were in the room. Out of the corner of his eye, Kyros saw his men surround the guards as he and Boreas walked to the two men near the thrones at the back of the large room.

"Which of you is Ampyx!" Kyros bellowed.

An older man, eyes filled with malice, stepped forward, his hand on his dagger at his waist. "I am. And you are?"

In the space of a heartbeat, Kyros pulled his sword and leveled the tip on Ampyx's throat, forcing the man to his knees. "Where is she?"

"Wh—who?" he stuttered, his hands raised and shaking.

"Jarina. Summon her immediately."

Ampyx looked helplessly to his friend, who Boreas held immobile with a dagger at his throat. Finally Ampyx returned his gaze to Kyros. "I cannot."

Anger flooded Kyros. He pushed the tip of his sword into Ampyx's throat. Blood welled and dripped onto Ampyx's red tunic. "Cannot or will not?"

"Cannot," Ampyx repeated. "She isn't here."

Jarina held her breath as she and the Pereth guard circled around Kyros's massive army outside her gates. Her guard had proven highly skilled, and they had covered the ground quickly as they rode to Hesione.

Suddenly he held up a hand to stop her; then he turned his mount around to come even with her. "We're at the gates. I don't suppose you want to go in the front?"

She smiled and shook her head. "It's time you followed me now," she said and nudged her horse.

She couldn't reach the palace quick enough. It took everything in her not to rush to the gates and shout her identity to all, but her need to see the shock on her uncle's face kept her quiet.

The trail to the hidden entrance to the palace was overgrown and barely discernable, and the only way Jarina knew her way was because her father had made sure she could get to the entrance blindfolded in case of an emergency.

She jumped from her horse when they reached the doorway. "This way," she said to the guard.

He followed close behind her as she pushed open the nearly hidden doorway in the stones. She closed the door behind them and pointed to the palace. "We'll go in through the side entrance."

After he nodded, she hurried toward the door and the guards. As soon as they approached, the guards blocked their way with their spears.

"Move," she commanded them.

They both hesitated as they glanced at each other. The younger one finally spoke. "I'm glad you finally returned, my queen."

Her heart fell to her feet. "What has my uncle told everyone?"

The soldier shrugged. "I know not."

"Then how did you know I was gone?" she asked. She was ever thankful she had one of Pereth's guards with her.

The guards exchanged another look. "We were two of the six that took you, your highness."

"Took me?" she repeated, unsure she had heard him correctly. "You would dare abduct your queen?"

"Aye," he quickly replied. "Lord Ampyx wanted us to kill you. Instead we took you to Pereth and the slave market. We knew you would eventually find your way back."

Jarina sighed as the full impact of what her uncle had done settled around her. "And my personal guards?"

"All dead, your highness. I'm sorry."

She waved away his words. "I need to surprise my uncle," she said as anger replaced her surprise.

"We'll come with you," the guard said.

Jarina knew the castle and all its secrets from many hours of childhood play. She led the Pereth guard and two Hesione guards through secret tunnels and doorways until she came to the throne room. On the other side, she could hear men speaking, though she couldn't tell what they said.

She nodded to her three guards, and they quietly slipped unseen into her throne room. She was shocked to find who she could only assume was King Kyros holding her uncle at the point of his sword. The king's helm covered all but his mouth and chin. Her gaze raked over him, from the tip of his helm's black feathers to his boots. He was tall and lethal looking as he held her uncle in place.

"Answer me!" Kyros bellowed. "Where is she?"

Jarina swallowed as she realized Kyros wanted her.

"I told you," Ampyx said. "I don't know where she is."

Jarina turned to her guards and took one of their swords. It was time she interfered.

"You lie!" Kyros bellowed and pulled back his arm as he prepared to plunge his sword into her uncle.

Jarina stepped from the shadows behind her uncle and waited until she felt Kyros's eyes on her. "He doesn't lie. Up until just a few minutes ago, I wasn't in my city."

Kyros slowly lowered his sword as his mouth fell open. Jarina found his reaction curious, but she was more concerned with her uncle, who whirled around on his knees to face her.

"Niece!" he cried out and tried to take hold of her hand.

Jarina lifted the sword and pointed it at his throat. "Tell me, *Uncle*, how surprised you are to see me. Alive."

He swallowed nervously and tried to smile at her. "I think there has been some kind of misunderstanding, Jarina."

"No, I finally understand just what a monster you are. If it hadn't been for the loyalty of the guards, I would be dead now. That is what you wanted, isn't it?"

The smile on his face vanished to be replaced by a scowl. "Yes!" he yelled. "The throne should have been mine!"

Jarina's eyes clouded with tears. "My parents weren't killed by Pereth soldiers, were they?" When he didn't answer but only stared at her, she shook her head and took a step back. "You killed them."

"I had to make it look like an accident," he said as he rose to his feet. "Besides, I needed to keep the battle raging with Pereth."

Jarina lowered her sword. "Guards, take him to the dungeon," she said. She turned on her heel to walk away, when she heard a scuffle behind her.

She turned in time to see her uncle lunging at her with his

dagger and Kyros stepping between them. Her eyes widened as she saw her uncle fall on Kyros's sword; his lifeless body fell to the floor.

With her heart hammering in her ears, she raised her gaze to the king of Pereth. "Thank you," she said and licked her lips. "You came here for me."

"I did," he said.

There was something about his voice that sounded familiar. Jarina took a deep breath and realized she longed for the man who had claimed her body and soul . . . and her heart. Would he still want her once he knew she was a queen?

She shook her head to clear her thoughts and focused on Kyros. "My uncle lied to me, and I'm sure he lied to my father. I don't know why the war between or kingdoms started, but I would like it to end. Tonight."

Kyros reached up and pulled off his helm. Jarina's breath lodged in her throat as she stared into eyes as black as midnight. Her mouth fell open in surprise as she took a step toward her master. Slowly her hand reached up to touch his cheek.

"Is it really you?"

"Yes," Kyros said. "Why didn't you tell me who you were?"

She smiled. "I needed to return here and confront my uncle. I feared if I told you who I was and you didn't believe me, you would keep me tied."

Kyros pulled her against his chest, his armor digging into her cheek, but she didn't care. "Thank the gods you found your way back."

For long moments they stayed silent as they held each other; then Kyros pulled back and held her at arm's length. "We signed a treaty to be married."

Jarina sighed. "I never signed it. My uncle must have forged my signature."

"That doesn't matter. I've realized something in the time we've spent together. I've never found another woman who has claimed my heart the way you have. I was so worried about you I had my guards take you from the palace to my manor in the forest."

"I know," she said with a smile. "What are you proposing?"

"That we marry."

"We don't know each other," she argued.

He took her hand and looked deep into her eyes. "What are you afraid of, Jarina? Think of our kingdoms. We've been divided by war; let's unite by love."

"Are you saying you love me?"

"I'm saying I'm falling in love with you. I want to know everything there is to know about you, and I want to share all my secrets with you. Marry me. We don't have to get married right away, but I have to know you're going to be mine."

Jarina couldn't believe Kyros was offering her everything she ever wanted. "I'm falling in love with you as well."

"Then let's spend more time together. Take as long as you want planning the wedding, as long as it isn't more than six months from now," he finished with a heart-stopping grin.

There was no reason for Jarina to refuse. She knew in her heart her future was with Kyros. "Yes." She nodded. "Yes, I will marry you."

Kyros let out a whoop as he lifted her in his arms and spun her around the room. Jarina's laughter joined his as the guards cheered with them. She looked down at her future husband and kissed him. The laughter died from his eyes and was replaced with desire.

"Where is your chamber?"

"Upstairs," she said breathlessly. She was as eager as he to find some privacy.

"Let's find it. And something to tie you with," he said as he pulled her from the throne room to their future.

In His Bed

Annalise Russell

1
———

"Are you agreed?"

Sitting back on her knees before the large Viking, Chessa
nodded. "Yes, I am agreed." Good, her voice hadn't faltered.
She clasped her hands in her lap and tried not to think. Too
much thinking would make her blush.

"Then repeat the terms to me, so you appreciate the weight
of this bargain you wish to strike."

Wetting her lips, Chessa lifted her chin, looking Bodin in the
eye. A bold action, yes. But, after all, she had been freed of her
servitude, if only since the dawn. "I agree to tend all the needs
of your body as payment for my place on your ship."

She waited, silently willing his agreement to the bargain.
Her heart lodged in her throat. If he refused her, denied her
passage home, what would become of her? The one thing she'd
learned well living these past ten years among the Vikings was
that a woman without protection lived in peril every moment.

Bodin took a deep breath. "Your home may no longer be as
you remember. Are you certain this bargain is what you wish?

Once made," his eyebrows raised in warning, "there will be no going back . . ."

Chessa tucked an errant strand of hair behind her ear. Fear burned in her belly, weakening her confidence and softening her words. "Please, I've nothing else of value."

Sitting in the large village hall, he leaned forward in the chair, bracing his forearms on his thighs. Her sweet face only inches from him, smudged with dirt from her first day of freedom—the first day she'd not had the protection of his father's name by serving in his household. He lifted her chin with his finger, thinking on what she offered him with this bargain of hers. "Tell me what you know of tending a man's needs."

Her mouth opened, then closed. Chessa pressed her lips into a thin line. Cowardice would not get the better of her now. She inhaled a deep breath. "It means I'm to share your quarters."

"Just my quarters?"

She shook her head, swallowing nervously. "No, I'll share your bed as well."

"And?"

"And do all you ask of me." Her stomach fluttered in anticipation. His ship sailed at sunrise, and already the light outside grew dim. He would have to give her an answer soon. Meeting his gaze with bold intent, she held her breath. . . .

Bodin let go of her chin and leaned back in his chair, stretching his legs out, ankles crossed. "Agreed."

Chessa beamed. "Oh, thank you! Thank you!" She scrambled to her feet, swatting the dust from her skirts. "I won't be any trouble, I promise. You'll see."

"Chessa . . ."

His voice commanded her attention, and she froze midstep on her way to the door. The tenants of the village were beginning to gather at the tables in the hall for the evening meal, and she had much to do in the kitchen yet.

"Yes?"

Bodin got to his feet. "Your service begins now. Conduct yourself to *my* quarters, not those of my father."

"And what would you have me do in your absence?"

"Wait." He adjusted his sword belt. "I'll join you shortly."

Chessa nodded. She hadn't realized he would mean to start immediately. Not that a few hours made much of a difference one way or the other. She'd had her day of freedom. And this bargain meant she got to go home, got to return to her family and take her rightful place among her people. "Of course, sir."

Her hand skimmed along the rough-hewn door frame of the massive hall where everyone but the sick and injured took their meals. She glanced back inside at the tables and benches. Much of her life had been spent in this hall. And now she would not come here again. Chessa sighed and looked away.

Outside, stars began to twinkle amid the cloudless twilight. Had her parents counted the days until the completion of her service? Were they looking out to the sea, waiting for her to return? They would be proud of her. She'd done her duty—to them and to her people.

As Chessa made her way along the worn dirt path, the past came to mind. *She* had been the price of peace for her people, the center of a bargain between her father and Bodin's father: servitude for the period of ten years, the time until she came of an age to marry, had been the deal. Nonnegotiable, she had been the old Viking's prize.

And she'd been lucky. As the daughter of a ruler, sent along to represent her people, she'd received much more gentle treatment than many of the others who were taken. She still held in her memory the names of the women who had been carried off, never to return. She'd been but a child then, and while she had not witnessed their manner of death, she knew they had died. Every part of her knew it.

She shivered, wanting to forget all that. She'd long since quit thinking about her first days and weeks in the village—so many frightening strangers, ways and words she couldn't grasp.

The trail branched, and she almost walked the way she had for more than half her life. But no longer. Tonight she would take a different path, one of her own choosing. And soon she'd wander the hills and shores of her father's land again.

Chessa stopped at the entrance to Bodin's quarters. She'd never been inside before. From time to time she'd left things for him at his mother's instruction. But never once had she been inside.

She looked over her shoulder. The evening had settled softer and quieter than usual. Most would be in the hall by now, having their fill of meat and mead.

Too late to turn back.

Chessa tugged at the heavy latch until the metal bar inside was freed and the door creaked open. Warm air touched the chill on her arms, but her underskirts were made of thick-woven wool and held back such comfort from her legs.

Chessa moved nearer the hearth and the faint heat of the dying fire. She thought to add another piece of wood but stopped. Bodin had instructed her only to wait. And it wouldn't do to anger him before they set sail. He might decide she'd be too much trouble after all and change his mind about their bargain.

Behind her the door banged open, and she spun around. Two servant girls from the kitchen lumbered in carrying a large metal tub. Others followed, filling the cistern with buckets of steaming water heated over the cooking fires.

Bodin strode in, eyes fixed on her. Had he almost smiled? She reached for one of the buckets.

"Chessa . . ."

She looked up at him.

"That is not for you to do." Bodin unbuckled the belt at his waist, draping leather and sword and knife over the back of a nearby chair.

He stepped over to the tub and dipped his finger in the water. "That'll do." He dismissed the maids. Grabbing the back of an empty chair, he turned it around and placed it at the front of the tub.

Chessa watched as Bodin sat, his long frame stretched, arms crossing over his chest. He said nothing. The air in the room turned dense and thick, making it harder and harder to breathe.

The door closed with a loud clank of metal and wood, startling her and freeing her from the confines of his stare. But her reprieve was temporary.

"Chessa . . ."

His voice—low and penetrating, as tangible as his gaze— sent a shiver down her spine. He'd done nothing more than speak, yet everything about him was as physical as a touch.

Tentatively she turned to look at him again.

"Undress."

For long moments she stood frozen to the floor, chest tight, palms sweating. A warm, fluttery sensation danced inside her belly. He intended to watch.

Chessa swallowed the lump of nerves climbing the back of her throat. She couldn't meet his ever-encroaching gaze as she fumbled with the brooch pinning the work apron over her linen gown. Her fingers shook, slowing her efforts to work the clasp free.

Doubt about the wisdom of this bargain crept into her chest as the second brooch snapped open. Chessa took a deep breath, trying to slow the many small breaths that were making her dizzy. She worked her arms free and then tugged the gown higher, pulling it over her head and off.

Bodin's eyebrows raised at the sight of her pieced under-skirt.

The women of the village wore no such garment, but Bodin's

mother had allowed her to make it from scraps to keep warm. The bulk of her gown threaded through her fingers, dropping onto the floor. She unlaced the side of the skirt, letting it puddle around her feet.

Nervous, her toes curled into the layer of packed rushes covering the dirt floor. She turned toward the tub. Steam rose from the smooth, glassy surface. She inched closer.

"Unh-unh." He shook his head. "Not yet."

His gaze roamed her body as she continued to stand exposed before him. She fought to keep her hands by her sides, her face growing warmer with each passing moment.

"Turn around. Let me see all of what you have bargained."

Chessa turned her back to him. Again she fought against the shallow breaths plaguing her.

Bodin reached forward and tugged at the single, weighty rope of red and gold tresses that always hung down the center of her back. "Free your hair."

She looked at him from over her shoulder. He sat upright, stiff. He was not relaxed as before. Chessa pulled the long strand of thick, unruly hair over her shoulder, untying the knotted leather strap that bound the ends together. Starting from the bottom, she began to untwist the hank of hair, freeing the tangled waves with her fingers as she worked her way higher, shaking the bulk of it loose.

"Very good, Chessa."

Had his voice gone deeper? She peeked over her shoulder again. The dark look on his face tied her stomach in knots. Beat after beat raced from her heart. Was he displeased?

"Get in." Bodin cleared his throat and nodded toward the tub. "But remain standing."

She braced her hands on the rim of the metal tub and climbed into the water. Her hair fell forward, offering a shield from his prying gaze. Embarrassment heated her chilled skin.

Hot water reached nearly to her thighs; the ends of her long, loose tresses mixed with the swirling steam. She looked around for soap and cloth but saw none.

Bodin stood. The sudden motion captured her attention.

Reaching forward, his calloused fingers traced the small bones that ran from her shoulder to the hollow at the base of her throat. Chessa held her breath. Did he plan to wash her? The idea made her hands tremble, and she swallowed. His touch was warm . . . distracting. . . .

Slowly he spread his fingers, moving up the column of her neck. "Tilt your head back."

She obeyed but tried to watch what he was doing. Bodin's thumb turned her head back to face forward.

A small stream of heated water poured over her hair, running rampant down her face and shoulders, over and around her breasts, and down the flat of her belly to drip into the tub from the tufts of curls centered at the juncture of her thighs. Chessa held her breath and wiped the excess water from her eyes.

Bodin set down the half-empty bucket and handed her soap.

Wet and shivering, she began to scrub at the masses and masses of hair plastered to her back and legs. Bodin poured the remainder of the water from the bucket, rinsing her clean of the thin lather.

Again, Chessa wiped the water from her face. The Viking leaned in close. The heat from his body warmed her skin, heating her with embarrassment again. She made an effort to swallow. From what little she knew, she thought men wanted to touch, not to look.

"Wash," Bodin's voice rasped, harsh in his throat. He walked around the metal tub, taking in the sight of her wet, naked body. His fingers dipped again into the warm water, brushing against the smooth skin of her leg. "And hurry, before you chill."

With the chunk of soap cupped in her palm, Chessa washed her neck and shoulders, pulling handfuls of wet hair out of her way to reach her back. Next, she soaped her stomach and legs.

"Don't forget the rest—" Bodin sucked in a tense breath as he reached inside his trousers and adjusted his blood-engorged cock.

Wide-eyed, Chessa looked at the large bulge. Her face burned hot. And even though the fire held little heat, she was plenty warm. An odd, fluttery sensation made her nipples contract and ache. She ran the soap over them, hoping to ease the strange feeling, but instead her belly reacted, the muscles quivering. She shifted on her feet, a slippery wetness joining the throb that had begun to beat between her thighs.

Tentatively she met Bodin's gaze. He stood there, watching, not saying a word as his gaze rolled over every inch of her. His lips twitched, jaw clenching tight.

Had she done something wrong? Was he angry?

"Fin—" he cleared his throat. "Finish."

His voice had changed from a ragged whisper to a low, commanding rumble that seemed to reach inside her and make her muscles obey of their own will. Her hands shook as she smeared her palms with a thin layer of the harsh soap.

Chessa lowered her gaze and rewashed her belly.

Bodin took a step closer. "Watch *me* while you bathe. Follow my instructions."

Her head jerked up. What would he want her to do? Rapid, shallow little gasps shook her breasts. She wanted to swallow, but her mouth had gone dry. As she was unsure what to expect, her heart thumped inside her chest.

Bodin's gaze dropped to her hands, her small fingers frozen atop her smooth, flat little tummy. "Slide one hand between your legs."

The harsh, strained expression on his face made her rush to obey.

"Slowly," he growled.

Chessa's heart jumped into her throat, robbing her of much needed air. The room started to spin. Her legs shook. She inched her hand lower along her soap-slickened skin, fingers reaching the nest of coarse red curls. She swallowed and continued deeper as he'd instructed.

"Ah—" Chessa's voice seized, her throat closed to air and words. A fire ripped through her, and she swayed forward.

Bodin grabbed for her, catching her small body as she lost her balance. His gut tightened. Keeping the weight of her pressed to his chest, he whispered in her ear, "Shall I finish the task for you?"

2

Bodin steadied Chessa back onto her feet. By the gods, she was beautiful. He cupped the side of her face, brushing back the long strands of wet hair with his thumbs.

Her fine-boned fingers curled into his shirt. She couldn't look at him. Bodin let out the breath he'd been holding. He collected her small wrists into one of his hands as he turned her around and braced her back against his chest. As a rule, maidens were damn skittish.

With her inconsiderable frame trapped against him, he bent and cupped his free hand into the tub. The scent of soap and wildflowers wafted from her hair. He closed his eyes and inhaled, letting the tincture of heady earth and sweet nectars fill his lungs. The smells still lingered fresh on her skin. She'd spent her day of freedom in the hills.

Bodin gritted his teeth. This bargain might take more control than he had. He brought the warm water to her waist and let it trickle down her leg. She tensed in his confining grasp. He further moistened the soap on her hip. Her bottom wiggled, rubbing against his already needy loins.

He clenched his jaw shut with a growl, tightening his hold on her wrists. "Easy, girl. This part won't hurt." *But it may damn near kill me.* His hand slid over the supple skin of her tummy.

Chessa held her breath, trying to stifle a whimper.

His trapped cock strained for freedom as her stomach muscles tensed and quivered beneath his palm. He spread his fingers, spanning the whole of her belly, hip bone to hip bone. She was almost insignificant against him.

He dragged in a deep breath. He'd hardly touched her, and already she maddened him. "Relax. Don't worm around so." Bodin continued to rub his hand over her ribs and stomach, sides and hips, to settle her to his touch. So unlike the other women he'd bedded—robust, healthy sized, anxious women. He would have to take great pains not to hurt this one.

And by the gods, he didn't want to hurt this one. He looked down over her shoulder. Her breasts, firm and soapy, rubbed against his hairy arm with every fractured breath she took. The pale globes, large on her small frame, fascinated him. He wished more than anything to seek out and explore the tight, pink nipples that bobbed up and down, teasing him, calling to him. But his balls pained him too much at the moment.

She moved backward, brushing against him again, and his cock throbbed, straining to reach her. He threw his head back, sucking in an impossible breath as he battled for control.

His fingers grazed over the triangular tuft of hair at her center. She arched against him, her small, firm bottom driving backward into his groin. Damnit, at this rate, her squirming would have him spilling his seed in his trousers.

Her breasts heaved, stiff nipples scraping his forearms as she panted in his grip, unfamiliar with the urgency of passion. His gut tightened, and he bared his teeth, hissing, "I'll not warn you again—be still, Chessa."

"Ah . . . I—" she gasped for air. "I—"

He leaned her backward, disrupting her balance so he could control her weight—and her innocent talent at driving him to the brink. He steeled himself as she struggled to free her hands and regain her footing.

Chessa whimpered, a deep, throaty half groan.

Bodin had had enough. If he didn't finish her bath now, he would regret it. And so would she. With the small, slippery chunk of soap still trapped between her stomach and his palm, he slid his hand to the top of her leg, brushing against the thatch of coarse red curls that hindered his view of her sex. His fingers moved to her inner thigh, opening her to his touch.

She continued to squirm, despite a grip he knew must be crushing to her. The tip of his finger slid easily into her wet, secluded juncture, smearing the evidence of her musky desire. Her head thrashed, gasps changing to sobs.

"By the gods," Bodin cursed. At this rate, he'd hurt her. He moved his hand behind her, cupping and squeezing the firm mounds of her buttocks.

Already engorged to the point of pain, his cock thickened and throbbed. He had to hurry.

Using the soapy water to ease his fingers between the cleft of her bottom, he made his way forward to her moist center. A single, calloused finger slipped into the slick, passion-swollen folds of her sex. He closed his eyes for a moment. How he wanted to taste her there, hear her scream his name. For now, this would have to do. Her writhing made his efforts to be gentle difficult as he coated more of his fingers with the evidence of her need. But before he could enter far enough to breech her virgin barrier, she cried out, her body convulsing as she shattered in his arms.

Bodin swore under his breath and tore at the laces of his trousers. He growled, his body frozen with effort as his seed gushed forth onto her creamy skin. His hand, slick from her copious moisture, jerked furiously at his cock, desperate to spend absolutely everything he had.

Out of breath, he bent forward, resting his cheek on the top of her damp head, panting.

Chessa struggled, shaking against the stranglehold of his arm around her body. Her wrists ached, hands and fingers tingling.

"Sorry," Bodin exhaled, standing her back onto her feet and turning her to face him. He looked into her wide eyes, still dark with passion and the shock of her first orgasm. Flecks of gold stood out atop vibrant green, sparkling in the dim torchlight. He brushed the backs of his fingers against her flushed cheek.

She shivered, the water long since cold on her skin.

Bodin took hold of her hands, turning them over to examine her fragile wrists, the obvious redness an ugly reminder of how gentle he needed to be with her. "Out with you," he ordered, his voice still edged with passion.

Chessa's legs trembled, weak, and she clutched at his shirt as she stepped onto the rushes.

Bodin grabbed the bathing cloth and dipped it into the water. He turned her around and cleaned his spendings from her pale, flawless skin. The sight of her, dips and curves and hollows, aroused him.

He tossed the rag away and looked down at his cock, almost half hard and well on the way to demanding satisfaction a second time. "By the gates of Valhalla," he hissed. This bargain just may be his undoing. Never had the need to satisfy his baser urges returned so soon.

Chessa turned around to see what was the matter. "Sh— shall I see to your bath now?"

Her small voice broke into his thoughts. "No!" His harsh tone startled even him. With closed eyes, he sighed. But it did no good. The vision of her, soft and sweet, lingered in his mind and on his fingertips. And he'd yet to taste the tiniest portion of her bared skin. The sound of her impassioned whimpers bounced around inside his skull. With a shake of his head and a deep breath, he nodded to the chair. "Sit."

She obeyed and reached for her clothes.

"No." He cleared his throat and put forth the effort it took to soften his voice. "You'll not dress again until the morning." His gaze dropped to her taut pink nipples, peeking through the veil of her long hair, straining for him with their daring presence. Every drop of blood in his veins changed direction, rushing below his waist. His cock demanded that he touch her, ready her to meet the full force of his flesh and sate the deepening need inside him.

Bodin reached out and brushed her long hair behind her shoulders so he could see all of her. His cock jumped.

Running a hand over his face, he bit back another curse and stepped into the icy bath water, desperate for refuge from his urgent need. His heart just might explode inside his chest if he had to endure such a necessity for control again.

She sat beside the tub, eyes focused on the floor, her skin a burnished pink.

He could see thoughts of confusion roll through her mind. "Keep your eyes on me, Chessa." She might as well learn from the start that he intended to make the most of his limited time with her. That is, if he could survive this night and the challenge of her sweet innocence.

Quickly he soaped and rinsed. The cold water had done little to diminish his desire. Only one thing would do that.

Her body.

3

Bodin stepped, dripping wet, from the tub, his manhood large and protruding.

Chessa swallowed. Her body warmed despite her state of undress and only embers left in the hearth. She watched him walk to his bed, scrubbing his hair and skin dry with the cloth.

Her stomach quivered. The warm wetness between her thighs urged her to squirm. The same tingling from before drew her attention.

"Chessa."

The command startled her, and she jumped, snapping her wide-eyed gaze to meet his. The beats of her heart slammed in her chest; she hadn't realized she'd been staring.

"Come here to me," he growled, sitting on his bed.

As she stood, her hair fell forward, covering her. She glanced down at her pile of clothes on the floor but left them. He wanted to see her, bared. He'd said so. And by the look of him, he wanted to touch her again, too.

Of that much she was certain.

The thought of his hands on her again, teasing places she

didn't even know she wanted him to touch, sent strange sensations churning in the pit of her belly. Her nipples contracted, tight and aching. She stopped, standing before him. His gaze roamed the length of her, heating her naked skin. A throb hammered between her slippery thighs, and she closed her eyes. She shifted on her feet, seeking some sort of relief, but moving only made it worse.

"Closer," Bodin rasped, his eyes fixed on her breasts.

As she inched forward, he brushed her hair to the side.

"Closer."

Chessa's eyebrows rose. How could she get closer? She was already well within his reach. He brushed back more of her hair, and she reached behind her neck, gathering and twisting thick handfuls of waves to tie into a knot.

"No. Leave it unbound," Bodin ordered. He spread his legs a little wider. "Now come closer."

A dewy sheen of sweat chilled her, rippling over her flesh in waves from the cooling night air. She started to ease between his thighs, but his knee intentionally interfered.

"No," he whispered. His hands grabbed her hips. "Like this." He pulled her forward so she straddled his leg.

"I—" Her throat constricted, choking off her words. His mouth was so close; his breath washed hot across her skin again and again. Bodin's mouth hovered only a scant distance away from her breasts. A thrumming fire burned between her thighs. Would he touch her there again? He licked at his lips.

A drop of moisture trickled down the inside of her leg, and she gasped. Why was this happening? Chessa wanted to close her legs, to cease the burning, to stop him looking, but he held her trapped, standing astride his hairy, muscular thigh, preventing any chance of that.

"Sh—" She cleared her throat and swallowed. Squeaking, her voice rose in pitch with each word. "Shouldn't I be tending to your—"

"You are." His mouth closed over one taut, pink, teasing nipple.

"Ahhh—" Chessa's stomach tensed as her knees gave way, fingers curling into fists on either side of his head, digging into the thick blond hair. She gasped for air as he did everything in his power to devour her. The throbbing between her thighs got worse. Had he not held on to her, she would have fallen.

Bodin sucked hard on her breast, taking as much as physically possible into his mouth. He trapped her hard nipple between his teeth.

Chessa cried out, hips jutting forward as her body shook. Just as she thought she'd lost her breath forever, his attention shifted to her other breast. But the chance to breathe was short-lived.

She tried to pull him closer, to give him more of her. But more of what? The need between her thighs grew more urgent. Her hips rocked back and forth, demanding attention elsewhere.

His large hands slipped lower on her hips, fingers covering her buttocks, thumbs lodged into the bend at the top of her legs. He drew her tender flesh apart. The friction racked her. Far from sating her need, he'd made it worse. Chessa melted forward, his manhood hard against her thigh. She heard him suck in a sharp breath.

He released her nipple from his teeth, cursing. He slid one hand to her lower back as the other pressed into the cradle of her belly, bracing her. "Look at me, Chessa."

"Ahhh . . . p—p—please . . ." She wormed in his grip, wanting him back at her breast. Wanting his fingers back closer to the pulsing need between her thighs. She let her head drop back, struggling for more air in her lungs.

"At me—look," he demanded, lust grating harsh in his voice.

Why didn't he touch her as he had before in the tub? Her eyes, half lidded and black as night, managed to meet his gaze. Tears of confusion rimmed her lashes.

"Do not take your eyes from mine," he breathed. "I want to see how much you enjoy my touch."

How could she act so? He'd done little more than touch her skin, taste her breasts . . . She shuddered. Never had she imagined she would be standing before a Viking, exposed to his every whim, and willing. Bodin's thumb slid into the moist, wet cleft of her thighs, and all thoughts ceased. She struggled to do as he'd commanded, to watch only him.

Her hips writhed, riding the firestorm of ache and want and need as his thumb delved deeper into the wet curls, stroking back and forth without reprieve. And without allowing her to catch the crest of desire as he had before. Eyes closed, her head dropped back.

Bodin's lips pulled back over his teeth as he warned again, voice low. "Do not hide your pleasure from me."

Chessa gasped for air, unaware he had maneuvered his other leg between hers until she sat open and vulnerable between his slightly spread thighs. Her feet dangled above the cold floor.

He continued to rake his thumb ever so slightly over the sweet, moist sanctuary awaiting him. He guided one of her arms around his neck as he held her balanced over his legs.

Panting, she leaned into his shoulder as her small body trembled and jerked toward his elusive, feathery touch.

Bodin bent his head, whispering against her ear, "And this bargain is what you wish, Chessa?"

The ominous need rose to a fevered pitch, and she clutched at him frantically, her voice managing only to squeak, "Yes! Oh, now, please now—"

Bodin ceased his brief, teasing caresses.

"No . . ." she groaned, gasping for air.

He gritted his teeth, speaking more to himself than to Chessa. "No help for it." He'd have to use her own body against her. Or she would reach completion again before he could take her maidenhead. He pulled her against his rigid cock.

Chessa sucked in a shocked breath. Yet she relished the contact of his warm body. Of the hard heat of his swollen manhood. Of anything that would ease this furious hunger. Free of his hindering grasp, she moved of her own accord, rubbing as best she could against him.

"That's right, sweet one," Bodin rasped. "Let the fire build inside your belly." He grabbed his cock, dragging the tip of it through her moist curls and across the surface of her honeyed sweetness, seeking the entrance to her slickened sanctuary. He lifted her a little, his mouth clamping onto her breast again, doing service to her need as well as to his own.

Chessa moaned as his teeth claimed possession of her swollen nipple. She arched her back, her body moving on pure instinct.

Slowly the tip of his manhood rubbed along the length of her and then back. She froze, torn between the opposing sensations in her body. Moving either way, up toward his mouth or lower against the urgent, parting pressure of him, would cease the pleasure of the other. Something she couldn't bear at the moment.

Bodin's arm wrapped about her waist, pulling her hips down to better meet the head of his cock.

Chessa's mind grappled for what to do. She held her breath, unable to decide between the raw, aching need searing at her breast and the invading heat of him pressing at her, parting her.

Bodin's hand slid beneath the long tresses of hair hanging down her back, wrapping the masses of waves around his wrist as an anchor. Fingers tightened around the nape of her neck.

Chessa's head dropped back as her body rocked of its own accord, seeking the semifamiliar urges he'd wrung from her body before. She panted, caring of nothing at the moment, not home, not duty, not consequence—

Bodin wiggled his thumb deeper into her damp nest of curls, adding influence to her indecision. She pressed her slim body downward a fraction, striving for more of his touch.

Chessa's eyes widened at the incursion of such an enormous pressure.

Bodin relinquished her breast, panting for air as he tightened his grip. He surged upward, sliding deeper into her body, filling more of her. "Good girl, Chessa." He gritted his teeth, enduring the tight heat of her innocent body, and gripped his cock harder in an effort for control. His thumb flicked over the wet, swollen nub her passion had exposed for him. "It'll hurt this time," he breathed in her ear. "No help for it." He widened his legs, using her own weight to bear more of him inside.

"Ah . . ." Chessa tensed, struggling between fear and desire. Her body burned, torn between the need of more and the ache of discomfort. Her nails dug into his shoulders.

Bodin's ragged, harsh breaths washed across her shoulder as he gently pressed her downward, impaling her ever so slowly. "Ah . . . ah . . ."

Bodin reached the barrier of her maidenhead.

A blur of sensations filled Chessa. Pressure and fullness. Pain. An urgency to move. She shook her head, pushing against his chest. "What do I—how—" His touch feathered along her tortured flesh, sending away all reason, all uncertainty and protest. She strained for him, for the completion he'd given her before, taking a little more of him inside her body as she did so. A harrowing ache threatened of pain, and she stilled.

"Here, let me help." Bodin raised her just a fraction, unwilling to relinquish much of the territory he'd gained. By the gods, he needed to bury himself deep and stay there.

He urged her back down, stopping when she tensed, and then repeated the small motion, showing her the means to gain what she sought. He squeezed his eyes shut; his own need demanded attention, and he grabbed ahold of the back of her neck, preparing to do what would have to be done.

Chessa groaned as his thumb returned to torture hidden

places. Her hips began to rock forward of their own accord, unable to resist greeting the wave of invading pleasure any longer. She panted.

"That . . . a girl. Give into it, sweet one."

His words were a warm breeze on her mouth as he brushed against her lips. He pulled her closer, nuzzling her ear, distracting her.

"All of it, Chessa. You must take all of my cock inside you if you wish to sate your body." His touch ceased, reinforcing his point.

"No, don't stop, please. . . ." She fought for breath, shaking her head as she clutched at his shoulders. "Please. . . ." He had to keep touching her; she needed him to touch her, but she just couldn't move down any farther. "I can't . . ." Sobs caught in her throat. "There is too much—"

"No." His gut tightened as he fought the urge to ram his body inside hers, teach her that he would fit, over and over and over again. Instead he sucked the chilly air through his clenched teeth. "You will see," he continued on a groan, "your body was made for this."

Chessa squeezed her eyes shut. Her nipples, raw and swollen, scraped against his chest with every breath either of them took, lashing her with a force of need she could not control. His thumb returned to the splayed, open center of her body. With swift movements, he demanded everything from her. And she welcomed it. A rise of pressure flooded her belly, heating her from the inside out, taking away reason.

Bodin claimed her mouth, tightening his hold as he helped her rock up and down on the head of his cock, showing her the way to seek her own pleasure. Just as she began to whimper and rush, her muscles clutching and contracting around the girth of him, he drove her down onto his shaft.

Chessa screamed as her body convulsed in warps and wefts

of pleasure and pain, disbelief and driving need. But Bodin's silencing kisses did not relent, did not let her think, did not forgive her of her innocence.

He held tight, his grip rough and possessive as he pressed the full length and breadth of his cock inside her, holding her body spread astride his, his claim on her never to be doubted.

Chessa tensed, eyes watering as she froze momentarily atop him, not daring to breathe, her mind unable to comprehend what had just happened. Though her body clearly did. Her hips began to rock forward, attempting to take more of him.

He broke the kiss. "Not yet." He tried to give her a moment to ease to the shock and size of him. His chest heaved for air, his own need nearly upon him. "Breathe, Chessa. The worst of it—" he tightened his grip on her as her muscles clenched around him, pulling at him, "—done."

She trembled. His forehead bent to meet hers, his lips laying tiny kisses at the corners of her mouth.

"The pain is over now, sweet one. Breathe."

"Breathe?" Chessa gasped as tiny intakes of air shook every inch of her. How could she ever breathe again? She squeezed her closed eyes even tighter.

"Look at me," he growled, baring his teeth. He tugged the handful of hair he held, tilting her face to his. "Chessa, look at me."

She opened her eyes. Bodin's lips twitched, a pained expression straining his features.

"You must relax and breathe," he panted. "I have to move inside you now. To finish."

4

Confusion clouded Chessa's thoughts as Bodin laid her onto the thin feather mattress of his bed. The last minutes of pleasure were nothing but a blur. Her mind struggled to catch up to the realizations her body already understood.

He bent, tugging a fur to cover her as his gaze scanned each feature of her face. The back of his hand wiped a tear from the corner of her eye.

"Have I hurt you much?" he asked, plucking strands of long hair from her flushed face, setting them off to the side.

Chessa shook her head. She didn't know what to say. But when he stood and walked to the door, the words rushed from her. "Where are you going?" She sat up, worried, and winced at the aching soreness between her legs.

Bodin returned to her, smiling. He leaned over the bed. Brushing the hair back from her shoulders, he pressed his lips to her soft, swollen mouth. He curled his hands into fists to keep from touching her further as he backed away, grabbing his sword belt. He reached the door and turned back to look at her, his gaze dropping lower to see her shape beneath the furs. "Do not worry, sweet one. I am not leaving you behind."

Chessa watched him disappear into the darkness. She fought back the confusing emotions rising in her throat. Surely he would keep his word. Unless somehow he thought she hadn't kept hers? She braced her back against the wall, watching the wooden door, waiting. But uncertainty wouldn't let her be.

After all, she hardly knew him, had never dared speak a word to him before this night. Had she been foolish to make this bargain?

Or perhaps he'd left because she'd failed to please him. She knew so little about coupling with a man. His mother had taught her to hurry from the hall when the mead began to pour into cups the second time around. . . .

Maybe Bodin had expected her to know more. She closed her eyes, swiping away the tears. She didn't want to cry anymore. Chessa wrapped the fur tighter around her naked body and eased to the edge of the bed. Outside, the village sat quiet, too quiet. The usual hurry of activity before a ship set sail was gone. She went to the door, pulling it open enough to peek out.

Moonlight blanketed the dark night, a bright white light that softened everything it touched. A cool breeze blew in her face. She scooted behind the door to keep hidden as a few men walked past carrying barrels and trunks toward the shore.

But no Bodin.

Chessa gathered up the bottom of the blanket so it did not drag on the ground and stepped out of Bodin's quarters. Her bare feet padded softly along the well-worn dirt path until she reached the hall. Stopping, she peeked inside. Everyone had gone.

She looked toward the shore. Moonlight gleamed on the surface of the water, sparkling as it broke into countless fragments. No ship.

A wave of sickness rose up from her stomach to lodge in her throat. She nearly choked on the bitter bile. One step and then two and three . . . she ran toward the shore. How could she have been so foolish? As she stopped on the soft sand, her hands balled into fists, gripping the blanket tight around her. She went to her knees. He'd said he wouldn't leave her. . . .

"Well, well," a slurred male voice spoke from behind, "what've we here?"

Chessa gasped. She hadn't heard anyone approach. Sucking back tears and anguish, she struggled to stand, the ends of the blanket tangling under her feet.

A visibly drunken, burley Viking grabbed ahold of her arm, pulling her near. "Just what every man needs the night before a long voyage." His hand went to his laces.

"No." Chessa tugged against his grip. "I—I'm under the protection of—"

"I know who you are, and you've been released from Kaol's service," he sneered. "Don't try to lie your way out of this." His grip tightened, and he shook her.

"No, not—ow!"

"Release her!" Bodin's knife gleamed liquid silver, reflecting the moonlight as the blade pressed against the man's thick neck.

Turned loose with a shove, Chessa stumbled backward. She stood there, stunned. Not believing her eyes, she turned to look out at the water again. If Bodin hadn't left, where was his ship. . . .

"She holds *my* protection now, Gavit," Bodin seethed, pushing the man away. "Do not forget that." The man held up his hands in capitulation as he grumbled, lowering his gaze as he went on his way.

Trembling, Chessa hurried to Bodin. She wrapped one arm around his waist as she held on to him, squeezing tight. Fear and relief bubbled up through her, dampening her eyes. He hadn't left her behind. She buried her face in his shirt. He hadn't.

Bodin's hand went to her back. "What are you doing out here, sweet one?" He slipped his knife back into the sheath at his belt and pried her arm loose. "Answer me, Chessa." He held her away from him. "Why are you here?"

Emotion clogged her throat. "I—I thought . . . you'd left me—"

He gave her a sharp shake. "I told you I would not leave you behind." Bodin gritted his teeth, staring at her. He pulled her to his chest, eyes closed in a silent prayer.

Chessa closed her eyes and buried her face against him. He smelled of wood smoke and sweat. She could stay like this forever, safe.

Bodin forced her back, a full arm's length away this time. And the distance hurt more than his rough-handed hold.

"Chessa, you must trust me." He looked her over. His grip tightened as he wiped the sweat from his upper lip onto the sleeve of his tunic. With a sigh, he spoke. "Tell me, did Gavit hurt you?"

The wind kicked up, whipping her hair into her face. She shook her head.

"Where did he touch you?"

The rise of anger in his voice made her cringe, and she tried to pull away.

"Where!" He gave her a quick shake.

"My—my arm."

"Where else!"

Chessa tried to brush the hair from her face, to look at him, but his grip on her prevented it. So she shook her head again. "Just my arm."

Bodin released her with a sigh. "By the gods, Chessa." He turned away for a moment and took a deep breath, running the back of his hand against his mouth. He spun back around to face her. "Do you understand what almost—what Gavit was about to . . ." His hand rubbed over his face. Under his breath, he cursed. "Of course you don't."

Fighting to get the mass of hair out of her face, Chessa wrapped the fur tighter about her body and faced the bay, letting the wind dry her eyes.

Bodin turned her so she faced him, and he brushed the back of his hand over her cheek and then ran the tip of his finger around the curve of her ear and along her jawbone. He tilted her chin upward. Clouds began to slip in on the ocean wind, defying the moonlight with shadows. He could not see into her eyes. "You have to trust me, Chessa. I will not break my promise to you. I will see your feet back on the soil of your birth. That is our bargain." His voice dropped, a low whisper. "But—"

"You don't have to say it." Chessa stepped back from him. "And I do know what, what Gavit . . ." The consequences of her actions began to settle in, and she turned away, looking back across the bay, unable to speak the rest of her words. The moon had begun to retreat, the light losing its foothold.

"Chessa . . ."

His voice conveyed disappointment. She hadn't pleased him after all. Would he tell her he'd changed his mind about their bargain? Board his ship and sail without her?

"Sweet one, on a ship of men, a slave—a *female* slave is considered . . ." Bodin pressed his lips into a thin line. He couldn't speak the rest, couldn't tell her his men would think her entertainment. He saw her tremble at his words and reached for her, his hands rubbing up and down her arms. "Then you do remember."

She nodded. So many of her people had come to this village. But only she remained now.

"I'm sorry for that," he whispered. "Father took great pains to protect you. I guess," he sighed, "I guess he did not do as good a job as I thought." He turned her to face him. "Come."

Keeping ahold of her arm, he led her toward the woods. At the base of a tree, in the blackness of wooded shadows, he retrieved a bundle. "My ship is in the next cove. It is too large to keep aground here," he explained, guiding her along the path back to his quarters. He stopped short. Stepping in front of her, he narrowed his gaze, seeking to read her face before the clouds drifted fully across the moon. "Chessa . . ." He paused for a moment. "I only left right after I bedded you because—"

She jerked away, turning to look at the last slivers of moonlight grappling for the ground. She couldn't bear to hear him voice words of dissatisfaction. "I will do better, I promise!" Confusion wrapped around her insides, a knot so tight she could hardly breathe. She had not expected to find his needs so tied to her own. Or such an unraveling of things in her mind. What had she done by making this bargain?

"Chessa." Bodin sighed, shaking his head. "You did not—"

"Sir!" A male voice carried across the quiet village. "Sir." Booted footfalls hurried toward them in the dark.

Bodin closed his eyes, dropping his head for just a moment. A growling sigh forced its way through his gritted teeth. "Go inside." He tightened his grip on Chessa's arm to strengthen the seriousness of his words. "And stay there this time."

Chessa looked up at him. The concern in his eyes somewhat eased her doubts over this bargain, but still . . . she had clearly done something wrong, failed his needs somehow.

Her fingers caught ahold of his tunic.

"I will be inside in a moment." He saw her lingering worry. "Chessa, I will not leave my quarters without you again. I promise." He glanced over his shoulder as the soldier approached.

"Sir." The young man neared, panting as he slowed his approaching pace. "It's your father, he—"

Bodin held up his hand to silence the young man. He turned back to Chessa, handing her the tightly bound bundle. He pulled the knife from his waist and set it on top. "Take this." He lowered

his voice. "You will find something new to wear inside. Dress."
He forced her through the door, securing it closed behind her.

Chessa stood just inside Bodin's quarters, staring at the large
dagger balanced on top of the bundle he'd given her. Never had
she been allowed possession of a knife before. Not even a small
one to use for eating. Slaves weren't to be trusted. Ever.

She looked back at the door. Muffled voices came from the
other side. With her eyes fixed on the sharp blade just inches
below her face, she walked over to his bed and carefully set
down the entire pile.

Was he testing her or trusting her?

She pulled the blanket wrapped about her bare body a little
tighter and held both ends with one hand. Loud, indistinguish-
able voices rumbled outside. She glanced back at the door.
Swallowing her worry, she touched the dagger just below the
blade, running her finger tentatively down the length of the
carved handle. It was still warm from his touch. He had said to
dress—

Thump. A ruckus erupted outside and startled Chessa from
her worries. She dropped one corner of the fur blanket covering her. Dress. He'd said to dress. Chessa set the heavy knife off
to the side and tried to untie the tightly knotted strings but
couldn't get them free. She glanced back to the knife. Had he
given it to her to use?

Thump. Something hard slammed into the heavy door again.
She had to hurry. Careful to slice into only the string, she freed
the bundle and unwound the roll of heavy fabric. Folded inside
a thick cloak, she found a finely woven linen bed gown. She
hadn't seen one since she'd been taken from her home.

She held it to her cheek. The fabric was smooth and soft.
And not worn in the least. She measured the fit of the garment
against her body. Perfect.

Slam. Chessa jumped. She rushed to gather her everyday

clothes from the floor beside the tub. No sooner had she pinned the work apron over the heavy wool gown, the wood holding the metal latch splintered. The door crashed open.

Bodin and his father stumbled inside. A knife hovered between them.

5

"Chessa!" Bodin shouted. "My dagger!" He and his father grunted with effort as they staggered about in the room—first one in control and then the other.

"Chessa!"

She jumped at the repeated command and turned to the bed, shoving the cloak out of the way. Both hands grabbed the heavy weapon, holding it out in front of her. She watched, wide-eyed as Bodin and his father continued to grapple with one another for control of the sharp blade that wavered between them. Their fight brought them almost within reach of her.

Should she try to give Bodin his knife? Stay back? The men fought their way around the dwindling fire in the hearth.

"That's enough, Father. Cease this." Bodin tried to reason between gritted teeth.

The old man stumbled back, knocking the empty chair beside the tub onto its side. "The girl is for me!"

The wrestling men closed on her. Chessa's hands trembled,

the weighty blade shaking in front of her as she tried to inch closer to Bodin's side of the argument.

"You stink of mead!" Bodin scolded. "Go back to your quarters—"

"No!" Kaol grunted, the fight beginning to take a toll on him. Spit sprayed from his lips as he carried on in drunken anger. "I did not grant her freedom for you to have! She was to warm my bed tonight!"

"Chessa *earned* her freedom from you." Bodin pushed his father against the wall, wresting the knife temporarily into his own control.

On wobbling legs, Chessa pressed herself into the corner, dropping her head back for a moment, swallowing the shock of Kaol's words. The old Viking was not the man of honor she'd thought. He'd planned to see her in his bed . . . this very night . . . when she returned from the hall. . . .

Kaol had planned to—

Her legs shook, bile churning in her stomach. She could scarcely grab ahold of the truth. He would have never agreed to return her to her home—that was never his intention. He'd planned to use the freedom she'd earned against her.

Kaol swung his fist at Bodin and missed. "Your mother only lived so long"—he gasped for air—"to spite me." The old man began to run out of steam. "She knew I wanted more children. . . ." He tried to breathe but could only cough.

Chessa's heart pounded in her chest. The lump in her throat thickened, cutting off most of her air. Kaol had had no intention of allowing her out of his household, not with any measure of real freedom. She sucked in a fractured breath. He would have allowed her to keep his protection by becoming a whore. His whore. Good only to bear his children and keep his house. Nothing more. Not far different than the women he kept imprisoned for the soldiers to take their pleasure with at any time, day or night.

Her bottom lip trembled. Tears rimmed her eyes, blurring her vision. If she hadn't braved to speak to Bodin when she did, to gamble herself as payment—

"Chessa! Look out!" The chair splintered as Bodin sprawled sideways.

Startled, Chessa stiffened at the unexpected blur of motion that loomed and then slammed into her. The jolt shook large tears from her lashes and onto her cheeks. Eyes wide, she looked into a face contorted with shock and pain. A rush of foul air hissed at her, and she squeezed her eyes shut.

Kaol slumped forward in silence, pressing with increasing weight onto her as she slid to the floor. The blunt end of the dagger's bone handle dug painfully between her breasts.

"Chessa!" Bodin pulled at his father's excessive body. "Chessa!"

As Kaol's crushing weight rolled off her, the handle of Bodin's dagger slipped from her hands. The blade had lodged hilt deep in the old man's chest. Chessa looked down, tilting her head to the side. She stared at the flats of her palms, covered in a liquid red.

Bodin dropped to one knee. "Chessa . . ." He pulled the hair out of her face so he could better look at her.

She continued to stare at her hands, turning them over and then back again. Blood?

"Chessa, look at me."

Bodin's words mixed with the loud buzz that filled the inside of her head. Something shook her by the shoulder. *Odd,* she thought as her fingers blurred. Her hands weren't usually this color. . . .

"Look at me!" Bodin cupped her chin in the palm of his hand and forced her to meet his gaze. "Chessa, are you hurt?"

Wide-eyed, she whispered, "There's blood . . ." A numb, tingling sensation crept down her arms and legs. Chessa looked back down, trying to find a place to wipe her trembling hands clean. But her skirt and apron were wet through with blood, too. She swallowed. Hers? Was that why she couldn't seem to move?

Bodin cursed and lifted her small, shaking body into his arms. He carried her closer to the fire, setting her beside the hearth. Not much wood burned, but the coals still glowed with a little heat.

He pressed his lips into a thin line, frowning as he plucked the fabric away from her skin. Chessa shuddered again, and he used the dagger he'd wrested away from his father to slice into her blood-soaked garments. Bodin peeled them off her and tossed them onto the coals. The fire caught and began to consume the dry edges of her skirts and apron.

Bodin rubbed his tired eyes and then gathered from his bed the clothing he'd bought for her. He paused. The soft bed gown had been chosen with special interest and purpose. Now he wondered if it even mattered. He turned around. Chessa sat on the hearth, naked and trembling, eyes fixed on his father's dead body.

"By the gods," he cursed under his breath, shaking his head. He moved to block her view of the gruesome sight. Clearing his throat, he kept his voice level and firm. "Chessa."

She leaned forward, her forehead coming to rest against his thigh. "I—I'm sorry." She wiped away the tears streaming down her cheeks. She slid to her knees before him, arms wrapped tight around his leg. "I didn't mean to . . ." She hiccupped. "To . . ." Her shoulders vibrated in time with her sobs as she struggled to explain. "He—he was just there, and, and the knife . . ."

Bodin put his hand on the top of her head. "I know, Chessa." He hooked his fingers under her arm and pulled her to her feet. Her eyes were red and swollen. How could he have been so foolish as to let this happen? He knew of his father's fixation with the girl—he just hadn't thought it went so far.

"I know you did not intend to kill him." Her body trembled

at his words. "Kaol was drunk and not of his right mind. You are not at fault."

"But I'm a slave. Killing a free man is punished with death." Her voice broke. "Or worse—"

"That is not going to happen." Bodin pulled her against him. "That is not going to happen." He would not let that happen. "Now, come. We must get you dressed and aboard my ship."

A storm skirted the horizon, wind and waves slamming against the sides of the ship. Bodin pulled at the oar alongside his men.

But his thoughts drifted below deck to a small room. And Chessa.

He'd purposely kept her by his side, keeping an eye on her shattered state, while he finished the necessary preparations for the voyage, until, finally, she'd fallen into a fitful sleep at his feet, clutching the bottoms of his trousers. She had not wakened from her haunted dreams when he'd wrapped her in the heavy cloak and carried her aboard the vessel in the early morning darkness.

He looked to the sky and the position of the cloud-covered sun. It was well past midday now. Had she wakened? The vision of her atop the small cot, the soft bed gown clinging to every female curve and dark hollow, filled his mind, causing his cock to remain a steady affliction beneath the leather laces of his trousers.

A cold mist of salty ocean sprayed over the side of the ship. Bodin wiped his face on the sleeve of his tunic and dug the oar deeper into the storm-swirled current, pulling with every muscle he had. But no amount of physical exertion seemed to distract him.

He needed to touch her.

"I'm going below. Keep your eyes to the horizon!" Bodin shouted above the wind to the old man beside him. "Beach the ship before the full force of the wind hits. We'll wait out the worst on land."

The elderly man nodded, putting his hand on Bodin's arm to keep him seated for a few moments more. "I was aboard the ship that brought the girl to our village, you know. Not one of us agreed with Kaol choosing one so young." He patted Bodin's shoulder in sympathy. "I'd known your father since we were but boys, and never had I seen him so . . . unreasonable." The old man paused, remembering. "Even then, he was unnaturally taken with the girl." Distaste in his tone, he shook the memory from his head. "She was but a child all those years ago, far from capable of giving your father what he wanted."

Bodin turned away. *More children.* Those had been his father's words. And, specifically, more children from Chessa.

The defiant, green-eyed girl of ten years ago came to mind. The littlest one of all the slaves, who'd stood steadfast, refusing to take orders until his father had whispered some secret threat in her ear. Chessa had never dared show defiance to his father again. Bodin's jaw clenched.

That very evening so long ago, Bodin had gathered his belongings and sought different quarters, despite the pleas and tears of his ailing mother.

Kaol had been no great hero, but the man had sired him. And for that, Bodin owed a debt. But Chessa would not be the one to pay—Bodin had seen to that before they'd left the village. No one would ever know his knife had been held by her hand. Bodin nodded to the old man and stood, making his way across the ship. Out of habit, he checked each rigging line as he went. Dropping to one knee on the deck, he pulled open the bow hatch, running a hand across his sleep-weary eyes.

Below, in the hold, the shipboards groaned and strained against the storm-tossed waters. Bodin pulled a key from beneath his leather belt, where no one could sneak it from him unnoticed.

The small room dimmed to pitch black as he closed the door behind him and secured the wooden bar, ensuring privacy. He'd spent many a voyage in this secret hold, but never with a woman at his fingertips. He adjusted himself against the chafing laces that held his trousers closed.

A rustling of blankets drew his attention. "Bodin?" Her whisper was almost lost against the sound of the waves crashing into the sides of the boat.

Her voice stirred his blood, heating him. He closed his eyes as his cock grew harder with each beat of his heart. His fingers ached to touch her, pull her small body to his and warm her as she did him.

"Is that you, Bodin?" Her voice wavered.

His gut tightened—had her mind settled from the horror of last night's events? "Yes," he answered. The air in the recessed room lightened noticeably at his answer. He unbuckled his belt. Bodin frowned as his cock continued to harden, demanding release and satisfaction inside her. His body tensed. He wanted her to have this one opportunity to afflict him with pained need—his own self-imposed penance for having had to breech her maidenhead.

"Are you still there?" Her voice rang of uncertainty and worry.

He moved forward with ease, familiar with where he'd placed his personal belongings for the voyage. "I'm here." He reached out, fingers brushing against her cool, wet cheek. "Are you well?"

"Yes," she answered, nodding into the warmth of his hand.

"The waves do not bother you, then?"

"No." She sucked in a quick breath, unwilling to yet return to the heavy silence. "Bodin?"

"Yes."

Chessa closed her eyes, leaning deeper into his large hand. After she'd wakened alone in the dark, she'd had no sense of time or direction—just motion. And even now, with Bodin this close, she could not tell if he suffered for her actions. Did anger or grief fill him? Her voice faltered. "What is to happen to me?".

His hand dropped away, and he sighed. "Not a thing."

Her eyes flooded with tears. "How is that possible after—"

"Shhh . . . put it from your mind." Bodin rubbed his tired eyes, dragging his fingers through his wind-whipped hair.

"Are you angry with me, then?"

Bodin sighed deeply. "No, sweet one." He shook his head in the darkness. "I am not."

"Then why have you sentenced me here?"

"I have put you here for protection, not punishment."

"I don't understand—"

"You'll remember what almost happened on the beach with Gavit?"

She did. And he knew it. Her head, still in the comfort of his hand, turned to the side.

"I have a dozen men twice over aboard this ship, Chessa. What keeps them rowing and not down here fighting for a turn with you is their duty to me. And I see no reason to tempt them further than the knowledge that you exist."

Chessa thought on his words as the ship pitched and rolled in the heavy seas. She relaxed a little.

"Now, tell me the truth." With her there in front of him, easily within reach, he would not be able to wait much longer. "Do you suffer from last evening?"

The reminder brought Kaol's pained expression to mind. The old man's horrible words and twisted face were something she would likely never forget. And more than anything, she wanted to forget, to disappear in Bodin's embrace and think of nothing but the smell of him, wood smoke and sweat. "Touch me." Her hand went to his. "Please."

Bodin caressed the side of Chessa's face. His thumb moved to skate across her bottom lip, tugging at the soft pad of flesh as he whispered, "Are you certain?"

She nodded her consent against the calloused tip of his thumb. "Yes, take him from my mind . . . please." Chessa's hand went to his muscular thigh; the leather of his trousers warm and supple.

Bodin took his hand from her face and grabbed the rafter above him. His fingertips dug into the rough wood, a distraction for control. His other hand threaded deep into the mass of wild hair at the nape of her neck.

Chessa closed her eyes and leaned her weight into him, her forehead resting against his hip as she wiped the tears of worry from her cheeks, inhaling a shuddered breath. He didn't hate her. A nervous relief rolled through her.

Tentatively her other hand went to his knee, palm inching upward along the salty, damp leather of his trousers. His fingers tightened into the tangled mess of her hair, holding her so she did not pull too far away, but not forcing her either.

Bodin took her hand and put it to his swollen cock, urging her to ease his need.

Chessa fumbled with his laces, the darkness making it difficult to find the ends and untie them. A long, deep groan rumbled from him at her innocent efforts, and he compelled her to move just a little higher. She was raised to her knees before him, the soft mattress of the cot a cushion. His fingers dug into the back of her neck, pressing her forehead to the hard muscles of his stomach.

The moment she freed the knot, his other hand slipped between them to hurry open the lacings and pull out his hard cock. Chessa gasped as he brushed it softly against her cheek. Deep inside her belly, a longing for the pleasure he'd given her before began to grow, warming her, taking the away the chill of worry.

He let go of her head, pleased she did not try to move away from him. "Take me into your mouth." The instruction was spoken on a tense, exhaled breath.

Chessa swallowed, nervous, as his manhood hovered against

the side of her face. She moved back, nearer the tip of him. Licking at her dry lips, her tongue accidentally grazed against him. He tensed, his breath straining loud and fierce from his lungs. Chessa froze. Had she done something wrong?

Bodin panted, desperate to control the need to press his cock past her full, moist lips and into the wet, warm depths beyond. "Suck my cock. But be gentle."

Wary, Chessa admitted the tip of him into her mouth. His body stiffened and pressed forward. He tasted of salt and sweat, the skin startlingly smooth. The contrast surprised her, all softness and hard strength at the same time.

"More." He strained to speak the word.

She braced her palms against the solid pillars of his thighs as he slid himself deep into her mouth until he reached the back of her throat. Shocked, she dug her fingers into the tense muscles of his thighs as she started to panic for lack of air.

Bodin backed off but did not remove himself completely from the sanctuary of her mouth. "Use your tongue," he encouraged and grabbed the base of his cock, holding it steady for her.

Chessa did as he asked, relaxing as she began to understand that her attentions pleased him. She found she liked this manner of tending him, of affecting his need without her own being so close to the forefront.

But no sooner did that conclusion come to mind than he urged her higher. His fingers raked down the side of her neck, dipping low, beneath the neckline of her bed gown to caress the outside curve of her breast. He pinched her nipple. A fiery need flashed through her, increasing her need for air.

In an effort to distract Bodin from touching her just yet and finish the first task he'd given her, she dared withdraw the attentions of her tongue and take him again to the back of her throat.

Bodin sucked thick, salty air through clenched teeth. He

groaned, struggling not to force the entirety of himself into her mouth. "That's it, sweet one ... faster. ..." His fingers dug painfully into the rafter seated just above his head as his balls drew tight to his body. "By the gods—" He snagged a handful of hair from the back of her head and forced her to still her attentions.

Chessa gasped for breath as Bodin pulled almost the entire length of his shaft from her mouth. Only the slightest bit of him remained poised between her lips. The sounds of his harsh, ragged breath made her nipples contract beneath the soft fabric of her bed gown. A throbbing heat pulsed between her thighs.

She swallowed, and her teeth grazed ever so softly against the tip of his manhood. His body tensed, fingers tightening their grip in her hair.

She so wanted to please him, to prove she could hold up her end of the bargain. But at the moment she didn't know just what he expected.

A groan roared from him seconds before a hot, tangy liquid pulsed against her lips and teeth and into her mouth. Frightened at the fierce suddenness of it all, Chessa whimpered, fingers curling and digging into his rock-hard thighs. But Bodin held her firmly in place.

He remained frozen in a state of disbelieving and uncontrollable release. "Ye gods, girl. ..." he hissed, finally releasing her. Bodin slumped forward, bracing both hands against the inside curve of the ship, trying to slow the pace of his heart. "Have the gods no mercy. ..."

A long sigh blew past Bodin's lips. He eased his considerable frame down onto the cot, trapping Chessa between his body and the wall. He was not done with her yet. Not in the least.

The ship heaved in heavy waves, rising high and then slamming down onto the frothy surface of the sea. Chessa sucked in a pained breath as her head bumped against the wall.

Despite his longing to take her slowly, enjoy every inch of her on his terms this time, his cock had been unable to wait. A surge of renewed interest began to afflict his loins. And she wanted him, too, he could smell it on her. He closed his eyes for a moment. No man could endure such sustained longing.

This must be punishment from the gods.

He reached toward her face, tucking behind her ear each unruly strand of hair he could find in the darkness. With each touch, his body grew ever more taut with want of her, unsatisfied with not having taken her fully. He pressed closer. He'd never relinquished his seed in such a manner before. And he did not like it.

The village whores were for such. Not his Chessa.

"Where did you learn to do that?" His voice rasped, jagged as broken stone.

"Do what?" The waves seem to ease, no longer slamming her back and head against the wall. The ship settled, moving more gently now.

Bodin's finger hooked underneath her chin, her shallow, nervous breaths proof that she faced him. "Make a man spend his seed in such a manner?"

"Have I done something wrong?" Her tongue darted out quickly to moisten her dry lips. "If you are displeased, tell me why. Next time I'll do better—"

"No!" Bodin pressed a finger to her mouth. All of a sudden he didn't want the answer to his question. He traced the side of her face. "Just do not do such again."

"But I only did as you—"

His mouth closed over hers, possessive and fierce, angry as he punished her for daring to question his wishes. His tongue forced past her teeth, demonstrating the fact that he was indeed to be obeyed. He pulled back slightly. "Defy me and I assure you, you will not like my wrath."

Panic began to set in at his volatile mood. Chessa struggled to worm away from him. But the support beams on either side of her prevented it.

"Cease." His hand went to her ankle. "Hold yourself still, Chessa. I am not done with you yet."

6

Chessa froze, with the exception of the air squeezing through her heaving chest. Bodin would have to catch each slippery beat of her heart with his bare hands to hold her still in that manner.

She tried to swallow back her fear and slow her breathing. She must keep her wits about her if she was to figure out what she had done to make him so angry.

His grip on her ankle tightened. "Just so we are clear: from here forward, *I* determine when and where to spend my seed, not you."

She blinked, trying to make sense of his words. She'd only done as he'd asked. Had she somehow caused—

"Do you understand me, Chessa?"

"Yes." Just for good measure, she nodded in answer as well.

"That was our bargain, correct?"

"Yes." His thumb raked across the very moist center at the juncture of her thighs, and she gasped. Heat melted her insides.

"That is your need." He took one of her hands and put it to his again straining cock. "And this is my need." He gritted his teeth and took her hand away. Taking a deep breath for control, he continued, his voice a harsh whisper. "And right now, I wish my needs to be tended."

A loud knock interrupted, and Chessa jumped at the sound.

"What!" Bodin snapped in answer.

"We've beached for the night, sir," came the male voice from the other side of the barred door.

Bodin pulled the hem of Chessa's bed gown up over her knees, out of his way as he gathered her wrists in his hand. "Spread your legs for me."

Chessa moved her drawn-up legs slightly apart, opening herself willingly. She wanted him to touch her more than she'd ever wanted anything in her life. Didn't he realize she suffered far more from the lack of him than she ever could because of him?

His fingers slid against the slick, heated folds cradling her passion. Chessa gasped, closing her throat to a whimper. Her breasts heaved with the need for more air than she could manage to get in the stifling darkness. Her cheeks burned with embarrassment. The last thing she wanted was for the soldier to hear Bodin's touch stirring her.

"Sir?"

Bodin's lips curled over his teeth as he whispered, "Do you like that, Chessa?"

She squeaked, unable to think. His words sounded thick in the muddled cloud of passion. Her body burned for more of him, all of him. The only thing that mattered at this very moment was that he not stop. He began to concentrate on one spot, and she no longer had control of her body.

Chessa's head dropped back against the wall with a loud thump as she arched into his touch, the tips of his fingers slipping just inside her. A groan of gratification and rising need erupted from her, the sound distant and odd, even to her own ears. She no longer cared what the soldier on the other side of the door heard.

The loud, insistent knock came again. "Sir, are you hurt?"

Bodin stilled his fingers, and Chessa began to pant in protest. She writhed, searching, seeking more of his touch. He closed his eyes and removed his fingers from her sex. His cock throbbed in protest. "I'm—ahem—" He cleared his throat, trying to dislodge the deep thunder of passion clogging his voice. "I'm fine." One more breath for sanity's sake. "Stake my tent a good distance from the camp."

Chessa tugged at his hold on her wrists, trying to bring him back closer to her. He couldn't stop, not just yet. If she could only touch him, maybe he would cease her need as he'd done before. She needed his touch so much at the moment, she could scream.

Bodin dropped his voice to a low, warning whisper. "If my needs must suffer to wait, Chessa, so must yours."

"Sir? Are you certain? How far away? Because . . ."

The voice continued to drone on about some trivial matter Bodin couldn't have cared less about. Chessa's breaths came in little moaning pants, disrupting his ability to think with any amount of clarity. She opened her legs wider, inviting him. Bodin gritted his teeth, determined this time that he would take her at his discretion, in his own good time. With a tight grip on her wrists, he pulled her to her knees.

Chessa took a deep breath, her breasts swelling as she tried to get closer, to lean into his broad chest. She pressed her hips forward, seeking relief from her need against his thigh. The friction drew a deep breath and a moan from her.

"By the gods . . ." Bodin cursed and then turned his head toward the door. "Just do as I said!"

"Uh . . . yes, sir." A hurried bumbling of feet signaled the end of that conversation.

Bodin took a step back from Chessa. He began to work loose a strip of cloth tied just above his boot.

She tried to press closer, to garner his full attention. Her fingers grabbed for his shirt, but he held her at a slight distance. "Bodin?"

He spun her around, releasing one of her wrists just long enough to pull them both behind her back. "You'll touch no part of yourself. Not this night." He tied her small wrists together and then pulled her backward against his chest. "I alone have discretion over your body." His hands closed over her linen-covered breasts, thumbs grazing her swollen nipples.

Chessa's fingers grappled to reach his straining appendage that pressed against her backside. Instead she could only manage to grab his shirt.

He pinched her swollen, extended nipples hard.

"Ahhh . . ." A heated flash of silvery need knifed downward from her breasts through her belly and pulsed wet and slippery between her thighs. Chessa's legs gave way as she sunk low to her knees. Her full weight came to bare against his chest. "Bodin, please . . ."

His hands began to roam her belly, the tops of her thighs, her breasts, everywhere but the place she wanted most. "My needs, Chessa . . . that is our bargain," his voice rasped, lips pressed against the curved outline of her ear. He sucked at the soft pad of flesh and let his fingers graze promisingly over the red curls nested between her spread thighs.

Chessa shuddered and moaned, unable to affect any control over where he touched her, what he did to her. Another wave of liquid heat prepared her body to take him. But still he denied her. "You," she licked at her dry lips and tried to swallow, "you are in need, though, I can feel—"

He pinched her nipples again, silencing her words of persuasion with the groan that rose from deep within her small body. "Need, sweet one, is not always about gratification."

This would be done his way, by his rules. Not hers.

7

Bodin draped the cloak over Chessa's shoulders, securing the clasp. He stood and slipped one hand beneath the heavy fabric, pinching her still-aroused nipples.

Chessa sucked in an agitated breath as her body arched, breasts swelling, longing for more of his touch. The wooden bar slid from the door, and she blinked in the flood of light. Bodin guided her toward the hatch. A pair of hands reached down as he gripped her waist and lifted.

Up on deck, the wind whipped all around her, pulling and pushing and tugging her in different directions. With her hands still tied behind her back beneath the cloak, keeping her balance was more than a little difficult.

Bodin stepped behind her, pulling her against him, making certain she had no doubt he was still very much aroused as he assessed the site his men had chosen for the night. The corner of his tent peeked from a rocky cove some distance from the boat and the main camp. He leaped over the rail and onto the soggy beach.

Chessa was handed down to him.

But Bodin didn't set her on the sand as she expected. His arm tightened around her, suspending her off the ground so their bodies were exactly aligned. His eyes, dark with steely determination, made her stomach flutter. He had plans. Plans that included her exclusively. Of that he left no doubt in her mind.

"You are very right, sweet one," he whispered in her ear.

Chessa's heart pounded, reverberating against her ribs. Could he truly read her thoughts? His free hand slipped beneath the folds of the wind-whipped cloak and cupped her buttock, rubbing her sex against his erection as he squeezed. She gasped at the friction, her body shivering in his arms, wanting him, needing release from the ever-present urges he stirred with intent, she tried to wiggle closer.

"We will not sleep much this night." With his gaze locked into her wide green eyes, he licked his lips in anticipation. A wicked grin curved his mouth. Tonight she would learn to submit to his wishes, his desires. His cock pulsed at the thought. Or did it pulse because of her? Bodin slid her diminutive body down the taut, straining length of his body.

The rough, wet sand enveloped Chessa's bare feet. Bodin's hand at the base of her back propelled her past the campfire and more than a dozen watchful, lingering gazes. The dissipating stares of his men came as a relief. She wanted to be alone with Bodin. Alone so he would touch her again.

Chessa tensed as Bodin's fingers tightened into the dip of her waist, digging into her sides. She stopped as he stepped around her, partially blocking her view.

"Will this do, sir?" An eager young soldier stopped adjusting rocks as a windbreak to the small fire. He rushed to stand, dusting off his hands on the front of his trousers. His gaze flitted up and down Chessa and then to the tent.

"Go back to the camp," Bodin ordered the young man, his voice heavy with warning as he spread his feet shoulder-width apart.

"But I was told to stand watch and keep the fire—"

Bodin's hand went to his belt, fingers no more than a hair's breadth away from the hilt of his dagger. "I will manage, Erek."

Casting a sideways glance at the tent, the young man lowered his head and scratched the back of his neck. "The—the others, sir." He nodded in the direction of the beach. "They don't think this is quite fair, you keeping a," he licked his lips, "a slave all to yourself."

Bodin's hand went to the oiled leather sheath slung over his back. He slipped the long, sharp blade free. "And what do you think?"

A lopsided grin broke through a sparse, white-blond beard. "I think," he looked at the tent again, tilting his head just slightly, scratching the side of his face, "that you better take care to watch your back, sir. And her." Erek's gaze went to Chessa.

Bodin stared at the young man. In a swift motion he pressed Chessa backward against the rock wall, stabbing the tip of his sword blade into the dry sand inches in front of her, trapping her. Already moving toward the tent, Bodin drew his dagger. He rushed inside.

Chessa blinked in disbelief. The wide hilt of the sword pressed into her stomach, trapping her against the cold, rocky cliff. The edges of her cloak snapped defiantly in the wind. Bodin reappeared in moments, his dagger pressed to Gavit's throat.

She stared, wide-eyed. Anger darkened Bodin's features, his lips pulled back over bared teeth as he twisted Gavit's arm behind his back and pushed him toward the main camp. Chessa glanced at Erek still standing by the fire. A look of jealousy and something else she couldn't be sure of crossed his face.

For the first time since Kaol had taken her as a child, she felt afraid. She tried to remain calm, but she began to tremble. If Bodin died, if his men overran him . . .

Erek took a step closer.

Chessa struggled to move sideways, slip out from behind the sword, but there was not enough room. Bodin had left her trapped like prey with nowhere to hide.

Hearing someone approaching, Erek smiled and straightened. He craned his neck for a better view, and then his shoulders slumped.

Bodin strode through the overgrown, sprawling bushes, single-minded and determined as he wiped the flat of the blade on his trouser leg, cleaning off the blood. He stopped, glancing sideways at Chessa, and then turned to face the young man. A slight nod indicated the owing of a debt.

Erek took his leave.

A dark, unreadable expression masked Bodin's thoughts. Half a dozen steps, and he was on Chessa, the width of his body blocking the storm winds, hands braced on the cliff wall just above her head as he loomed. Her body tensed, and some instinct from the depths of her gut demanded she acknowledge his dominance. She lowered her lashes and looked to the side, not daring to meet his gaze.

Bodin bent his head beside hers, his breath ragged with a mixture of subsiding anger and pent-up desire.

A ripple of anticipation betrayed Chessa, and she closed her eyes. She ached for the rough touch of his calloused hands, for his fingers skimming along her skin to find hidden places, his fiery, heated kisses bringing the truth of her wants to the surface for him to see.

"That's right, sweet one." His voice grated harsh as rough gravel. "Submit, for tonight I enforce this bargain of ours to my full satisfaction." Bodin pulled the sword out of the sand as he took half a step back, releasing her from confinement. He strode to the tent and pulled open the flap, giving her one opportunity to obey.

Chessa swallowed, careful not to meet his dark gaze. He

seemed in an odd mood. Not angry, exactly, but not to be trifled with either. She ducked through, shrugging her aching shoulders, hands still secured behind her back.

Out of the corner of her eye, she could see him unrolling several large, thick furs. Bedding? It didn't matter, she'd find out soon enough—at least, she hoped she would. The slippery friction between her thighs made every movement far more torturous than anything his touch could inflict.

Bodin turned and faced her, one knee holding him balanced on the ground. "Come here to me, Chessa."

The tent flap snapped in the rising winds, a sharp, cracking sound.

Her stomach quivered at his command. And that's exactly what his every word was: a command. Negotiation not allowed. Their bargain had been struck, and, as she'd agreed, there would be no going back.

Her nipples tingled with anticipation, erect and nearly raw from such prolonged need. Even the soft fabric of the bed gown tormented her, provoking her to boldness. She could stand it no longer. "Bodin—"

"Be silent. And bring yourself to me."

Restless, rapid breaths swelled in her chest with each step she took until, finally standing before him, her head spun. His large, tanned hand wrapped around her small ankle, pulling her into a wider stance.

Bodin's fingers slid slowly up the back of her calf. The warmth of his touch nearly melted her. He reached the back of her knee and drew his thumb to the inside of her leg as he continued upward. Eyes closed, she took a deep breath, anticipating.

"Look at me. Look into my eyes," he demanded. "Think only of me."

Chessa bit her lip. Tentatively she swallowed and drew her gaze to his. The color of his eyes darkened in the dim light of the tent. His languid exploration of her only fueled the crisis between her thighs. As he reached the undeniable evidence of her need, she could not help but moan in pleasure. His thumb glided over the slick opening.

Chessa inhaled a desperate breath, biting down harder on her lip to keep her words of begging silent as he'd commanded. Unable to take the intensity of his stare any longer, she squeezed her eyes shut.

His questing finger pried a little deeper as he growled in warning, "Do not take your eyes from me again."

Her legs trembled, threatening to buckle beneath Bodin's attention. But she bit into her lower lip and managed to meet his gaze again.

"Much better, sweet one."

Bodin withdrew his touch, and Chessa whimpered, trying to stifle the sound of disappointment as she swayed toward him. She'd been wrong. His touch could inflict a more tortuous need than she thought possible to endure. And at will, it seemed. How could his needs affect her own so? And what of his needs would he have her attend with hands bound behind her back?

A dark, pleased chuckle rumbled from him as he stood. "That is right, Chessa. You debted yourself to me, and tonight you will learn just how much it takes to satisfy my needs."

Hazy fantasies of acts she'd yet to experience shimmered just beyond her imagination. A shiver of anticipation rippled through her sensitized body. He knew her every thought.

Bodin swept back the stray hair covering part of her face and then unclasped the brooch that held the heavy cloak closed. Erect nipples, dark and persistent beneath the almost sheer fabric of the bed gown, bewitched him. The gods willing, he could spend endless days at her breasts. His cock swelled, pained with an urgent necessity to be inside her.

He gritted his teeth, attempting to delay his desire and take her with a slow, punishing pleasure this time. He needed to consume each anguished wobble of her full lips and revel in every moan that escaped her sweet mouth.

Chessa's tongue skated over her tortured, swollen lower lip.

Bodin cursed under his breath and pulled his laces open with violent speed. He yanked the bed gown up to her waist, fingers digging into the small circumference of her hips as he lifted and plunged.

The moment he entered her, solid and deep, Chessa cried out. But the ferocious pleasure that ripped through every inch of her did not explode and fade. Instead his arm wrapped tight around her, pressing her down even farther, filling her to the point of pain. Her head dropped back, and she cried out a second time.

Bodin bent his knees slightly and flexed, pushing even deeper as a roar of frustrated relief accompanied the pulsing release of his seed deep inside her belly.

Pleasure and pain assaulted Chessa's senses. Instinct took control as her trembling legs clamped tighter around his waist, desperate to hold him trapped inside her body. The world blurred from existence as her insides convulsed again and again and again, unable to stop. As the clawing pleasure slowly subsided, she shook, tears streaming down her cheeks.

Bodin eased down onto his knees, keeping his cock well seated inside her. Not a difficult task, given how tight she was. He stroked the great mass of wild hair hanging down her back, comforting himself as much as her.

He squeezed his eyes shut, but it made no difference to the distressing crush of guilt in his chest. Chessa shivered and tried to worm closer for warmth. Bodin buried his face into the soft column of her neck, breathing in the flowery scent of her hair. With a soul-deep sigh, he freed the knot binding her wrists.

He had not meant to risk a child.

8

On shaky legs Chessa waded naked into the pool of heated volcanic water. Bodin led their way, holding her hand. The storm continued to bluster, dangerous and vengeful. But, so far, the rain had not come.

Hair blew in Chessa's eyes as she struggled to keep pace with his confident strides. She watched the muscles of his back and shoulders flex and give, stealthy beneath his tanned skin. How different their last coupling had been. She hadn't been able to get enough of him. Even now, so soon after, she wanted more.

Chessa shivered, her nipples tight and tingling despite the warm water. Would he take her here, out in the open or beneath the water?

Bodin pulled her against his chest and dipped them both under the surface of the heated water, disrupting the serious thoughts that had her brows furrowed together. Strong currents swirled beneath the black water tugging at them as he tucked wet strands of hair behind her ears.

"I adore your hair. Do not ever bind it in my presence

again," he whispered, continuing to play with the long, wavy tresses that floated on the surface all around them. Many a night since she'd grown out of girlhood, he'd imagined those red and gold waves spread across his cot, his chest. Or his belly. He gathered as much of her hair as would fit in his hand and held it up. "I took a lashing from my father because of this." A weak smile crossed his face as he weighed the handful of wet strands in the water. "But you got to keep it, all of it."

She looked up at him, eyes wide with surprise. But Bodin wasn't watching her; he stared at his palm, lifting some of the tangled mass out of the water, watching it warp into curls before his eyes.

"Why? I wouldn't have thought . . ."

"Thought what?"

She shrugged her shoulders. "That you'd have been old enough to defy Kaol."

He grinned. "You showed me the true meaning of courage that first day when he put you on display. You were arguing with him." He let out a brief chuckle. "And in front of the entire village, at that. I took the lesson to heart. And you kept your long hair."

"Your mother never told me."

"She confided in you, didn't she?"

Nodding, she answered, "Some. Enough to keep me out of trouble with your father and the other men."

Bodin released her hair and returned his interest to her face and eyes, continuing to smooth down strands the wind worked to corrupt. "You were but a girl when my father took you. I knew you had lost too much at one time. And when you threw a fit over having it cut, as they'd done to the other women taken that voyage, I knew you needed to keep it. Needed to hold on to something of yourself."

Chessa looked down into the dark, murky depths of the water. Her old life . . . that all seemed so long ago. Her memories held so little of her home. Mostly she knew only a life among the Vikings. And just like the depths of the dark, volcanic water, her journey to her rightful home held much uncertainty.

Chessa sighed. Had she made the right choice to return to her parents? Had she been wise to leave all she really knew for a place that, for all intents and purposes, may end up existing only in her mind? What if the few memories she had of her father's home were wrong?

Bodin stroked her back, easing his fingers up and down each bump of her spine. Did she worry as he did over the possibility that his careless action had added to their bargain?

"Bodin?"

He touched his forehead to hers for just a moment. "Yes?" He turned her around, sweeping her hair to the side and started to massage her shoulders.

"Mmmm, that's nice." Chessa sighed and leaned backward into his diligent attentions, tilting her head to the side, inviting him to expand the scope of his touch. Her eyes closed as strong fingers dug deep and probing, softening the muscles in her back and neck. A soft moan puffed from her lips. She could stay here forever, if only he . . .

"You've a question, sweet one?" he reminded.

She inhaled a luxurious breath. "Does it take long? I don't remember." Would the storm delay them? By days, maybe? Staying here, alone with Bodin, would be so nice. . . .

"Does what take long?" He put an end to the slight distance between them as his fingers slipped beneath her arms, grazing the sides of her breasts. When he reached her waist, he pulled her body against his, nuzzling her damp neck. One hand slid across the flat of her tummy, his thumb rubbing in slow, small circles beneath her navel.

"The voyage."

Bodin's lips tightened into a thin line. "Why?" His hands dropped away, and he moved back.

Chessa spun around but saw only the broad expanse of his back as he made his way to the shore. Had she done something wrong? She started to follow in his wake but could not move through the deep water with the same balance and speed.

He climbed out of the volcanic pool, grabbing his clothes from the top of a boulder.

"Bodin—"

"Stay there. Have your bath, Chessa," he said over his shoulder, not bothering to pause.

She stopped, blinking in confusion. He'd used her name, not called her *sweet one*. A twinge of hurt twisted in her chest. He was just going to leave her here? Alone? And what about his men—would they come to bathe, too?

Her breath shuddered, her eyes growing moist. This time with him, their bargain, was not supposed to be about her, had not been made with the intention of forever. She'd debted herself to him as a slave. And that, undoubtedly, was how he saw her. How he'd always seen her. Nothing more. Had he read her thoughts as he'd seemed to do before? Did he know she longed for more?

For the first time in her life, "more" was almost a possibility. "But not with him. . . ." she whispered to herself. Tears dampened her eyes.

Bodin would never seek a slave for a wife.

Chessa scanned the rocks and trees, hoping he would be there. But he wasn't. She sighed and took the cake of soap he'd left and moved back into the deeper water. If his leaving now was so unpleasant, what would it be like when he sailed away forever?

A tear slipped down her cheek. She scrubbed at her arms and back with the soap, rubbing until her outsides hurt as much as her insides. Bodin was a man of honor. He'd keep their bargain. Of that she had no doubt now. He would sail her home and then be on his way. Had he wanted her as a wife, he would never have agreed to their bargain. Well, it didn't matter. It would *have* to not matter. She'd take the days and hours this bargain allotted her and make the most of them with him.

From high on a cliff, Bodin watched, hidden behind a tree as she scrubbed her hair clean. The scent of flowers would be gone now. Just as she would—all too soon, for his taste. "That's just the cock talking," he whispered into the wind.

The drying cloth lay draped over his shoulder, damp. He rubbed the corner of it over his face, the harsh stubble of his beard scraping against the stiff cloth. He'd meant to take down his beard for her at the bathing pond.

He dropped to his knees, watching as she climbed out of the water. Her small hands took the cloth he'd left for her, drying every covert hollow and visible rise of her soft body, touching all the places he wanted to touch and kiss and touch again.

She slid the cloth across the small span of her belly, drying the supple skin he knew to be there. He cursed under his breath. He'd made a bargain. He'd have to keep it.

Chessa held the front of the cloak closed over her naked body as she struggled over the rock-encrusted deer trail, trying to reach the tent before the rain. Thunder rolled through the air above her head, the lightning threatening to tear open the sky and release an angry rain.

The wind pushed against her back, urging her to hurry.

She pushed through the tent flap and into the candlelit sanctuary, scanning each corner. Disappointment pricked at her. She'd hoped Bodin would be waiting.

A shuffle of booted footfalls accompanied wild, swaying shadows cast by the dying fire outside. Hope lightened her mood, and she moved back toward the tent flap, peeking through the opening.

Erek stood there, talking with several other men. Where was

Bodin? Clutching the cloak tighter around her, Chessa moved as far back from the flap door as she could. Bodin hadn't wanted his men near the tent. Had they come for her, as Gavit had tried to?

Her chest constricted, her throat suddenly dry and unforgiving. She couldn't breathe. Where had Bodin gone? Rain began to pour down, a solid, rhythmic thumping that drowned out what the men were talking about. Or who.

The tent flap opened a crack, held stationary by the blade of a knife, and then fell closed again. Chessa drew up her knees and wrapped her arms tightly around her legs. Had they harmed Bodin? Found him and killed him because he'd kept her from them? A cold wave of fear rolled through her, turning her stomach and numbing her limbs. Erek had said the men resented—

A deafening clap of thunder boomed as the dark, hooded figure of a man burst into the tent.

Chessa gasped.

Rain doused the last remnants of the fire outside, and darkness dropped like a stone. Her lungs burned for breath, hands and knees trembling as she launched to her feet at a run.

She ducked for the flap. Too late. An arm caught her across the stomach like a wall, stealing what little breath she had in reserve. She was swung off her feet and held by an iron grip as she kicked and struggled. Blackness began buzzing inside her head.

"In the name of the gods, Chessa, what is the matter with you?"

9

Startled, Bodin sat upright, the blanket falling to his hips as he listened to make sense of the sound that had woken him. From the branch of a nearby tree, a bird screamed. He rubbed his face, beard scratching his palm. He sighed, and his heartbeat began to slow.

A dream, just a dream. The sound that had woken him had come from a bird, not a crying child. Not his child. His gut tightened. It had all been just a dream.

He sucked in a chestful of damp air, catching his breath as he looked at Chessa, asleep on the thick layers of fur beside him. He rubbed his tired, dry eyes. He hadn't expected her to bolt or for his arm to catch her quite so hard. And he certainly hadn't meant to frighten her into fainting.

Bodin cursed under his breath, remembering. Even after she had come to, she was still frightened and near hysterical but would not tell him why. She'd shadowed him for hours until he'd finally lain down and made her do so as well. And all this because of him, because of his selfish behavior. He clenched his jaw shut. Her question about how long it would take to reach her home had stung his pride. Had he really thought she might change her mind and ask to stay? In her place, he would do no differently.

And now, with the possibility that she carried his child, the idea of leaving her on the shore of her father's land was becoming more and more distasteful by the minute.

Rain started to fall again, but softer and without the wind this time. Bodin pulled the blanket from his lower body, shedding the layer from Chessa as well. She lay mostly on her stomach, her soft, pale body bared, willing, open to him. If honor would force him to keep his part of her bargain, then at least he could take the time he had with her to create memories that would warm him in his bed on the long, cold nights of winter.

His cock reared to life. Bodin fisted the insistent appendage, slowly stroking up and down as he shook his head. With her, it took so little to want more. To need every inch of her.

The sun would not rise fully for a while yet, and then they would set sail on the tide. The currents would spirit them along, past the lands of the Saxons to the Gaels. To her home.

Chessa let out a soft moan, shifting slightly in the cool, predawn air. Her fingers curled into the thick fur where he had been lying, the sides of her breasts peeking from beneath her body.

Bodin clenched his teeth and stroked his cock a little faster. No, not again. This time he would take her slow, punish them both with pleasure. He reached for one of the drying cloths that lay beside his sword. Twisting the thin fabric into a soft rope, he slipped it beneath her wrists and gently tightened the noose. He knotted the ends around a staked iron rod securing one side of the tent.

Bodin eased behind her, not ready for her to wake yet. He intended for that to come when he entered her. But first he'd have to quell his fast-approaching desire to spend. If he didn't have forever with her, he'd make the most of every minute he did have. Bodin urged her legs open.

Chessa sighed in her sleep, drawing one knee higher through the fur.

The breath caught in his throat. She lay open to him completely, in view and access. He wadded the blanket he'd taken from over them, easing it beneath her tummy to keep her buttocks raised. He stared at her and shook his head. Unbelievable—the gods had given him a temporary mercy for his sins in this innocent temptress he had promised to leave ashore with the Gaels. He ran the tip of his middle finger along the entrance to her haven and deeper into her feminine folds.

Muffled words of sensual, sleepy dreams crossed her lips on a deep, breathy sigh.

Bodin made a concerted effort to slow his own breathing as he released his cock and knelt between her spread legs. And just in time, too. She shifted her body, turning her head to the other side and attempting to close her legs as she moved her hips to lay on her side.

Her pale bottom swayed and wiggled as she resettled, belly down, hips tilted up toward him, thanks to the wadded-up blanket he'd placed beneath her pelvis.

But still she did not wake. Apparently the gods had granted him some grace, at least.

He continued to slide his finger gently into her quickly slickening sex. Her sleeping body responding ever so willingly to him, liberally coating his touch with the evidence of her desire. He eased one finger inside her and was well rewarded with even more of her moisture. His cock grew thicker. He would spend soon. Too soon.

Bodin eased his finger from inside her, bringing with it as much of her sweet, wet heat as he could to coat his pained cock. He stroked fast and hard, his hand sliding easily, taking only moments to spend his seed into the wadded blanket supporting her hips.

Time, he thought, catching his breath. He'd just bought himself time.

Still between her spread thighs, Bodin leaned back on his knees. She had such beauty, such sweetness. His heart ached. No. He shook his head. He'd have to put all that from his mind. He couldn't just keep her. No matter how much he wanted to. Why in the name of the gods had he agreed to her damn bargain?

She stretched, her back arching her tummy into the furs. An offering, a pleading? Even in her sleep she wanted him. And that drove him to need her again. Already his soft cock was beginning to revive.

She was his dream, and here she lay for the taking.

He ignored his growing appendage. He wanted to hear her cry out for him. Beg his name in her sleep, in her pleasure.

Restless in her dreamy state of growing arousal, he remained between her thighs. The nest of curls between her legs shimmered, moist, waiting for him. And his cock grew a little harder, urging attention, but Bodin refused to oblige his body yet.

Instead he waited a few moments for her to fall back to sleep, enjoying the sight of her spread open before him, better than any meal he'd ever tasted, or would ever taste. He knew that.

Unable to wait any longer, he skimmed his fingers along the soft skin of her inner thighs, retreating when he neared his desired goal to start back up from her knee. Each time he neared her sex, her body quivered and she would open a little wider for him.

Inviting him.

This time his fingers did not retreat from their destination. He slipped easily along her opening and through her saturated curls to tease the surface of her sensitized folds.

A moan exhaled from her chest, the air puffing from lips. Her hips began to writhe, her dream more real than she realized. Her tongue skated across her lips as she worked to form words in her sleep.

He leaned forward, bracing his body over hers with one hand to whisper in her ear while he continued to stroke and tease her. "That's right, sweet one. Say my name," Bodin urged, skimming his fingers along the opening of her slick sex but not giving in to what she so obviously needed. "Yes, say it," he urged on an exhaled whisper. "Cry out my name. . . ."

Chessa's back arched again, seeking more of him. A sobbing whimper accompanied her insistent squirming.

Bodin kept his touch light and haunting. Every muscle in his body yearned to give in and slide deep inside her hot sex. "Call my name, sweet one." He heard the echo of urgent need rasp through his own voice. "Let me hear the sounds cross your lips."

Her frustration grew, her body struggling to obey him in her dreamy arousal. Through pursed lips, another moan coursed through her body as she arched and wormed and struggled, pulling against the restraints to gain more of his touch.

Her bottom wiggled, wanting, just beneath his straining cock, her need torturous to him. If she didn't say his name soon, his heart would surely explode from the confines of his chest. He took his cock in hand and dragged the tip through her wet curls, readying them both. Dropping his head next to her ear, he rasped, "Beg for me, Chessa."

Her body arched, needing. "B—Bodin—"

Panting, his chest constricted. He drove the full length of his cock into her heated sex. One arm wrapped around her waist, rocking her hips with his as he pressed against her womb.

Chessa gasped awake, eyes wide and body burning for more. Confused, she tried to make sense of what was happening, but her body was already well aware and demanding more. Bodin rocked his hips into hers again, burying his shaft deep inside, and she needed no further explanation.

She wanted to reach for him, touch him, but her hands were stretched out in front of her, bound. She had no way to encourage more from him. "Bodin . . ."

He braced his weight on one hand and leaned over her stretched, straining body, sweeping her hair out of his way. "Yes, sweet one?" One hand slid over her hip to her waist and down until he reached her swaying breast; the soft, fleshy mound more than filled his hand as he cupped and squeezed. "Do you need something?"

"Bodin, plea—ahhh—" He pinched her yearning nipple, sending a burst of fire down to her belly to further fuel the need pulsing between her spread thighs. She wanted his hand to follow the same path, to cup the place between her legs that would send her into blinding pleasure.

"Please what?" he panted in her ear, holding himself motionless and fully encased deep in her small, straining body.

Her chest heaved as she tried to speak, his fingers still poised at her nipple. She knew as soon as she spoke, he would send that fire burning through her body again. "Touch me. . . ." He pinched again, and her body burned.

"But I am touching you."

"Not there. Please . . ."

He chuckled, his breath soft and warm on her ear.

Bodin moved the hand he'd been using to keep the bulk of his weight from crushing her and cupped her other breast, pinching the swollen nipple it so willingly offered. "There?" Her head shook in answer, and her breathing picked up, the muscles of her sex tightening around his cock.

"No, Bodin—"

"Where, sweet one, where do you wish for me to touch?"

Her body throbbed and clenched, seeking the relief he refused to allow. "Between my legs. . . ."

"You have grown bold, sweet one. And I find that most pleasing, but this bargain is about me, remember? I will let you know when such boldness is what I wish." His hand moved to the base of her throat, turning her head, stretching her neck so her lips met his mouth as he pulled his cock from her heat.

Just as she cried out in protest, he claimed her mouth and rammed his shaft back inside, striking her womb.

Chessa's legs trembled, spread wide and holding herself open for him. Never had she known such need, such want. And he was right. As his slave, it was not her place to ask for pleasure; she was meant to give it.

His hand moved to her belly, fingers skimming, teasing the patch of coarse curls before spreading across the flat plain, digging into the soft flesh. "How is this?" he taunted.

Just the proximity of his hand so near the crux of her need sent spasms of want through her belly. Chessa bit her lower lip and nodded.

"You would not lie to me now, would you, sweet one?" He dipped his fingers deeper into her moist nest but did not go low enough to touch her where she needed him most.

The throbbing between her thighs intensified. Chessa could hardly breathe, hovering on a knife's edge of pleasure. His shaft filled every inch of her insides, and her muscles contracted around the girth of him of their own volition, urging him to move, to satisfy.

"That will not work this time, Chessa. I've seen to that."

"What do you—"

"I am not ready to spend. I want to hear you cry out my name," Bodin informed as he moved back to his knees, pulling all but the head his cock out. "And you *will* cry out my name, over and over, Chessa. Before you have your release."

He began to rock forward and backward, stroking his shaft into her in small increments—tiny tastes of the blinding pleasure he commanded. Chessa's thoughts swirled behind her eyes. She cared not for anything, would promise him anything if he would only permit her just that one touch, that one moment of searing relief. Her arms and shoulders trembled, having strained so long against the soft cloth binding them.

Bodin pulled his cock completely out, taking a few moments to let the cool air ease his ardor.

She ached inside, empty without the full length and breadth of him filling her. Chessa began to sob. Being devoid of him, robbed of any form of touch from him, sent her into a desperate spiral. "Bodin, I beg you! Please don't make me suffer so." She tried to see him from over her shoulder. "Bodin!" Her voice broke.

His name, begged from her lips with such desperation, shredded his willpower. He bore deep into her, filling her in a single, effortless stroke.

Chessa convulsed from the inside out, a white light filling her head as her body gripped tight around him. His hands dug painfully into the flesh of her hips, holding her body to his. But all too soon he left her again, his seed hot and thick and splashing against the inside of her leg.

Stiff and strained, her muscles wouldn't move. She rested her forehead in the furs, gasping. Her body couldn't stop shaking. She didn't even flinch as Bodin used a damp rag to clean his spendings from her thighs.

He reached around the front of her and released her wrists from the noose.

Chessa closed her eyes as he eased one of her arms down to her side and rolled her onto her back. His fingers skimmed over the slope of her cheeks, brushing the hair from her flushed face. Her skin rippled as a tingle of anticipation betrayed her. He was not done with her yet.

A wicked smile curved his lips. "You are right about that, sweet one," he confirmed.

She shook her head. "I—I couldn't possibly. It's not—" He pressed his finger to her lips.

"Do not be contentious with me."

She tried to speak anyway, but his mouth claimed her words as his hand did the same to her aching, neglected breast. She couldn't help but moan. Fuel for his fire.

Bodin shifted his body, planting first one knee and then the other between her still quivering thighs. He broke the kiss. "I have not heard my name begged from your lips enough times yet this morn, Chessa."

He suckled one taut nipple into his mouth, his tongue laving and teasing as she arched beneath him. He released it and blew a cooling breath over her warm flesh. "I will have every inch there is of you, as was our deal." He turned his attention to her other breast, affording the sweet, soft mound the same attention he'd lavished on the other.

Chessa's fingers threaded through his thick hair as her shoulders lifted off the furs, offering herself up as sacrifice. Yes, he owned her, as well and as truly as though he'd bought and paid for her. And that had been her free choice. But now it had gone further than that. Now he possessed everything that was her, everything that made her who and what she was.

And his command was absolute. She inhaled a fractured breath. He ruled her, body and soul. Master. She trembled as his tongue laved her sensitized skin. And the thought of leaving him stung her heart and filled her eyes with tears.

Bodin would not allow her mind to wander. He dipped his tongue into her navel, swirling circles, bringing her thoughts back to her body. And to him. His teeth grazed a line the rest of the way down her belly.

Chessa gasped.

"Keep your hands at your sides." Bodin ordered, pushing her thighs open wider. "Do not disobey me."

"What are you . . ." His mouth closed over her exposed center as his tongue answered her question. No discussion. No argument.

Chessa body all but levitated as she gripped the fur blanket in her fists. Her body alternately seized and writhed at the intimate invasion, pleasure scalding her cheeks, the very air she needed to survive deserting her.

And so Bodin's lesson began. A necessary chastisement of what it meant to live under his command, his rule, in the searing permanency of his soul.

10

The sun steamed the fallen rain from everything, returning the moisture to the clouds. Chessa inhaled the heavy air. "Bodin?" She rolled onto her back, relishing the soft, warm furs layered beneath her, blinking to adjust her eyes to the light. Her body tingled, her mind racing to delicious and improper thoughts of what Bodin had done, of where he'd spent so long kissing her. And how much she'd enjoyed his attention.

"Awake now, are you?" He turned to look at her, eyebrows raised, a wide grin showing straight, white teeth.

Her cheeks burned at the blatant enjoyment on his face. She clutched the blanket to her chest as she reached for her bed gown and cloak.

"We have a little more time; the tide has not filled the bay yet." Done with his laces, he knelt beside her, his hand cupping the back of her head as he studied her face. His eyes settled on her full lips. "You obeyed well," he whispered.

Chessa closed her eyes as his breath washed across her cheek, moving from her ear to her mouth. Her breasts swelled in anticipation, her body arching, offering.

He smiled and pressed a series of soft, tender kisses to her mouth before slipping his tongue past her teeth, exploring her mouth.

She couldn't help but recall how his tongue had felt lower, between her thighs, doing the very same things. Her nipples hardened, the breath catching in her throat.

Bodin pulled back, admiring her ready response. He tugged away the fur blanket covering her.

Chessa sighed as his warm hand cupped one breast, calloused thumb scraping the raised nipple that betrayed her thoughts. Her body, still raw with the needs he'd so easily brought forth, was still more than willing to submit to his every demand. To revel in it. Her hand went to his wrist, urging his touch lower.

"No, not so soon." A pleased chuckle accompanied his words. Dropping his voice to a whisper, he added, "Besides, there won't be enough time before the tide to do what I have in mind."

Still, she pulled his hand to her belly, wanting but not brave enough to speak the words and ask. Her other hand went to his thigh and upward.

Bodin halted the progress of her fingers and pulled her to his chest, nuzzling her neck as she clung naked to him. "Later, I promise." He gave her another soft kiss and released her. "Right now I have a job for you. So dress." He moved to the rear of the tent and dropped to one knee beside a leather bag of supplies, searching through the contents.

Chessa quickly slipped her arms through the linen bed gown, pulling the bodice over her aching breasts. She struggled to shift the material and smooth out the bunched front, but for some reason it was snug up top, almost too tight.

As she draped the cloak over her shoulders, Bodin took the brooch from her hands to fasten the clasp himself. "Here." He handed her a small pouch. "By the trees are raspberry bushes. Pick some for us."

Chessa frowned.

"Don't you like raspberries?" he asked.

"Yes." She looked down. "Very much, but . . ."

"But what?" He lifted her chin.

"I've never been allowed—"

"*I* will say what is or is not allowed." He grinned. "Besides, I have a particular use in mind for them." Bodin turned her toward the tent flap. "So do as you're told."

Conceding to his orders, she bent to exit through the tent flap.

Bodin swatted her backside with a firm strike.

"Oh!" Chessa squeaked in surprise.

"But stay where I can see you!" he called to her back.

Chessa stepped into the fresh morning air just beginning to warm from the sunshine. She drew her fingers through her hair, pulling the raucous mess out of her face.

Berry bushes formed a barrier around most of their private encampment. She started toward the nearest one. Picking the first plump, red berry she saw, she turned it between her fingers. What use could he possibly have in mind for them other than eating? A shiver rippled down her spine, spreading through the rest of her in waves. She glanced back at the tent. He was watching.

Chessa smiled and turned back to her task, gathering each berry within reach. She couldn't help but glance over her shoulder again a few minutes later. But he'd returned inside the tent to pack.

Determined to surprise Bodin, she ignored the prickly thorns and picked as many berries as she could. With such abundance, the bag was full in no time. She cinched the drawstring closed and then sucked her fingertips clean of the sweet juice from the overripe berries. Chessa turned and froze. She hadn't heard anyone approach.

Erek stood there between her and the tent. Between her and Bodin. He grinned, leering at her. An odd look crossed his face as he licked his lips. His hand slipped inside the front of his trousers and moved up and down.

Her grip on the small bag of berries tightened as her heart raced in her chest. She glanced down to make certain the cloak covered her and then inched backward as far as the thorned bushes would allow. The sharp sounds of calling birds began to fade behind the loud pounding of her heart.

Erek took a step toward her.

The side of Chessa's foot struck a rock as she tried to scramble out of his reach. She yelled out. Flocks of birds launched from their perches in a winged rush to take to the sky as she landed hard on the damp ground. From the corner of her eye, a hand reached for her, and she cringed.

The hand touched her shoulder. "No!"

"Chessa," Bodin scolded. "Calm yourself. What is the matter, are you hurt?"

She looked over his shoulder. Half a dozen men stood beside the rained-out fire pit, watching.

The small crowd of men stood waiting, Erek prominent among them.

Bodin cupped her chin and forced her to face him. Dropping his voice to a whisper, he pressed for an answer again. "Chessa, what upsets you so?"

She shook her head. "I—I was startled. They startled me." She glanced at Erek again and swallowed. Would he have hurt her, or . . .

"Come." Bodin lifted her from the ground, handing her back the bag of berries. Keeping himself between her and the small party of men, he escorted her back to the tent and pushed open the flap. "Wait for me."

Chessa's heart still pounded as her eyes misted with tears. She would never be safe among them. Kaol must have had tremendous influence to have kept them from her in the past. But wanting to stay with Bodin, even as nothing more than a slave he used to warm his bed, would never work. She'd never be safe outside of his presence. And just how long would they tolerate his presence?

The men stepped away from the tent, their voices deep and muffled as they spoke. She wiped away the tears that moistened her cheeks, and she knelt beside the bed furs, folding and stacking them neatly together.

A pair of heavy boots tromped beside the canvas walls of the tent. The flap opened. Bodin entered, a scowl etched deep into the features of his face.

The moment she saw him, all her anguish and turmoil bubbled to the surface. And quiet tears became sobs.

He knelt beside her, silent.

Chessa threw her arms around him and cried. How could this have happened? When had it happened? Her arms tightened around his waist, tears soaking into the rough fabric of his shirt. She loved him.

Bodin wrapped his arms around her, comforting her. "Are you certain you are not hurt?"

Chessa nodded against his warm chest, her fear fading. Here in his arms, she was safe. Here, alone with him, she was happy.

He kissed the top of her head as he pulled her arms from around him. "I must pack, sweet one." He kissed the backs of her hands. "The tide fills the bay as we speak."

Reluctant to let go, she nodded as Bodin stood, already moving to the back of the tent, gathering things as he went.

If only the storm had raged for weeks instead of hours, there would be more time with him. She looked at his broad shoulders. His body was far too large for this tent. He filled the whole of the space, the whole of her heart. She closed her eyes for a moment and sighed. If she wasn't a slave, his slave, then maybe she could tell him she loved him. And maybe, just maybe, he could love her back.

Chessa wiped her cheeks dry, blinking back the threat of more tears. Crying would not change a Viking man's mind. She'd learned that lesson as a child. And as before when she was just a girl, she had a duty to fulfill. She had to return home to her people, to her family. What she wanted didn't matter.

A shadow flickered across the side of the tent. "Ahem." Outside one of the men alerted them to his presence.

She straightened, her stomach coiling into a knot. She recognized the shadow.

Bodin turned toward the sound and then glanced down at Chessa. "Erek will take you to the ship."

"What? Why?" She stood and hurried beside Bodin.

His eyes narrowed on her. "I have much to do before we sail, including meet with my men. And I want you out of the way, safe." He glanced down at her hand, which was gripping a fistful of his tunic. "Not clutching at my shirttails and cloak."

"But why can't you take me to the ship?" She turned slightly to see over her shoulder. "It would not take long." The shadow paced, kicking at the charred wood from the rained-out fire only a few feet from the tent opening.

Bodin took her by the arm, turning her body so she faced only him, watched only him. "Why are you afraid?" He scanned her face, narrowing his gaze to study her reaction. She had been in much the same state when he'd arrived back last evening. Only then, she'd refused to tell him why.

"Sir." Erek called out.

Chessa startled and tried to get closer, but Bodin kept her where he could see her. He lowered his voice. "Has Erek touched you? Harmed you?"

"No, but—"

"Tell me the truth. Now!" he growled, giving her a slight shake.

"No, he hasn't, but—"

"But what, then?" he snapped, trying to get an answer quickly.

"Last night . . . during the storm, before you returned . . . he—"

"He what?"

"He was here." Chessa tried to see behind her, see the shadow she knew hovered just on the other side of the canvas wall.

Bodin tightened his grip on her arm. "Erek was here? Are you certain?"

She nodded, lowering her gaze to the ground. "I'm positive it was him." She swallowed.

"Sir? Are you in there?" Erek pressed. "I'm here to take the girl to the ship."

Bodin rubbed at his rough beard. "When?"

Chessa spoke in a whispered rush. "Just after I arrived from the spring. I—I heard a noise and thought it was you." *Hoped it was you,* her heart screamed inside her chest. "I peeked out and saw him by the trail." Her heart began to race, the memory of her fear returning. She shuddered, voice wobbling as she continued. "A few moments later, the blade of a dagger opened the tent flap like someone was peeking in, but they went away as the group of others approached."

Bodin puzzled on her words for a moment. Erek had not been amongst the men at the beach camp, nor had he been waiting here with the others at first. The young man had arrived late. Needing to get to the bottom of all this, Bodin pulled Chessa through the tent flap and kept a tight grip on her arm, not allowing her to take shelter behind him as she wanted. "Where were you last night, Erek? Before you met me here with the others?"

Erek looked at Chessa only for a moment before responding. "Me?" He shrugged his shoulders. "Just scouting around the area, making certain all was as it should be." A big, sloppy grin lit his face as he raised his eyebrows. "Wouldn't want anyone else sneaking into your tent uninvited."

The hinted reminder of a debt owed was not lost on Bodin. He relaxed. It was likely just curiosity feeding the boy's actions or eagerness to rise in the ranks by taking on extra duty. Besides, there were far more likely candidates among his men for any additional trouble that might be caused over Chessa.

Erek stared at Chessa. "Didn't you want her secured aboard the ship as soon as possible?"

"Change of plan. I'll take her." Bodin let go of Chessa's arm and pressed his hand to her back, hurrying her toward the trail leading onto the sandy beach. He'd already been forced to slit Gavit's throat. No point in tempting the boy beyond retribution.

"Sure," Erek called to Bodin's back. He lowered his voice to a whisper. "As you wish."

Out of Erek's presence, Chessa sighed with relief. But, still, she wanted to cry. Getting back aboard the ship meant Bodin was that much closer to taking her home and that much closer to leaving her. She ached, raw inside and out, vulnerable to every hurt she knew would come when she watched his ship sail off into the distance. Bodin's hands gripped her waist as he lifted her to one of the men already aboard. On deck, she turned and looked back at the trail they had just walked. Erek stood there, watching her, chewing on a long strand of grass. He would come after her. It was only a matter of time and opportunity. She had no doubt.

"Come, Chessa." Bodin waited beside the open hatch.

She placed her hands in his, letting him lower her down for the remainder of the voyage. This time she was grateful for the small room below deck, grateful for the lock on the door.

Bodin waited until she'd entered the hidden space inside the drop hold. "I'll be back soon." He pulled the door closed, turning the key in the latch.

Chessa dropped onto the cot, the blankets soft beneath her. Overhead, metal-strapped trunks thudded and slid as booted feet shuffled to secure possessions and supplies. She closed her eyes, tugging the cloak to cover her bare feet. They would sail soon. Already the bay had filled with enough water to rock the beached ship with waves. She curled onto her side. Nothing to do but wait. Wait and wonder.

So much would happen in the next few days. Or would it be hours? Bodin had never said. He'd not answered her question about how long the voyage would take. Chessa sighed. Soon she'd see her parents, her home. . . .

The door handle rattled, the lock clunking again and again as someone attempted to pull it free. Chessa sat up, heart racing. A dull thud jarred the heavy wooden panel. Slits of light flashed between the planks with each impact. She drew her knees to her chest, resting her chin on top of them, eyes wide and watching. Where was Bodin? *Thunk. Thunk.* With his key, Bodin wouldn't need to break through the door. . . .

11

An almost imperceptible clink of metal against metal resonated in the small room. Chessa jarred awake. When had she closed her eyes? She couldn't remember, couldn't quite catch hold of her fuzzy thoughts. Her stomach turned, threatening to be sick from the motion of the ship. She dropped her head back against the wall. Had she really fallen asleep? The thought plagued her.

The door creaked.

Chessa closed her eyes again, her stomach insistent on the concession. Maybe if she just listened. Weapons clunked against the floorboards. A large, cool hand cupped the side of her face, thumb stroking softly against her warm cheek.

"Are you awake?"

The sound of Bodin's voice soothed her. She nodded in his hand.

"Then come here to me, sweet one." Bodin pulled her to his chest as he lay back on the cot, taking her down with him.

She sighed and smiled, snuggling deep into his warm shoulder. One of his large hands drifted down the length of her spine as the other guided the rest of her body atop him. He widened her legs so she straddled his hips.

Aroused, Bodin centered her over his cock and worked the fabric of her bed gown up and over her head, out of his way, dropping it in a heap on the floor. He pressed a plump, ripe raspberry into her mouth and then cupped both sides of her face, pulling her lips to his, tongue delving, sharing the berry between them. He explored the inside of her mouth as he soon would other places.

Chessa moaned, her body as hungry for him as he was for her. Bodin's engorged manhood twitched against her bared, open sex, but he did not move to enter. Her body needed no further urging, nothing more to wake her and sway her into action. Pressed against his chest, her belly ached, needing, wanting, and she wiggled her hips, trying to take him inside her body.

Bodin broke their kiss. He filled her mouth with several more berries and lifted her so he could taste her breasts, sucking one hard nipple deep into his mouth.

She panted for breath, struggling to swallow the sweet offerings. The fire between her thighs flared as she squirmed against his firm hold. But in this position, she could not make contact with him, and she wanted the feel of him, the heat of him more than anything. She reached behind, hoping to touch him, to stir him into satisfying her desire, but his grip wouldn't relent. Moisture leaked down the insides of her spread-open thighs, her need more than evident.

Bodin switched to her other breast, taking the nipple between his teeth, clamping down on the hard bead until she whimpered. Her hips hovered above his torso, squirming, longing for his cock. He popped several berries in his mouth, swallowed, and then ran his tongue between her breasts and down, lifting her as he tasted his way lower. "You are far sweeter than the berries."

"No, Bodin. . . ." Chessa breathed. "Please, I need *you*."

"Later," he mumbled against the soft, spongy flesh of her belly. His fingers dug into her hips as he lifted her higher until she kneeled, straddling his face.

Chessa could go nowhere. Bodin's commanding grip bordered on painful. She was at his mercy and wanted it no other way. His tongue swept upward along her inner thigh, tasting her desire and inflaming her more. Her cheeks burned at such boldness, but her body was unwilling to protest as she reveled, without shame or reproach, in the hot need he stirred inside her belly.

Bodin chuckled, speaking between nips and kisses, "You have turned into quite the naughty wench, sweet one."

She twisted slightly, able to at least help balance her trembling body by bracing one hand against the muscles of his hard chest. Her legs shook and quivered as he kept her at his discretion, open to his brand of teasing.

He ran the tip of one finger along the hollow of her inner thigh, coating it as he followed the trail of heated moisture to the open entrance of her sex. He spread the liberal, searing liquid of her desire through her fleshy folds, seeking and finding the hard, swollen nub that throbbed for his attention.

Chessa gasped. She bit down on her lower lip, trying hard not scream her pleasure with so many men above them able to hear. "Bodin—oh!"

He pressed her down to his mouth, silencing her desperate plea as he tasted the sweet, salty pleasure of her need for him. His cock jerked each time she shuddered and whined.

Her eyes grew wide, sobs choking the air from her lungs as his tongue pressed into the cavern of her desire. Inside, her muscles contracted, desperate to catch and hold on to his elusive, slippery demands.

He lifted her easily, running his tongue along the passion-swollen flesh of her sex before blowing cool air to contrast the growing heat. "You are a very tasty wench indeed." He continued to tease her with soft bites of his sharp teeth.

"Bodin . . . please . . ." She grabbed for him, ready to spiral past the point of control, ready for him to ravage her again and again as he'd done before. But Bodin pulled her back down to straddle his hips, pressing her moist, open flesh against his thick manhood.

His hands closed over her breasts, rough and consuming. She groaned, his shaft hot on her tender skin. Chessa rocked her hips forward and then back, taking him inside her body. Gaining at least part of what she wanted, she pressed her body down as far as she could, closing her eyes, letting the hot, hard length of him fuel the fire in her belly.

"Don't move, sweet one." Bodin pinched her nipples hard to make certain he had her attention. "Just hold still for a moment." Her inner muscles clamped tight around him, and he gritted his teeth. His gut burned with the urge to press deeper inside her heated, wet sex.

She started to raise up, her body desperate for more of him, for the whole of him to fill her, to press so deep inside he could go no farther.

He pinched her nipples harder. "I said not to move yet, Chessa," he growled in warning, bracing his feet on the cot's small mattress.

So close. Her completion was so close. "Why?" Unused to baring her weight in this manner for so long, her thighs waivered.

Bodin's cock jerked in response. Sucking a breath through clenched teeth, he pulled her down onto his chest, flattening her full breasts. One arm wrapped around her back to hold her in place. "Because I want to kiss you, that is why." He threaded his fingers through the hair at the back of her head, pulling her mouth to his. He raised up, taking her weight and forcing his tongue past her teeth as he rammed his cock against her womb.

Blinding pleasure consumed every part of her as she shook and tried to scream, but Bodin didn't let go. He held her to his body, rocking himself deeper and deeper as her body clenched around him, begging for more. Chessa's fingers curled into the hair on his chest, desperate he not stop as she shuddered and seized in his grip, wanting all of him, taking all of him. And still she needed more.

Bodin broke the kiss with a gut-wrenching groan. Giving in to the insistent demands of her sweet, soft body, he had no more control. His hands pressed her hips deeper onto his as a growl rumbled from his chest. His cock throbbed and pulsed, exploding his seed deep inside her belly for a second time.

Panting, he held Chessa tight to him, his swollen cock still buried inside her wet heat as he turned the both of them onto his side. He brushed the hair from her face and from between their sweating bodies. She nuzzled into his embrace.

Bodin closed his eyes. He took a deep breath and sighed. "You are far, far sweeter than any berry I've ever put to my lips." Unable to let her out of his hold, his hand caressed her back and hip, pulling her thigh up to rest over his on the small cot.

How would he let her go, let them go?

Every instinct he had told him that withholding his seed was pointless. She carried his child. Bodin kissed the top of her head as his body finally began to relax, his cock sliding slowly from her sex on the mixture of their spendings.

His eyes misted. Where would he possibly find the strength it would take to leave her with her people as he'd promised to do? He pulled her tighter to his chest, his hand dipping between her slippery buttocks.

Reluctantly he whispered the truth to her. "Chessa, my men will anchor in the bay at dawn. You are home." Those words cut deep. Worse than any blade that had ever cut into his skin.

*   *   *

Chessa moved forward at the urging of Bodin's hand low on her back. She didn't remember the bay or the landscape. Nothing seemed even vaguely familiar. She turned to him. "Are you certain we are in the right place?"

He nodded, wary as he pressed her farther up the shore toward the cliff trail. "Yes."

"Where is everyone?"

"That's what I was just wondering." Bodin nodded to a couple of the men who had accompanied them ashore, indicating they should take a look around.

Chessa lifted the hem of her cloak and bed gown to better walk up the steep hill. Where were her parents? Her people? No one was on the shore. Anxious to see someone, anyone, she hurried along the trail to the top. Chessa stopped dead in her tracks.

Keeping pace, Bodin nearly ran into the back of her.

Abandoned, collapsing cottages dotted the top of the cliff. The strong sea air continued to lash at their remains. No one was there either. "Where are they?"

Bodin frowned, uncertain what to think. He scanned the closest of the hills. "Perhaps they saw the ship and are hiding."

"But the cottages are falling in on themselves. No one lives here anymore."

He shook his head.

The people who once populated this part of the coast were gone. Chessa's bottom lip quivered as she whispered, "Bodin, where are my parents?" A cold chill turned her stomach.

"I do not know, sweet one," he said on a sigh. "We've not returned here since my father took you . . . and the others. That was the bargain."

"Sir." Erek approached. "The men have returned from searching along the coast." He shook his head in answer before the question was even asked.

A movement caught Bodin's eye. He tensed, pulling Chessa

behind a run-down cottage. In the distance someone emerged from the trees.

An old woman tottered downhill along a rough footpath, one hand clutching a bundle of twigs to her bosom, the other using a crooked walking stick for balance.

Erek skirted low along the sparse trees, quickly covering the hilly ground to creep up behind the old crone and catch ahold of her rather large stick. He held it from her reach.

"I—I'm not afraid of you—" she stuttered, forming the words with few teeth. "Kill me if ye wish, jus' gi' me back my s—stick!"

The old woman wobbled on uncertain limbs. Bodin walked up, purposely keeping Chessa alongside him. "Erek, return it."

With a frown, the young man reluctantly handed back the crooked but sturdy stick. The old woman turned to Bodin, scowling as she glanced back over her shoulder at the boy. She planted the walking stick into the damp ground, shifting her weight onto the wood. Relief eased her pained, wrinkled face. She looked at Bodin and then turned to Chessa, lips pressing into an angry line. She hobbled a little closer, still keeping a tight hold on the armful of twigs and sticks as she squinted, looking close to be sure. Lifting the point of her stick from the ground, the old woman stabbed toward the battered cottages. "You! You did this!"

Bodin snatched the sharp end of the stick before it could reach Chessa. "Put it back on the ground." His eyebrows rose in warning to the old woman. "Or I will snap it in two." He released his hold.

"You know who I am?" Tears welled in Chessa's eyes. Had she found her people?

The old woman sneered. "Ye were the king's daughter, the one he sent to keep the raiders away." She teetered closer. "But yer not'ing but a traitor." Leaned forward, she raised her stick to strike.

Chessa stumbled back, bumping into Erek as Bodin twisted the wood from the old woman's hand and began snapping it into pieces over his knee.

Chessa turned back to the old woman. "What do you mean 'were'? Where is my fath—"

"He's dead!" The old woman grunted a sound of disgust. "Dead and buried beside yer mother!" She narrowed her gaze on Chessa and pointed a crooked finger at Bodin and Erek. "It is yer fault the king is dead! Ye chose to seek out their beds."

Chessa's stomach rose into her throat, leaving a sick, bitter taste in her mouth. She had failed. All those years of servitude were for naught. She had still failed her people. Trembling hands rose to swipe the hair out of her face as she swayed forward, her legs shaking too much to support her any longer.

Bodin caught her, holding her tight to his chest. His cheek rested on the top of her head as she clutched at his shirt, squeezing her small arms tight around his torso. He whispered, "I'm sorry, sweet one." Bodin raised his head and looked at Erek. "Have the old woman take you to the others. Camp the men on the beach."

When Erek had taken the woman far enough away, Bodin pulled Chessa back, wiping the hair from her wet cheeks. "Chessa . . . sweet one, look at me." He cupped her chin, tilting her face to meet his gaze. He searched the depths of her green eyes. "The old woman is wrong. You are not to blame."

Her chin quivered. "Of course I am. You heard her." She inhaled a ragged breath. "My father is dead, my people all but gone. I failed! And—and I did go to your bed—willingly." Her lips trembled. "And she knows, Bodin, she can see it in my face!" Chessa tried to pull away.

"Stop it!" She refused to look at him any longer, and he gave her a gentle shake. "Listen to me. Coming to my bed was a bargain between you and I. It had nothing to do with your people or what happened to them. You are not to blame, Chessa. Do you hear me? You did nothing wrong!"

Numb, she stood motionless, not believing his words. She'd wanted in his bed. The passage home had just given her a reason. How could he think she was not to blame?

Bodin led her to the door of the nearest cottage. "Stay here." He stepped inside the run-down hut, using the side of his boot to clear a path through the debris as he shook the remaining timber supports, testing them. Stepping back outside, he took Chessa's hand. "Come here, sweet one."

With little resistance, he tugged her inside out of the wind and sat, pulling her down onto his lap. Bodin tucked wily strands of hair behind her ears, dropping his voice to a low rumble. "You did nothing wrong."

"But—"

He pressed his finger to her lips long enough to silence her protest before he traced the delicate outline of her jaw and continued down the column of her neck. "If you believe nothing else in your lifetime, believe this: Your parents did not die because of anything you did. You were a child, Chessa, you never should have been expected to carry the responsibility of your people's fate."

The wind picked up, carrying a light rain and promising more to come. Chessa shivered but not so much from the chill.

"Do you wish to stay on the ship tonight . . . or here?"

Taken aback by the question, she took a deep breath. "What do you mean?"

Bodin pressed his lips tight together for a brief moment. "I know it is not the homecoming you wanted, Chessa, but you *are* home. The terms of our bargain have been met. You are free—forever this time. Your fate is your own."

His words sifted through the quagmire of her emotions. "Oh." A fresh wave of anguish churned in her belly. He would leave now. He *wanted* to leave now. She slipped off his lap, kneeling in a pile of musty thatch that had fallen from the roof some time ago.

Chessa raised her gaze to meet his and tried to steel her insides to the hurt clawing at her. She swallowed. "Here is fine."

Bodin got to his feet. "I'll get your things from the boat."

"But there isn't—" She looked over her shoulder. Bodin had left. Her head dropped forward. Chessa fought back the tears burning her eyes. Somehow she had to find a way to help her people. This was her fate, her place since birth.

Perhaps not all her people thought as the old woman did.

She looked up at the darkening sky. The storm sent a shiver down her spine. Would Bodin hurry to sail tonight? She had no possessions. . . . Had that been his way of saying good-bye?

Chessa scrambled to her feet and rounded the door frame. But Bodin was already descending the trail with his men. Her heart wrenched in her chest, and she held the cloak tight around her as she stepped out of the scant shelter of the cottage. She couldn't let him leave. Not this way. "Bodin! Wait!" The wind blew rain in her face, forcing her to shield her eyes to keep going.

"Well, now, it seems you are no longer under the protection of any man," a deep voice stated.

Chessa whipped around. The wind blew against her back, fluttering the ends of her cloak about her legs. She took a deep breath and then swallowed.

Erek.

12

Erek's eyes glowed with ill intent as his gaze roamed down to Chessa's feet and then back up, holding steady at her breasts.

A chill shuddered through her. She glanced over her shoulder, but there was no one to call for help. Her tongue skated nervously across her lower lip. She had to buy some time. "Bodin is—"

"Not coming back," Erek asserted. "This little bargain between the two of you is over. He's done with you." He snatched her wrist, yanking her soft body against his. "Now it's my turn."

Chessa struggled to get free as he pulled her back inside the crumbling cottage and out of view. His fingers pressed between the small bones of her wrist, sending a shooting pain up the length of her arm.

Chessa cried out and dropped to her knees.

Erek chuckled. "You are anxious to get started, aren't you? But that's not what I had in mind. Yet." He released his hold.

Chessa rushed to get to her feet, but that was all she could do. Erek's arms blocked either side of her. She swallowed. He didn't intend to let her leave. She balled her hands into fists, gripping the sides of her cloak tightly.

Erek's head bent forward as he whispered, "How about striking a little bargain with me?"

Chessa turned her face away in refusal.

"No matter. I'll just be the next of many more to come."

Her heart pounded fiercely in her chest; so loud were the beats she could hardly hear the wind. But Bodin's quiet words came to her—*you are free—forever this time*—and gave her courage. She shoved the unsuspecting young man back. "Leave my land."

Erek laughed, shock and surprise dissipating almost instantly. "*Your* land? This is no more your land than mine. You're a slave, nothing more, a kept whore, no matter what you were led to believe."

He moved closer again, but this time Chessa scrambled over the knee-high pile of debris in the corner to stand beside a gaping hole in the cottage wall. "This is my land and my home. And I will help my people through whatever tragedy has happened. But you are not welcome here."

"They do not want you here, these pitiful excuses you call your people. You are a traitor to them."

"They will think differently when they know the truth—"

"They know the truth." The words were growled through clenched teeth. "You have betrayed them in the bed of their enemy. They will not care for what purpose."

His words cut deep. And resounded with truth. A sickening chill ran down her spine to twist in her stomach and clog her throat. The old woman had somehow seen into the depths of her heart at a mere glance. So, likely, would the others. And no amount of reason or logic would justify her willingness in Bodin's bed. Not even as the only means of returning to her family. Tears rimmed her eyes, blurring her vision.

Erek stepped within reach. "You serve but one purpose." He snatched her arm and yanked.

Off balance, Chessa gasped, stumbling forward, trapped in his painful grip. Her foot broke through a piece of brittle wood on the top of the pile, and she went to her knees. Sharp pains seared along her legs as debris gouged into her shins. Another forceful jerk on her arm, and she was dragged back to her feet.

"Turn me loose!" Her arms soon ached from the effort of trying to push Erek away. Some dark thought moved from his eyes to settle in his mind as a plan of action. Chessa braced for more pain.

Distant voices wafted along the wind, and Erek paused, glancing up to see a small group of armed Gael men heading toward the cottage, led by the old woman, who had another stick. Erek grabbed Chessa's wrists and turned her so she was visible to them through the hole in the wall. "Do not think of crossing me again," he warned, grabbing hold of her chin. "Or what little is left of your people will be no more. This time their fate really is up to you."

She sucked in a breath to protest, but the words she tried to form were cut off as his mouth slammed into hers in a violent, one-sided kiss. Then, just as quickly, he turned her loose with a slight shove, sending her backward into the heap of cottage wreckage.

By the time she managed to sit up, Erek had disappeared through the open door. "Good riddance," she whispered, wiping his spit from her mouth. She began assessing the new gashes on her arms and the still-bleeding ones on her leg. She needed to get the wounds clean.

Chessa eased back onto her feet, picking her way out of the rubble with care. Closing her eyes for a moment, she strained to remember. Which way was the river?

"Seize her!" a male voice shouted.

Before Chessa could react, two men rushed forward and

grabbed her by the arms. "Wait! Please, listen. You don't understand."

The oldest of the men spoke. "Words will do you no service, girl. We saw you with him." He spat on the ground at her feet, "Kissing him."

"With who? Kissing who?" The words stuck thick in her throat. They'd seen Erek kiss her. She squeezed her eyes shut. They'd never believe her now.

"That 'a right, girl. We saw ye evil deeds firsthand." The man turned to the rest of the group, nodding approvingly toward the old woman, who stood there wearing a pleased, justified expression on her face. "Morna were right about the girl." He turned a scathing, loathsome gaze to Chessa. "The offspring of our great king prefers the bed of savages who plunder and murder us at every turn of the wind."

"Please, you must listen." Chessa twisted, trying to pull free of the men who held her. "You're wrong about what you saw. It is not as it looks."

The old woman scoffed and raised her chin. "She must pay for her crimes."

A chorus of agreement and nodding heads erupted, joined by shouts. "Bring her!"

Chessa stumbled along the rutted trail, trapped in the clutches of two unkempt men. She glanced back toward the cliff, but Bodin still had not returned. Her heart sank. Erek had spoken the truth. Perhaps Bodin had no intention of returning to the cottage as he'd said he would. Chessa inhaled a shaky breath. She should not have expected him to share the twisted knot of emotion in her heart. After all, he'd kept his part of the bargain. She had no right to want more than that.

Yet, somehow . . . she did.

Sheltered against a cliff wall, a collection of small stone huts came into view. Smoke from several open-pit fires hung rancid and gray in the damp air. Chessa winced as the stench of decay and rot and mud hit her with full force. Her home was nothing like she remembered. Dozens of blank, empty eyes stared at her as she was hauled through the center of activity. Could this harrowed, ragged klatch of souls really be all that was left of her people?

"Ge' down there."

Chessa landed in a deep pit not much wider than the span of her outstretched arms. Her feet sank ankle deep in thick mud. The men disappeared from her view. "Wait—"

A flat slab of rock scraped against three half-buried boulders overhead, darkening the opening of the hole, closing off all but a small ringed space around the edges.

"Wait!" Chessa reached toward the fracture of remaining light and grabbed a clump of grass clinging to one side of the wall in hopes of gaining her captors' attention, but the soil was slick, too saturated with rain, and the roots gave way easily in her hand. "Please—" Her voice broke.

There would be no climbing out.

"Please listen to me." The hopeless, whispered plea hardly reached her own ears. Why wouldn't they at least listen to her? They were her people—people she'd given away most of her life to protect.

Tears spilled over her lashes and down her chilled cheeks. She looked up at the small cracks of damp, gray light. This was not how her father had punished wrongdoers. What had happened to make her people behave this way? Chessa sank to her knees, leaning her shoulder against the sticky, muddy wall for support. She closed her eyes and shivered, the cold beginning to seep through to her bones.

These men—people who shared the same blood that ran through her veins—made serving under the Vikings look almost easy. But that all seemed a lifetime ago now. How could mere days stretch in the mind to feel like years? She sighed. Well, if she was trapped down here, she wouldn't have to witness Bodin's ship sailing from the bay. And her heart with it.

Chessa shivered. *Small graces,* she told herself, *be thankful for small graces.*

"I say we punish her now!" a male voice shouted.

She watched as a pair of dirty hands gripped one side of the stone slab briefly. A scuffle erupted.

"No! We'll wait for Dairmid to return."

"Wait! The bastards are sitting in the bay! How long do ye think they'll wait this time 'afore they take the last of the women and boys, the last of what little we have? If we wait, they'll be nothing of us left! I say we make an example of her; then maybe they'll leave us be!"

"We'll wait for Dairmid. The others will find him by nightfall."

"No!"

A resounding thud blocked the light on one side of the pit. The slab slid back, rock grinding against rock until it tilted into the mud, balanced on only two of the boulders.

An angry man stood on the lip of the hole leering down at her with hatred in his eyes. He knelt and grabbed for her.

Chessa cringed, but there was no place to go. The hole was not deep enough to keep out of his reach. He pulled on a handful of her hair until she got to her feet. Anger fueled his strength. He grabbed her arm and dragged her out of the pit with one hand. "Time to show them Vikings we won't cower no more!"

Chessa glanced back at her temporary quarters and saw a man lying on his side next to the slab of stone. Blood trickled from the corner of his mouth, thinning as it mixed with the rain. She struggled to keep up as her new captor yanked her hard, forcing her to keep pace with him.

"Please, I am the king's daugh—"

"I knows who ye are."

"Then surely you know I was given over to the Vikings by my father in service to protect—"

"You didn't do no protecting of us. You served only yerself and yer whoring ways. If you'd done like you was supposed to, we wouldn't be living like this."

The winds rose to battering gusts as they neared the cliff's edge. She looked out into the tide-filled bay. She might be forced to watch Bodin sail from her life after all. A surge of anguish and tears fueled her fading strength. "You must listen." She jerked against his iron grip. "I tell you that is not true. I don't know what happened here, why the village has been destroyed, but it was not because of me!"

The man stopped less than two steps away from the sharp drop of the cliff ledge. " 'Course it were cause of you. They never stopped their raiding and killing, cause you didn't do as you was supposed to do."

Chessa winced as the man's grip tightened on her arm. He moved her closer to the edge. "Enough!" she shouted, managing somehow to twist free of his hold. She took a distancing step back. "I don't know who did this, and right now I don't know how to help, but I swear"—she pointed to the Viking ship still beached on the sand—"that the men who made the bargain with my father are not the men who did those things."

"You would say that, wouldn't you? After all, you bedded with all of them."

"One! I went of my own choice to the bed of one man. Only one!" Chessa stopped short of adding that she also happened to love that one man. She raised her voice, partly to be heard over the rising wind and partly because she was so angry. "I did it as a means of earning my passage back here, to take my rightful, hard-earned place in my father's household." Her words shook as she spoke through clenched teeth. "I did it to return to my people!"

"I don't believe ye. And neither do they." He pointed to a small crowd who had followed and crept closer to watch.

Chessa glanced over her shoulder. Her stomach roiled. The faces of the villagers confirmed the truth of his words. They did not intend to listen to her. Or believe anything she said. "So what . . . you intend to throw me from the cliff? You think killing me will frighten them away?" On the shore, men were loading Bodin's ship, readying to leave.

"Aye, that's right. Getting rid of ye will get rid of them." He jerked his head in the direction of the bay.

"Not so!" With dagger drawn, Bodin strode through the fast-evaporating crowd. He pulled Chessa clear of the cliff ledge. "If you harm her, my wrath will echo off every stone and hill and blade of grass on this island for years to come." Using his body as a shield, Bodin blocked any attempt the man might make to rush at Chessa. "She speaks the truth! My father struck the bargain with your king, and my father upheld his end. My men are not the perpetrators of your hardship."

The man blinked, looking out to sea and then back toward his village and then over the top of the rocky cliff to the sandy shore below. Keeping an eye on the well-armed Viking, he eased farther away from the edge.

Bodin gripped harder the handle of his blood-covered dagger as he watched every last villager retreat, unwilling to challenge him. He turned to Chessa. Covered head to toe in a stench of mud, she stared at the blade of his knife coated in blood. She trembled visibly in the salt-laden mist. He took a step toward her, hand outstretched in invitation. Her eyes widened as she stumbled backward, keeping out of his reach. "Chessa . . ." His voice held a dangerous warning. "Do not attempt to run from me."

"Stop." She took yet another step back. "You do not own me any longer. No man *owns* me. You can no longer demand actions from me." Shock and cold began to numb her limbs and tint her lips blue. "You even said so." She gasped for air and turned her head to the side, staring at the cliff ledge. To watch him walk away would be more than she could take at the moment.

Bodin gritted his teeth, fighting to dissipate the adrenaline still heating his veins from battle. He forced a deep breath into his lungs and struggled to soften his voice. "You *are* free, sweet one. I am not here to dispute that."

She stared at his hand. The wind blew a drop of blood from the tip of his knife. Tears rimmed her lashes. "Then why are you here? To kill more of my people? To kill me before you sail?" Determined not to cry in front of him, she clenched her teeth, lips quivering with cold.

"Never." He sheathed the bloody dagger. "I could never harm you, sweet one," he admitted. Bodin raked his fingers through his hair, dislodging the accumulating droplets of mist before rubbing his jaw, easing tense muscles. "The blood on my dagger is that of Erek and the three men who chose to follow him." The dark red spatter of proof was visible on his clothes. "I do not abide betrayal."

The words of his violence trembled through her. Chessa blinked, staring at the waves lapping onto the shore, one after another.

"Chessa. Come back with me."

Slowly she turned to face him, chin raised as she dared her fate. "I am done being a slave." She turned on her heels, her back to him. Tears spilled over her lashes, racing one another to mix with the rain. Bodin's hands gently gripped her arms. She shivered, wiping at her cheeks.

"I do not wish a slave."

Unable to control her constant shivering, Chessa could only manage shallow breaths. Might he really want her? *Not likely*, a little voice inside whispered. She stared out at the rough water of the bay. Thunder rumbled, spilling a line of rain onto the frothy surface of the sea. She didn't know what to believe anymore. Nothing had turned out like she thought it would.

"Chessa, did you hear me?" Bodin turned her to face him, his grip tightening. "You will never be a slave again. Ever. I swear it." His gaze narrowed on her, watching. "Do you understand me?"

She stared at the laces of his tunic, unable to meet his determined gaze. Her brows furrowed. "Then what do you want of me if not to warm your bed?" His fingers caressed her cheek— fingers so warm her numb skin began to sting from his touch. His thumb tilted her face upward, giving her no choice but to meet his gaze.

Bodin dropped his head forward, lowering his mouth almost to hers as he spoke in a low, growling whisper. "I wish a new bargain with you. One that allows me to hear your laughter and share your tears, to watch the sun rise in your eyes every morning and the moon set on your skin each night. A bargain that secures me the whole of your heart, Chessa."

"And what . . ." She tried to swallow away the growing lump constricting her throat, but it would not go. "And what would be my part of this bargain?"

"To be happy." He smiled, his lips brushing against hers in the barest of touches. Her body shuddered, and she swayed into him, sending his gut into spasms. "And, if you wish, to bear my sons and daughters." Through a sheer force of will he did not truly possess, Bodin released her and straightened. If he continued to touch her, there would be no bargain, just his will. He fisted his hands in an attempt to control the plaguing doubt that sickened him, and then he glanced down at her stomach. His knuckles went white.

Chessa stood frozen as the rain poured unnoticed from the sky. Had she really heard the words, or had she heard only what she'd wanted to hear?

"My men are awaiting word, sweet one. Will you sail back to the village as my wife? Or do I remain here, skulking about in the cover of the woods, longing for glimpses of you?"

Chessa's head spun. So precarious was her state of balance, she sank to the muddy ground to keep from falling. Bodin dropped to one knee in front of her. But he did not touch her.

Impatient, he pressed, "Have we a bargain, Chessa?"

Dazed, she looked into his eyes—serious, truthful, longing eyes. Wishes did come true. "Yes," she breathed. The word barely crossed the threshold of her lips when his mouth closed over hers.

Bodin wound his arms around her back and beneath her knees, lifting, possessing as his lips refused to relinquish claim.

She clutched at him, wanting to be closer, though she could hardly breathe. His grip was crushing as he carried her quickly down the trail and onto the beach.

Hefting her aboard his ship, he steered her across the deck boards to the hold.

"When do we sail?"

"Now."

The ship was already free of the shore. She smiled as he took her hands, lowering her. "And when does this new bargain begin?"

He dropped down behind her. "Now." He nuzzled her neck, making her squirm and squeak as he nipped at the soft, pale skin that was now his to touch at will. "I intend to have a son growing in your belly before the dawn—if there isn't one there already."

Chessa wormed closer into Bodin's side, snuggling deeper into the very male scent of his warmth, his hands already roaming her body again. She smiled, closing her eyes with a deep breath as his touch roused her yet again.

Watching her, Bodin whispered against her salty skin. "What

has you smiling so?" He moved atop her small body, urging her thighs apart with just a touch.

She laughed softly. "You."

He paused in his attentions and lifted his head to look into her eyes. Raising his eyebrows, he asked, "Me?"

He positioned his thumb to dig into her ribs, a warning. He would tickle her, if necessary.

Chessa squeaked, her eyes wide as she tried to squirm sideways out of his reach, but he lowered more of his weight onto her, preventing any escape.

Bodin grinned, growling as he taunted, his thumb skimming lightly along two of her ribs. "Tell me why you laugh, sweet one." His finger pressed a little deeper.

"Bodin! No!" she squealed, her body jerking involuntarily beneath him.

"Last warning." He smiled, sucking one of her nipples into his mouth.

Chessa's body reacted, arching, straining. "It's just that you're so determined."

He released her breast long enough to ask, "Determined?" Then he lavished attention on the other soft, pale mound of flesh.

"Yes," she panted, her fingers threading through his hair, urging him lower. "To have a son."

Bodin chuckled. "I always keep my bargains, sweet one."